Livvy gasped with shock and realization.

Colton Cassidy. One of the newly discovered relatives of the Havens from Ranch Haven. An uncle the matriarch, Sadie Haven, had never told her family about, and cousins that apparently Sadie hadn't even known about.

Livvy had already determined to stay out of that, so instead she asked, "Oh, no, is everyone okay after the fire?"

Colton nodded, and the black cowboy hat slipped a little lower on his forehead. "Collin's burns are the worst of the injuries. My older brother had a few small burns and, like my dad, a bit of smoke inhalation, but nothing serious."

"And you?"

He grinned. "I'm a firefighter, so I know not to go into a situation like that unprepared." His voice dropping to a gruff whisper, he added, "If only I could prepare for everything..."

She had a strange urge to reach out to him then. To comfort him...

Dear Reader,

I'm so excited to bring you a new book in my Bachelor Cowboys series! If you've read the previous books in the series, you know all about the Haven family and their trials and tribulations and secrets! Matriarch Sadie Haven had a big one she was keeping from her family—a son who ran away years ago. She never brought him up because she didn't think he was still alive. But it turns out Jessup Haven was living close by as JJ Cassidy and has four sons of his own. So Sadie has a lot more matchmaking to do because all these grandsons are bachelor cowboys, too!

First up is Colton Cassidy, a firefighter and paramedic with the Moss Valley fire department. He has enough on his mind dealing with all the recent revelations about his family and with a big secret he's keeping from all of them. But when he *somehow* gets transferred to Willow Creek, where the Havens live, he finds himself falling in with Grandma Sadie's plans and falling for a certain ER doctor.

If you're new to the series, don't worry, you'll be able to jump right in, and if you're a returning reader, I hope you enjoy this new branch of the Haven family as much as I am. The Cassidy brothers fit right in with the family with their banter and their brotherly love. Coming from a big family myself, I love writing about them and hope you love reading about them!

Happy reading!

Lisa Childs

HEARTWARMING

The Firefighter's Family Secret

—

Lisa Childs

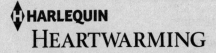
HARLEQUIN
HEARTWARMING

HARLEQUIN®

HEARTWARMING™

Recycling programs for this product may not exist in your area.

ISBN-13: 978-1-335-58505-9

The Firefighter's Family Secret

Copyright © 2023 by Lisa Childs

For questions and comments about the quality of this book, please contact us at CustomerService@Harlequin.com.

Harlequin Enterprises ULC
22 Adelaide St. West, 41st Floor
Toronto, Ontario M5H 4E3, Canada
www.Harlequin.com

Printed in U.S.A.

New York Times and *USA TODAY* bestselling, award-winning author **Lisa Childs** has written more than eighty-five novels. Published in twenty countries, she's also appeared on the *Publishers Weekly*, Barnes & Noble and Nielsen Top 100 bestseller lists. Lisa writes contemporary romance, romantic suspense, paranormal and women's fiction. She's a wife, mom, bonus mom, avid reader and less avid runner. Readers can reach her through Facebook or her website, lisachilds.com.

Books by Lisa Childs

Harlequin Heartwarming

Bachelor Cowboys

A Rancher's Promise
The Cowboy's Unlikely Match
The Bronc Rider's Twin Surprise
The Cowboy's Ranch Rescue

Harlequin Romantic Suspense

Hotshot Heroes

Hotshot Hero Under Fire
Hotshot Hero on the Edge
Hotshot Heroes Under Threat
Hotshot Heroes in Disguise

Love Inspired Cold Case

Buried Ranch Secrets
A Cowboy's Justice

Visit the Author Profile page
at Harlequin.com for more titles.

With so much love for the matriarch in my family who never meddles like Sadie but is always there when we need her—Sharon Ahearne!

CHAPTER ONE

THE SMOKE WAS THICK, the flames hot and rising high, eating at the wood that crackled and sparked as the fire consumed it. "Where are you?" Colton Cassidy shouted the question but doubted anyone could hear him through the protective gear he wore as a fireman. The other men who'd gone into the burning house didn't even have a mask.

Those men were his brothers and his dad.

He had to find them. Had to get them out. Before the fire consumed them along with the house where they'd all grown up. His boot struck something, and above the roar of the fire, he heard a loud grunt. A body. He'd found a body.

He pulled the man up from the floor and dragged him toward the door. The porch was nearly gone, the boards weakening and cracking beneath him, but he got across it with his brother.

His twin. Collin's shirt sleeves were scorched,

like his arms. Panic gripped Colton. Collin was a doctor. He needed his hands.

A paramedic rushed up from the rig that had pulled into the yard. Colton yanked his mask aside to tell his coworker, "He needs oxygen and his burns treated." At fiftysomething, Ed Meyer had been a paramedic firefighter longer than Colton had at thirty-two; Ed knew what to do without his input.

"Marsh and Dad are still inside," Collin said between gasps and coughs for breath.

Colton affixed his mask again and rushed back inside the house. Like with the porch, the floor shuddered beneath him, the joists, weakened from the flames, threatening to give out. The whole two-story farmhouse was about to collapse. Colton tore through the house, searching in the smoke and flames. Finally on the back porch, he saw them.

His older brother Marsh, a sheriff's deputy, was dragging his dad out the back door. Their clothes weren't as scorched as Collin's. He rushed out after them, pulling his mask aside. "Get to the paramedic rig. Get oxygen."

Dad couldn't be without it for long, not with his new heart. He'd only had it four months or so, and his body hadn't rejected it yet. Not like

it had his first kidney transplant. But now…
with the smoke…

"Find the boy," Marsh said. "The nurse's
kid. Mikey. He's missing. That's who we were
looking for."

He knew that already. The boy's mother,
Sarah, had been frantic when the fire truck
had pulled up. Darlene, Colton's late mother's
best friend, had been holding her back from
rushing headlong into the fire. Darlene obviously hadn't been able to stop Colton's dad and
brothers, too. They'd already been inside the
burning house.

After watching Marsh lead his dad away
from the fire, toward the rig, Colton headed
back inside. Through the radio in his helmet,
he coordinated with his team. Every room of
the house had been searched. No bodies found,
living or not.

The kid couldn't be inside. But Colton did
one last walk-through, searching all the places
he'd hid as a kid. The cupboards. The tub. The
cellar.

He didn't have to find the door to it; he was
able to drop down through a gaping hole in
the floor. And as he searched, he found no kid
in the smoke. But he did find something else,
something sparkling beneath a fine sheen of

soot. He grabbed it up from the ground. The metal was hot yet…even through the thickness of his gloves. And even through the thickness of his gloves, he could feel the distinctive engraving on the silver: horseshoes that spelled out CC.

He hadn't seen this lighter in seventeen years. Since his oldest brother, Cash, who'd been gifted the lighter, ran away. How had it showed up now? And what the heck had it been used for? To start the fire? Since the flames had already burned through the floor in this area, the kitchen might have been the point of origin.

The house creaked and groaned above him.

"Everybody, clear out!" The order came through the headset in his helmet. "It's going to cave!"

And where Colton was, in the cellar, the rest of the house would fall on him, burying him under burning debris and flames. This wasn't the first time he'd been in this dangerous a situation and it wouldn't be the last. That was why he'd vowed to never have a family of his own. To never have a wife and kids worrying that he wasn't going to survive the next time.

He was going to this time, though.

He grabbed at the edges of the hole, pulling himself back out of the low-ceilinged cellar. But as his weight hit what was left of the kitchen floor, it shook beneath him and began to give way. He rolled himself across it, through the kitchen and into the living room. Then he regained his feet and ran out the front door. The porch was nearly gone now, more gaping holes than structure, but since it was narrow, Colton stretched his long legs across it and hurried down the stairs to the security of the ground.

Darlene must have still been holding Sarah outside the house, but now the younger woman broke free of Darlene's arms and ran up to him, her dark eyes wide and as wild as the blond hair that curled around her pale face.

Colton dragged off his helmet and mask and shook his head, sweat rolling down his face. "There's nobody inside." Not anymore. Not since he'd gotten his dad and brothers out. "He's not in there." Her son had probably never been in the house. The five- or six-year-old was rarely inside; since she'd moved to the ranch to help with his dad, Sarah's son was always in the barn.

"We'll find him," Darlene assured the crying woman as she helped her up from the ground. Darlene was great like that; since she'd showed up at the ranch shortly after Cash had left, she'd spent most of her time comforting and taking care of them all.

Before he could tell Sarah where he thought her kid had safely been this whole time, a firefighter, from a Willow Creek rig, ran up to him. "Where do you need us?"

Colton blinked a moment to clear the smoke from his eyes, but it hung thick in the air all around them. There was no clearing it away, no making the image before him any sharper. Maybe that was why the guy seemed to look so much like him and his brothers. The same dark hair and chiseled features but his eyes were a lighter brown.

Was this the Willow Creek firefighter Colton sometimes got mistaken for? The same one Colton had seen at that horrific accident four months ago?

That accident made Colton think of his dad, and he turned his attention back to the paramedic rig parked a safe distance from the fire. His dad was his number one priority, had always been his number one priority.

"If you guys can finish up here, get the flames out, make sure it doesn't spread to the barn," he said, which was most definitely where little Mikey was, "I'm going to get my idiot brothers and my stubborn dad to the hospital." He headed toward Ed's ambulance rig with its back doors standing open.

The other firefighter followed him instead of heading toward the house with the rest of the Willow Creek crew. "I'm a paramedic, too," he said. "Maybe I can help."

With all of his family injured from trying to find the kid in the burning house, Colton could use the help, so he nodded. "Do you have idiot brothers, too?"

"Four…" The guy's voice trailed off before he cleared it and amended, "*Three* of them."

This was definitely the firefighter Colton had first thought he was, the one whose brother and sister-in-law hadn't survived the crash four months ago.

A pang of guilt struck Colton, and he couldn't look at the guy. He peered beyond him to where Darlene and Sarah stood. "We'll find him," he assured them. After clearing the house, the rest of his crew was spraying down the area around it, the grounds and the barn and other outbuildings. This late in July in Wyoming, it was so hot and dry that the fire could easily spread. "Her son is missing," he told the Willow Creek firefighter. "I'm betting he's in the barn. He likes the mare."

"Sounds like my nephew," the guy remarked.

"Did you check the barn, Darlene?" Colton asked her. She had to know how often the kid visited her mare. She visited it as often. Putting it up for sale had to be as hard on her as putting up the ranch had been on all of them; she'd given up a lot for their family. Colton wasn't sure why. If she was just that good a person or if she figured she owed her friend's family a debt of some kind...

Darlene's hazel eyes widened with surprise, probably because she hadn't thought of it. Then she and Sarah rushed off toward the barn.

"I'm sure he's fine," Colton said, but he was speaking into the ambulance now where his two brothers and father were crowded. "He'd rather be in the barn than the house anyways. He probably was nowhere near the fire. Unlike you idiots..." He couldn't believe they'd gone back inside after the fire had started, that they'd been so close to the flames...to death. Panic gripped him at the thought of losing not just one of them but all of them. He'd already lost Mom to cancer and Cash to whatever had made him so angry that he had disowned them all and run away. He'd vowed then to never return. But that lighter...

Despite the heaviness of his gear, he could almost feel the silver heirloom inside his pocket.

The weight of it, the heat of it…the implication of it…

Cash was back. But where?

"We need to help her search," Marsh said, then he dissolved into a coughing fit.

Collin reached for an oxygen mask for Marsh, but his hands were so heavily bandaged that he fumbled with it. Colton took it from him and fixed it over Marsh's face, which was red from the heat and probably from struggling for air. Their dad was the opposite, deathly pale, as he'd been so often while Colton was growing up. So sick…so close to dying…

The panic that had already been gripping Colton tightened its grasp now. His dad and brothers needed to get to the hospital, and obviously Colton's partner knew it since Ed had already climbed into the driver's seat. "I got this," Colton told the Willow Creek firefighter. "You can close the doors. I'll have my partner drive us to the ER."

The guy hesitated for a moment, staring at them all with such an odd expression in his pale brown eyes. Then he stepped back and finally shut the doors.

"Hurry!" Colton urged the driver. Moss Valley ER was the closest, but it was still too far away. That was partially why Dad and Darlene had put the ranch up for sale; so they could move closer to town, to medical help. Something they should have done years ago. But Colton suspected Dad had held off because of Cash, because he'd thought he would come home one day.

But seventeen years had passed with no sign of him.

Until now…

Until the lighter, the one mom had given him that had belonged to her father, had turned up in the fire. Even though Cash had never smoked, he'd always carried that lighter on him. And Colton was certain he'd had it with him when he'd left. So why had he returned now…after all these years?

Had he found out Dad was selling the ranch? Colton could imagine how he might have learned about the sale. There was one person that Cash might have stayed in contact with… the realtor who'd listed the ranch for sale.

But none of that mattered now. Only Dad mattered now while they waited for news of his condition in the Moss Valley ER.

The little boy had been found safe and sound in the barn. Darlene had confirmed it when she'd showed up at the hospital a short while after they had. And Colton's brothers had been treated and released to wait with Colton for news about their dad.

Hours passed with them pacing the waiting room floor. Darlene had gone to find them something to eat and drink while they waited for the doctor. They really hadn't learned anything yet. Even Collin, who had used being their dad's medical power of attorney to demand access to their father's charts, didn't know any more than the rest of them did. And he was a doctor. He could read the labs and all the reports and tell them his father's prognosis. For so long, it hadn't been good, but things had changed now.

Their father had a strong new heart, and since receiving it four months ago, he had been getting stronger, too.

Then the fire had started.

Colton's stomach flipped again with that fear he'd felt when the call had come into his firehouse, when he'd learned the location. He'd known there were oxygen tanks on hand in his father's room, tanks that could blow up...

He cringed as he imagined how much worse it would have been had Sarah and Darlene not acted as fast as they had in getting the tanks out of the house. But then Sarah hadn't been able to find her son. Despite the danger, JJ

Cassidy, Colton's dad, had gone back into the house. And Marsh and Collin, who'd arrived before Colton and his crew, had gone in after him. They all could have died. Dad could still die.

So Colton didn't want to think what he was thinking…about that lighter, about Cash.

"Hey, Colt," his older brother Marsh called out to him, his already deep voice a little gruffer than usual. Probably from smoke inhalation.

Marsh wasn't the only one who'd rushed into the flames without the proper gear. Colton glanced over at his twin. They looked exactly alike, but only their outward appearances were the same. In every other way, they were different. Collin was brilliant and driven, always had been, while Colton was laid-back and liked to joke around and have fun. Collin could never relax; even now he was struggling to hang on to his cell phone since both his hands were heavily bandaged. The burns were bad, but they would heal. Colton had seen worse.

That was what he kept telling himself. He knew how hard Collin had worked to get through college, med school, his residency and fellowship to become a cardiologist at thirty-two. But his bandaged hands weren't keeping him from consulting, as he barked medical orders into his cell.

For Dad?

No. Collin couldn't treat their father. He must have been consulting for someone else, probably at the hospital where he'd recently been hired in nearby Willow Creek. Thinking of Willow Creek brought that firefighter back to Colton's mind, the one who looked so much like him and even had the same job as a firefighter and a paramedic. He had brothers, too, but had changed the number of them because he had lost one recently. Colton remembered his name now: Baker Haven.

"Colt!" Marsh said, his voice louder now.

He shook his head and focused on his older brother. "Sorry. What?"

"Are you okay?" Marsh asked with concern. He could have been a triplet with Colton and Collin; he looked that much like them. But he wasn't the only one who looked so much like them.

Colton nodded. "Yeah, yeah. I'm fine. I wasn't an idiot like you guys were when you rushed into a burning house with no protection."

Marsh flinched but didn't deny it. "If you're fine, why are you so quiet?"

Colton tensed. He was usually the loud one,

the funny one, the one who broke the tension in all the tense situations in which the Cassidy family had found themselves over the years. And there had been so many of those...

The lobby doors swished open, saving him from having to answer as everyone turned to see who was entering the small-town hospital. It was so small that there was only one waiting room right there in the lobby. The Willow Creek firefighter he'd talked to earlier walked through the doors with a tall, blond-haired woman at his side.

The woman gasped and murmured, "It is like looking at Jake and Ben, but there are three of them..."

"Is something else happening at the ranch?" Colton asked. "Did the fire spread from the house to outbuildings?" If not for Darlene's horse being in the barn, Colton probably wouldn't have cared; it wasn't like the place would be theirs much longer. Unless the sale fell through before the deal closed, and then it would be their problem again, as it had been the past several years when they'd struggled to keep it afloat while trying to keep their dad alive. They should have sold it years ago and moved him closer to town, to medical attention.

"No, we didn't leave until all the hot spots were out," Baker said.

Colton's stomach began to knot with the tension that had already gripped him. "Then why…" What was the guy doing here? And why did he look so much like them?

"I wanted to check on you all," he said. "How is your dad?"

Not good. That was Colton's fear, the reason the doctors had to be taking so long to tell them how he was doing. Colton clenched his jaw so tightly that he felt a muscle twitch in his cheek. Before he could say anything, Collin called out, "Darlene! Are you okay? Are you burned?"

Colton whirled around to see his twin rushing toward the woman they treated as their surrogate mom, after Colleen Cassidy died. Darlene stood just within the doorway to the hall that led to the cafeteria. At this hour, it would have been closed, but she must have gotten some coffee from the vending machines. She'd just dropped those cups onto the floor, splashing the contents onto her jeans. But she didn't even seem aware of what she'd done as she stared at the man from the Willow Creek Fire Department.

"What's wrong?" Colton asked, his heart

beating fast with concern for her and for that strange look on her face.

Marsh stepped closer to the Willow Creek firefighter and asked, "Who are you?"

"Baker Haven," the younger man replied. "Darlene's youngest son."

Marsh turned toward their mother's friend and gruffly asked, "Darlene?"

She said nothing, just continued to stand there, staring…at the stranger. With her sandy hair and hazel eyes, she looked nothing like the man who looked so much like them.

"I'm your cousin," the man told them. "Your father is…was…my dad's brother."

"Are you crazy?" Collin asked. "What are you talking about? My dad doesn't have a brother. And Darlene is…was…my mother's friend."

"Baker Haven…" Colton murmured as that knot in his stomach tightened. He had gone out on that call four months ago that had been personal to this firefighter. The scene of the man's brother's tragic car accident.

"What are you trying to pull?" Marsh asked Baker.

Darlene's last name wasn't Haven. It was Smith. But Colton couldn't remember ever seeing anything with Smith actually on it. In the nearly seventeen years Darlene had been living at Cassidy Ranch, she'd never received mail at the house. Nothing with her name on it. Colton had never even seen her driver's license.

"He's telling the truth." The woman who'd accompanied him spoke up in Baker Haven's defense. "Ask her…"

When everyone turned back to Darlene, she remained silent but managed a faint nod.

"She might be hurt," the blonde pointed out, and Baker Haven rushed toward the woman he claimed was his mother. He pushed aside Collin, who'd been clumsily trying to help her. After Baker's friend steered Darlene into a chair, Baker rolled up Darlene's jeans and examined her skin for burns.

"I'm okay," Darlene assured him. "It's really you…" And she took his face in her hands and added, "It's my baby…"

Whatever else they said was just a buzzing sound in Colton's ears as he reached into his pocket and clenched the silver lighter in his fist. He caught bits and pieces of the conversation, something about a grandmother and a heart attack, and then Darlene shared the news about their dad's heart transplant.

Colton watched Baker's face pale as the other firefighter came to the same realization he had. Colton knew whose heart his dad had and now he knew why it had been such a perfect match, since the donor had been his dad's nephew. Colton also realized something else— that it wasn't just the ranch that had burned down today. His entire life had. Everything he'd thought was true had been a lie. And for the first time, he understood his oldest brother running away.

For a second, just a second, Colton was tempted to run, too, because he had a feeling that it would be smarter and far safer than facing the truths he'd just learned.

He was a Haven.

LIVVY LEMMON PEEKED through the crack in the doorjamb and tried to ignore the small twinge of guilt she felt over spying on her grandfather. He'd been so upset when he'd gotten the call that had brought them to the hospital that Livvy was nearly as worried about him as Grandpa Lem was worried about his friend.

When Livvy had seen him earlier today at her father's house, she'd been struck by the fact that he hadn't changed at all since she'd seen him last over a year ago. He looked the same as he always had which, with his white hair and beard, was old. But not a feeble or fragile old.

His blue eyes were bright with intelligence and humor, and his full cheeks were flush with color. With his round belly and his short height, he looked like Santa Claus, which was the role he'd played in the town square every holiday season for as long as Livvy could remember.

She had inherited his short height as well as his red hair. Or at least she'd been told his hair had once been red but a much darker shade than her strawberry blond. She had her mother's green eyes, though, instead of his bright blue. She wished she'd inherited Grandpa Lem's outgoing, jovial spirit and his forcefulness, too. But Livvy had always been an introvert except when she was working. She must have inherited his work ethic, though, since he was still working at eighty years old. But she suspected the mayor had convinced Grandpa to run as his deputy so that he had a distraction from his grief over Grandma Mary dying.

The only thing that had struck her as being different about Grandpa Lem was that his beard and hair had been freshly trimmed, and his usual wrinkly, ill-fitting suit had been replaced with one that looked custom-fit and cleanly pressed. He looked good. Or he had until he'd taken that call on his cell at her dad's house.

Then all the color had drained from his face and he'd started to shake as he'd suddenly aged really fast, which had worried her. So she'd stuck around the hospital, just in case...

The Haven family had gone home, and she probably should, too. But she hadn't seen Grandpa often over the last several years, so she wanted to make sure he was okay before she left. She peered through the door as her grandfather leaned over and pressed a kiss to the forehead of the white-haired woman lying in the bed.

So that was the formidable Sadie March Haven.

Her grandfather's archnemesis since they were little bitty kids attending Willow Creek Elementary. The woman turned toward Grandpa Lem and stared up at him with such a soft look on her gently lined face, with so much love in her dark eyes that love flooded Livvy's heart.

The octogenarians weren't enemies anymore. And they were more than the friends that Livvy's grandfather claimed was all they were. With a pang of envy and another of guilt,

Livvy pulled the door closed to give the eighty-year-olds their privacy.

That was what love was supposed to look like. She glanced down at her bare left hand, at the faint indentation on the finger that had held her engagement ring.

She hadn't had a love like that. She'd known it even before Steven had given her the ultimatum. She might have known it even before he gave her the ring. What she hadn't known was how to say no to the ring, to the proposal and to the life *he* had envisioned for them... until the ultimatum.

When she'd said no to that, she'd known then that she'd done the right thing. And now, being back in Willow Creek, watching her grandfather with Sadie Haven, Livvy had no lingering doubts.

She was where she belonged. She was home.

Willow Creek was where she'd been born, but her family had moved away when she was six or seven. They'd returned for holidays and some summer vacations. Livvy's dad had moved back earlier this year, and her grandfather had never left. And a part of Livvy wished her family had never left either.

Then she would have had more time with Grandma Mary before Alzheimer's disease had so slowly taken her away from Grandpa Lem. Livvy's mother was gone, too, to breast cancer. She and Dad had been living in Michigan then, at their lake house, but as close as they'd been, Livvy had been too busy to see them often. She regretted not being there for her grandpa and dad like she should have been.

That they had had to lose the loves of their lives and all without Livvy's support. She'd been so busy, first with college and then med school and residency and Steven. He had kept her busiest of all. She would rather be alone than ever lose herself like that again.

Earlier this evening, one of Sadie Haven's grandsons, who was actually the mayor of Willow Creek, had offered Livvy a strange warning: *"You might want to make yourself scarce. I think she has plans for you, too."*

Ben must have just been teasing because clearly Sadie Haven had too much going on to give any thought to Livvy, let alone make plans for *her*. Heat rushed to her face with embarrassment and guilt that she'd overheard so much of the Haven family business while she'd been in the waiting room with Grandpa Lem and Sadie's family.

Some of her relatives…

Apparently there were more Havens, a whole

other branch of the family that Ben and his brothers hadn't known about.

But that wasn't Livvy's business, and she didn't want it to be, which was what she'd told the waiting room attendant who had tried to interrogate her when she'd asked the older woman for Sadie Haven's room number. Livvy didn't want to gossip with people with whom she would soon be working.

And she especially didn't want to gossip about the Havens. While Grandpa Lem had a relationship with them, she didn't want one.

She didn't want a relationship with anyone but her own family. Her focus was on Dad and Grandpa and the new position she was starting as an attending ER physician.

Pride suffused her that finally *her* dream was coming true. And she was going to make certain this time that she didn't let anyone and anything hijack and derail it.

CHAPTER TWO

FOR THE PAST two days Colton had felt as if he was trapped in an episode of the *Twilight Zone*, but he never felt more that way than when he drove his brothers out to Ranch Haven and arrived at the same time as his dad and Darlene who'd driven separately from them.

The property stretched for miles and miles along the road that led to it and down the drive between the barns, an old schoolhouse and up to the enormous cedar-sided two-story farmhouse. They walked across the wraparound porch to the front door, which Colton's father seemed reluctant to just open and walk inside even though he'd grown up there at the ranch.

Once they'd been able to see him in the hospital, Dad had shared his story with them. His real story. His real name. He'd said he'd been so sick as a kid that it hadn't looked like he would survive into adulthood. Not being able to handle how much his mother worried about and tried to coddle him, he'd run away

after high school. To the rodeo…where he'd
met their mother. When they'd married, he'd
taken her name instead of the fake one he'd
been using, and he'd come home with her to
her family ranch. While it was only about an
hour from his home, he'd made certain to go
to Moss Valley instead of Willow Creek on
the rare occasions he left the ranch, so he had
never run into his mom or other relatives. With
his health so touch and go all these years, he
hadn't wanted to worry her all over again.

Colton felt a pang of concern that his father
might worry about him like that because he'd
chosen to become a firefighter. He'd been so
careful to never fall for and get serious with a
woman, so that he wouldn't have a wife worrying about him. But Dad…

Dad already had too much to worry about
with his own health and the money pit of a
ranch and Cash…

"It's changed so much," JJ Cassidy, aka Jessup Haven, murmured, sounding as awestruck
as Colton was.

Darlene had lived there, too, with her late
husband, the uncle Colton would never meet.
And with her kids. For some reason she seemed
to blame herself for Michael Haven's death in
a ranch accident and she'd taken off after his

funeral…to find their dad, to bring Jessup back to his hurting family as if he could make up for the loss of his brother. But he'd been so sick when she'd showed up and Mom had just died and Cash had taken off…

Darlene hadn't been able to leave them when she knew they had nobody else, so she'd made up the story of being their late mom's best friend and she'd stayed. His heart swelled with love for her, for the sacrifices she'd made for *them*. She'd lost so much. Even though she'd lived there, too, she rang the bell instead of opening that door.

Only seconds passed, with a little dog yipping somewhere inside that enormous house, before the tall blond-haired woman from the ER opened the door. Tears shimmered in her blue eyes even though she smiled. "I'm so glad you're here," she said. "You're *all* here."

But they weren't all here. Cash wasn't. Was this why he'd run away? Had he found out the truth? Colton remembered him shouting something about living a lie.

Now he knew that they'd all been living a lie.

"They're waiting for you in the kitchen." The woman led the way down a wide center hall that passed through formal rooms on either side, rooms that from the untouched look of them were probably hardly ever used. After passing another hallway that branched off that one, they stepped inside an enormous kitchen with green-stained cabinets and a brick floor and tall brick fireplace, a back staircase on one side and on the other, a wall of French doors that opened onto a patio.

While there were quite a few adults and four young boys, the three he'd seen in that crash and another little blond boy, in that room, it was eerily quiet as everyone stared at them. And Colton stared back.

Meeting Baker Haven had been surreal enough. Seeing a stranger who looked so much like him and Collin and Marsh had been unsettling to say the least. But the two other guys standing around the kitchen island looked even more like them. Then, in addition to Baker, there was a fourth, and he, with his sandy brown hair and hazel eyes, looked so much like Darlene.

When she'd told them about this meeting, she'd intended to go alone, but Dad had insisted on joining her and so had Marsh and Collin. Colton wanted to support Darlene like she'd supported them and their dad all these years, but he hadn't really wanted to come here.

He could just about hear the spooky music

playing in his head, and a chill of foreboding chased down his spine. If what he'd found in the fire meant what he thought it did, he had more than enough to deal with; he didn't need this, too.

He didn't need *them* in his life.

Dad had slipped behind Colton and his brothers somehow, and he made a strangling noise in his throat. And that foreboding inside Colton increased; he'd thought this was a bad idea for so many reasons, Dad's health being the biggest concern. But the doctor had assured them that he'd suffered just a small amount of smoke inhalation in the fire, and after two days of monitoring his vital signs, he'd been released.

He seemed strong now as he pushed past them and rushed toward the woman sitting at the end of the long kitchen table, her back to the fireplace hearth. Even sitting, she was tall and imposing with chiseled features and long, white hair. It was hard to believe that her heart had stopped a few days ago, but her grandson had gotten it started again and medication had been prescribed to regulate her arrhythmia. The white-haired, white-bearded man sitting next to her, his hand on hers, stared at her with concern, though.

"Mom…" Colton's dad murmured as he dropped to his knees in front of the woman and wrapped his arms around her. "I'm so sorry," he said. "I'm so sorry."

She leaned back and cupped his face in her big hands. Then she pressed kisses against his cheek, her voice cracking with emotion as she said, "I thought you were dead…"

"I know," Dad replied. "And there were many times I nearly was. That I would have been… and I didn't want to put you through all that."

Remembering all the times *they* had been put through that, all the times he and his brothers had nearly lost their dad, had Colton's pulse racing even more than it had already been. That was why he'd vowed to stay single just in case he developed the health problems Dad had, or in case something happened to him while he was fighting a fire, Colton didn't want to have a family, people he loved, worrying about him like he and his brothers had worried about their dad and mom. No kid should have to live with that constant fear.

His dad continued, "…after you lost Michael and Dad, I didn't want you to lose anyone else."

Michael. His dad's younger brother. An uncle Colton had never met and would never have the chance to meet. And Big Jake Haven, Sadie's husband, who'd died of a heart attack twelve years ago...

Even in Moss Valley, Colton had heard stories about the Havens, and whenever he'd been in Willow Creek, people had talked about them. Some claimed Big Jake Haven had been seven foot tall with fists the size of watermelons. The man was a legend, and Sadie Haven was a living legend. To protect the calves on the ranch, she'd reportedly killed wolves with her bare hands. Colton had heard so many stories about the Havens...from everyone but his father. JJ Cassidy had never said anything about them. But then he'd never even told his kids that his real name was Jessup Haven until they'd talked to him in the hospital after the fire.

Colton might have been angry with him if he wasn't so happy that Dad was alive and, for once, he was healthy. Thanks to his new heart...

"I lost my grandson and his sweet wife," Sadie Haven was saying. She had to be talking about Dale and Jenny Haven who'd died four months ago.

That chill gripping Colton intensified until he was cold to the bone. He remembered showing up at the crash site as backup to the Willow Creek Fire Department. The rolled-over SUV, the injured and terrified little boys and their parents…

He shuddered again.

"I think I might have his heart," Dad confessed, his voice cracking. His hand was on his chest, over that heart, and the old woman covered that hand with hers. While her hand was big and looked strong with calluses, the knuckles were swollen with age and arthritis.

Tears filled her dark eyes as she said, "Dale would have liked that…"

A sob broke out of Darlene, and she began to shake uncontrollably. Colton wrapped his arm around her shoulders, trying to comfort her over the loss of her son and the daughter-in-law she'd never met.

She'd made so many sacrifices for his dad and for them. Missed out on so much with her own family. But she'd sworn, when she and Dad had finally revealed the truth, that her family hadn't needed her like Colton's dad and his boys had needed her. Her own children had Sadie. And she'd thought they'd all blamed her for Michael's death, like she blamed herself, because she'd been on the tractor with him when he'd fallen. In her grief and guilt, she'd convinced herself that they all hated her.

The old woman stood up and walked over to them. Then she pulled Darlene away from Colton into her arms, and she held her close, saying, "Welcome home, honey…"

As the two women talked, Colton felt as if he was watching a movie. Strangers on a screen. Even his dad, who joined in the conversation, reciting lines about being a rodeo bullfighter and a fool…

It was surreal to Colton that people he'd thought he'd known so well he really knew very little about. Then Dad mentioned Cash, how he'd run away just like Dad had from his mom all those years ago.

And it all became too real to Colton, just like it had when he'd found that lighter in the house. Cash's lighter. That he'd not seen in as many years as he'd not seen Cash. Seventeen years.

"I'm not going to live a lie anymore!" Cash had yelled at Dad just before he'd thrown his duffel bag, with the lighter in it, into his truck and drove off. He must have found out the truth somehow.

Colton reached into the pocket of his jeans and closed his fingers around that lighter. He'd cleaned off the black soot, and he could feel the engraving on the silver. Two horseshoes turned sideways to spell out CC.

Dad claimed he hadn't seen Cash since he'd run away. And Marsh and Collin had said the same. But after learning that everything he'd thought was true—Darlene being his mom's friend, his dad an only child, even his own last name—was a lie, Colton wondered if anyone in his family spoke the truth.

THE ER IN Willow Creek was so far removed from the ER at the hospital where Livvy had done her residency in Chicago that she felt as if she'd stepped onto the set of some old sit-com…from the black-and-white television era. With no patients on the actual floor of the ER, she was hanging out at the front desk, waiting to see if anyone might come through the front doors. No ambulances had been dispatched and so far no paramedics had called to say they were on their way with patients.

Where were the gunshot wounds?

The crash victims?

She sucked in a breath as she remembered Grandpa telling her about the tragic crash four months ago and the two people who hadn't survived it, leaving behind three orphaned little boys.

No. She didn't want a crash to happen or for any gunshot victims to arrive. After three years in that Chicago ER, she welcomed the quiet of the Willow Creek Emergency Department. This was what she'd wanted. A perfect first day on the job.

The staff had warmly welcomed her and shared stories with her about her grandfather. Old Man Lemmon was definitely beloved in Willow Creek. And in her heart. She smiled, thinking of him, but then she felt a twinge of concern, remembering that everyone expressed how sweet it was that he and Sadie Haven were keeping company. With everything going on with the Haven family, was that good for *him*?

Other people, bored with the slow day, gathered around that front desk as well, and asked her about the Havens.

But Livvy shook her head. "I don't know them. I've just moved to town."

"It's too bad you and your dad didn't move back sooner," an older nurse commented, and she pursed her lips into a tight frown of disapproval. She was probably Livvy's dad's age, with silvery blue hair and eyes nearly the same color as her hair and just as cold. "Your grandfather had a lot to handle on his own with your grandma Mary's Alzheimer's. Good thing

Sadie Haven was there for him then. Maybe that's why he's there for her now."

Remembering how he'd reacted to the news of her heart attack, Livvy suspected there was more to their relationship than gratitude. And maybe she wasn't as concerned as she was jealous that her eighty-year-old grandfather had a better relationship than she'd ever had. Actually Grandpa had had two of them because he and Grandma Mary had been so happy as well.

But a relationship was the last thing Livvy wanted right now. She wanted to focus on her family and on herself for once. Not lose herself again.

"Do you mind watching the desk while I grab some coffee?" the intake desk attendant asked. "I'll bring you back a cup if you tell me how you take it."

Other doctors, especially one she knew all too well, would have refused to watch the desk, but Livvy smiled and nodded. "Sure. And I take it with a splash of cream and a sprinkle of nutmeg and cinnamon. I brought some and left them by the pot."

The older nurse and the other staff that had gathered around the desk headed through the authorized personnel only doors into the back with the attendant. Maybe for coffee. Maybe for the gossip Livvy had refused to take part in regarding the Havens.

That was fine with her. Livvy was not going to do anything she didn't want to, just to make someone else happy, ever again. Her cell vibrated in the pocket of her scrubs, and she instinctively knew who was trying to contact her, as if thoughts of him had conjured him up. She should have left the cell in her locker, but she'd carried it with her in case Grandpa Lem needed her. When she pulled it out, the message on the screen wasn't from Grandpa as she had already suspected. It was from Steven.

We need to talk.

He meant that *he* needed to talk, and she needed to listen. Well, she was done listening. She dropped the cell back into her pocket, leaving the text unread. And when the lobby doors to the ER swished open, she breathed a sigh of relief that she had something to do besides think about her ex-fiancé and how much of herself she'd lost during their engagement.

She would not make that mistake again.

Then she looked up from the check-in desk to see who'd walked through those ER doors. And her heart did a crazy little flippy thing in her chest at the sight of the two handsome men who were totally identical except for one having bandages on his hands and the other wearing a black cowboy hat.

She stepped out from behind the check-in desk and asked the one with the bandages, "Can I help you?"

"No," he said shortly and, to Livvy's ears, dismissively.

Her pride prickly with righteous indignation, she drew herself up as tall as she could stretch at five foot and stared down the men who towered over her. She should have been used to this by now: people assuming she was too young or inexperienced to do her job. In med school, her intern year and residency, it hadn't bothered her that much. Then, she had been learning; now, she knew very well how to do her job. She had the knowledge and the experience. "I assure you that I am capable of helping you."

The man with the bandages shook his head. "I'm not here for your help—"

"What my idiot brother is trying to say is that he's not a patient," the man in the cowboy hat interrupted him, his dark eyes bright with warmth while his mouth curved into a wide grin.

And Livvy's heart did that strange little flip again.

"Collin here is the new cardiologist on staff," the man in the cowboy hat explained. "And what he lacks in bedside manner, he makes up for in brains."

She knew that type; she'd been engaged to that type for too long. With that easy grin and charm of his, she would have been more interested in the cowboy brother if she'd had any interest in another relationship. She certainly didn't right now and wasn't sure if she ever would. After her two-year engagement, after two years of dating, she wanted to be single for at least that long...maybe forever.

"I'm new to the staff, too," she said. "This is actually my first day. I'm Dr. Lemmon, an ER attending."

"I'm Colton Cassidy," the man replied. "And this is—"

"I can speak for myself," his brother Collin interrupted. But he didn't say anything more, just headed across the lobby toward the elevators. Maybe he was heading to the administration office or maybe to a room to check on a patient. Either way, she didn't care.

"He's usually not such a jerk," Colton said

with a sigh. "It's just been a rough couple of days."

"I saw the bandages…" she murmured with sympathy.

"He was treated at the Moss Valley ER. The burns aren't too bad," Colton said. "He should heal quickly, just not quick enough to suit Collin."

She'd seen more than her share of burns in the ER, and her sympathy grew. "I'm sure it must be difficult for him to not have the use of his hands."

Colton nodded. "Yeah, but he should have known better than to rush into a burning house like my dad and my other brother had done."

She gasped with shock and concern and a sudden realization. Colton Cassidy, he'd said his name was, so he was probably talking about the Cassidy Ranch. She'd been in the Willow Creek ER waiting room with her grandfather two days ago when Baker Haven had told his brothers about it catching fire and what he'd discovered there: family. An uncle Sadie had never told them about and cousins that apparently Sadie hadn't even known about.

Livvy had already determined to stay out of that, so she quelled her curiosity but not her concern. "Oh, no, is everyone okay?" she asked.

He nodded, and the black cowboy hat slipped a little lower on his forehead, casting his face in shadow. "Yeah, Collin's burns are the worst of the injuries from that day. My older brother Marsh had a few small third-degree burns and, like my dad did, a bit of smoke inhalation, but nothing too serious."

"And you?" she asked as the curiosity about him refused to go away.

He grinned. "I'm a firefighter, so I know not to go into a situation like that unprepared." His voice dropping to a gruff whisper, he added, "If only I could have prepared for other things…"

He was definitely one of the Cassidys Baker had talked about finding. Baker hadn't known about that branch of his family, and from the pensive look on Colton's face and Collin's attitude, she suspected the Cassidys hadn't known about their relationship to the Havens either. She could only imagine how shocked and devastated Colton was. Despite not wanting to get involved, she had a strange urge to reach out to him. To comfort him.

Just like her curiosity, she fought to quell that as well, curling her fingers into her palm to physically restrain herself.

She wasn't sure if Colton had intended for

her to hear the last part, but she found herself whispering in reply, "I don't think there is any way to prepare for everything." She hadn't been prepared to lose her grandma, even though she'd known she was sick, or her mom or herself...

Colton uttered a ragged sigh and bobbed his head in agreement. "True. Very true...unfortunately." And he stared at her speculatively, those dark eyes intense, as if he wondered what she hadn't been prepared for.

Her heart did another little flippy move in her chest. Him. She hadn't been prepared to meet Colton Cassidy.

SADIE'S HEART WAS so full that she felt as if it was about to burst. She really hoped that didn't happen now, not when she was so happy.

"You're here," she murmured as she stared at her oldest child through a sheen of tears. She'd been so certain for so long that he was dead that she hadn't allowed herself to hope to see him again. And while she could have been angry that he'd stayed away so long, she wasn't going to waste a minute on anger, on anything but gratitude.

After his sons had left, they'd retired to the easy chairs in the sitting area of her suite, leaving Darlene in the kitchen with the others so she could reconnect with her sons and connect with her grandsons. All these years, the poor woman had believed that they all blamed her for her husband's death because she'd been on the tractor with him when he'd gotten hurt. Darlene was lucky she hadn't been killed as well, and she never should have blamed herself. Sadie certainly never had, and she knew Darlene's sons hadn't either. Hopefully they could convince her of that and they could all heal.

"You're really here…" she murmured, as she stared at her oldest son.

Jessup's lips curved into a faint grin. "Are you talking about at the ranch? Or the fact that I'm alive at all?"

"Both," she admitted.

"I've missed your blunt honesty," he said.

"I've missed you."

"I missed you, too," Jessup said. "But I was sick so many times, close to death, that I didn't want to reconnect with you just for you to watch me die, especially after you just lost Michael and then Dad."

She reached across the space between their chairs and clasped his hand. "Even if it would have been for just a minute before you passed, I would have treasured that minute I could have spent with you…"

He released a ragged sigh and nodded. "I should have realized that, especially after Cash took off."

She hated to pry but she had to ask, "Why did he leave?"

Jessup's shoulders sagged. "He found out something that he couldn't handle knowing…"

"That he's a Haven?" she asked.

"That's the thing…" Tears brimmed in his eyes but he blinked them back and shook his head. "I can't talk about that…until I can talk to him again."

"You don't have any idea where he is?" she asked with concern for this child she hadn't met. But he wasn't a child. He was a man now.

Jessup shook his head. "I hope he went on to college. He had some scholarships. He was a smart kid, but he was so mad when he left that he might have thrown it all away to spite me." His voice cracked with emotion. "I'm sorry for how I treated you when I was a kid. I know now that you were just worried about losing me. That's why you were so—"

"Overbearing," she interjected. "I'm sorry that I was—"

"Protective," he said as if correcting her.

"And worried. I hated seeing how worried and scared you were all the time, every time you looked at me."

She gave him a pointed look now, one she infused with love and gratefulness and hope. "But you're home now. He might come home to you, too."

"The home he knew is gone," Jessup said, "And I haven't seen him in seventeen years."

Her smile slid away as sympathy for him overwhelmed her. "That's a long time."

"Not as long as I've been gone," he said. "I am really sorry, Mom."

Her heart ached thinking of all the lost years, but she pushed those thoughts from her mind and forced her smile back. "Let's not dwell on the past," she said. "Let's focus on the present and prepare for the future."

His jaw dropped open for a moment before his dark eyes brightened. "I've always focused only on the present because my future was so unknown. But now..." He pressed his free hand against his chest.

And she knew, because of dear, sweet Dale, Jessup had a future now. "I am so glad that something good came of that senseless tragedy," she said, blinking against the sudden sting of tears in her eyes. She should have been all cried out by now, after all the sobbing she'd done, albeit in private, over the many losses in her life.

But again she was going to focus solely on the present and the future. She couldn't change the past; she could only learn from it. And that meant not pushing Jessup too far again, not pressuring him or trying to protect him as obsessively as she had. She'd tried to keep him out of school, home in his room where she'd thought he'd be safe from germs and a flare-up of his lupus. But she'd driven him away instead.

"I know your house burned down," she began softly, trying to figure out how to make an offer without it sounding bossy or controlling.

He shrugged. "We were going to have to move anyway," he said. "We were in the process of selling the ranch."

She nodded. "To my grandson Dusty."

He chuckled. "I had no idea he was a Haven. I thought the buyer was some rodeo rider by the name of Chaps."

She swallowed a sigh. "Yes, that was the name Dusty used when he was with the rodeo. It was some kind of branding-marketing ploy." While she hadn't been happy he'd changed his name, she knew it had been a successful strategy in getting him endorsements. He'd earned enough money from those to pay for the ranch. And earlier today he'd assured Jessup that he still intended to buy it. He wanted the acreage, barns and Darlene's mare; he'd never intended to use the house.

"I used a different name when I was with the rodeo, too."

"As a bullfighter..." She shuddered at the thought. "And here I was worried about your illness."

"My lifelong battle with lupus has been tougher on me than any of those bulls or broncs were," he said. "Seventeen years ago I had a kidney transplant, but my body rejected it and I needed another one. But now specialists think that the new heart put it in remission. So finally I am going to focus on the future."

"With Darlene?" she asked with curiosity.

He chuckled. "She's like my sister."

"Sister-in-law."

He shook his head. "No. We're closer than that. She kept me alive. She kept my boys on track. If only she'd found me before Cash left..."

"I want to get to know your boys," she said. "They left so quickly..."

Jessup nodded. "I know. This has been hard on them to find out I kept so much from them. And I should have known better. I should have been honest with them. But I was worried that they would react like Cash had over secrets, and I was scared that I might lose them, too."

Sadie squeezed his hand in commiseration. She'd kept secrets, too; she'd kept *him* secret. She'd told Michael not to tell his kids about his brother. He'd agreed because it had been hard for him to talk about Jessup, too; like her, he'd worried that he was dead. And after Michael had died and Darlene left, it had been point-less to tell her grandsons that they might or might not have an uncle. She hadn't realized that Darlene had left to find him…for Sadie, to replace the son she'd blamed herself for taking from her. "You were doing what you thought was best."

"I thought wrong," he said. "It was wrong to stay away from you and wrong to not tell my sons everything years ago."

"Then don't stay away any longer," she said. "You and Darlene and your sons should move to the ranch."

He chuckled again. "You haven't changed."

"I'm sorry," she said. "I was really trying not to push."

He grinned. "Really?"

"I was trying, but I really do want you all to stay here. I missed you so much. And I'd love to have the whole family together, to get to know my grandsons."

"It's still early days for me with this heart transplant," he said as if warning her.

A pang of fear struck her heart. "Is everything okay?"

"Yes," he said. "But the Cassidy Ranch was closer to the hospital than Ranch Haven is. I need to make sure that I'm close to medical help."

"I can hire a home health aide—"

"Darlene and Collin already hired one for me," he said. "There's only so much Sarah can handle, though. I need to be in town. Right now Darlene and I are staying at a hotel in Moss Valley."

That small town was even farther away from Sadie than the Cassidy Ranch. She implored him, "At least move back to Willow Creek. The hospital is great and has a wonderful new cardiologist on staff. And even though he can't treat you, there are other ones in Willow Creek."

"I'll think about it," he said.

"And Darlene and your sons could still move to the ranch," she persisted.

He chuckled. "They might be called Cassidys, which was my wife's last name, but they are Havens through and through with their stubbornness and their independence. They've all had their own places for a while."

"Do you have daughters-in-law? Grandchildren?" she eagerly asked.

He shook his head. "The boys are all still single."

"They're older than your nephews," she pointed out.

As if she hadn't spoken, he continued with a smile, "And determined to stay that way, which might have been why they hightailed it out of here when their cousins warned them about your penchant for matchmaking."

She snorted. "Like any of Michael's boys has reason to complain."

"They do seem very happy," Jessup said with a wistfulness in his deep voice.

"You want that for your sons, too," she said.

He nodded. "Of course. That's what you want most for your children. Health and happiness."

Those traitorous tears stung her eyes again. "I wasn't able to give you either."

"You gave me love," he said, turning his

hand over to clasp hers. "So very much love. And I thought that leaving was giving that love back, saving you from having to worry about me being sick all the time. But I know that it doesn't matter where your kids are, you worry about them. You want them to be happy."

"Love makes you happy," she said. And for some reason, she thought not of her late husband but of that old fool Lem. He'd been there for her for the family meeting earlier today, supporting her as he'd been since they'd buried their old rivalry and become friends. But that was all they really were. Right? They'd both already had their great loves. She wanted all of her grandsons to find their great loves.

She'd found them for Michael's sons. She would for Jessup's as well. But she had to acknowledge they might give her a bit more of a challenge. Since they were older, they were definitely true bachelor cowboys.

Sadie had never backed down from a challenge, though. In fact, the greater the challenge, the more determined she was to succeed.

CHAPTER THREE

COLTON COULD HAVE gone back outside to where Marsh waited in the SUV for him and Collin, but he preferred to hang out in the Emergency Room waiting area. He could have mentally used the excuse that, as a paramedic firefighter, he had a professional curiosity about the place since he occasionally transported patients here. That was the initial reason he'd come inside with Collin, but it wasn't the reason he was staying. *She* was.

He had to admit that because he was always honest with himself, even though he couldn't quite be honest with everyone else right now. At least not over what he'd found in the fire.

But in all honesty, the only curiosity that was keeping him in the ER, standing close to the intake desk while he waited for Collin to come back down from checking on a patient, was his curiosity about the new ER attending doctor.

Strawberry blond tendrils that had escaped

from the clip holding up her hair, curled around her delicately featured face. And her eyes. They were so heavily lashed and such a stunning green, but when her gaze met his, she quickly looked away and her pale skin flushed. Was she as curious about him as he was her?

He'd checked out her hand earlier to see if she was married, and he'd noticed the indentation on her ring finger. She might have been recently divorced, or maybe she just took off her jewelry at work.

She was probably only hanging out at the intake desk because she was bored. Nobody had come into the ER in the long minutes he'd been waiting for Collin to come back down from the in-patient floor. His twin had convinced Colton to come by the hospital after they'd left Ranch Haven.

Because of the burns on his hands, Collin wasn't able to drive yet, so Colton had offered to play chauffeur for the journey out to Ranch Haven earlier today. While Marsh was physically able to drive himself, he'd tagged along with them, probably not wanting to go alone to face this secret family they'd never known they'd had.

His stomach knotted with anger over being kept in the dark for so long. But then he also felt guilty for being angry when he should just be grateful that his dad was alive. They'd come so close to losing him so many times. And what if they had? Would they have ever found out who they really were, that they had this whole family they'd never known about?

That day in the hospital, after the fire, Dad had apologized for screwing up so badly, for not knowing how to tell them, for being worried that they'd be so furious that they would leave.

Like Cash had...

Dad hadn't said that, but Colton suspected that was what he'd been thinking and had held him back from telling them all the truth. Was finding out he was a Haven the reason that Cash had left?

It seemed like an extreme reaction, but Cash had been a teenager. And even though he'd seemed mature as the oldest, he'd really just been a kid. They weren't kids now. Worrying about Dad as much as they had growing up, maybe they'd never really been kids.

Colton quelled his anger over the secret, though, because he was keeping a secret of his own. And for the same reason his father had kept his: to make sure nobody got hurt.

He reached into his pocket and ran his fingers over that silver lighter again. It might not be the only one like it, with those sideways horseshoes spelling out CC, but it was the only one Colton had ever seen. Though it had been many years…

So many years. Sadness rushed up on him, overwhelming him, and he closed his eyes to hold it in, to force himself beyond it.

Someone touched his arm and asked, "Are you all right?"

Startled, he jerked back a step and opened his eyes to Dr. Lemmon's beautiful face turned up to his. She was so petite that she didn't even come to his shoulder.

She studied him with concern in her green eyes. "Are you all right?" she asked again.

He nodded. "Yeah."

"You said you weren't hurt in that fire, but that must have been hard, emotionally, losing your family home like that," she said with sympathy.

Sympathy that confused him. He wasn't sure that he'd told her where the fire had been that had injured his dad and brothers. But maybe she'd just assumed since they'd all been there.

"It was being sold anyways," he said with a shrug.

"But sold and destroyed are different," she

said, and she touched his arm again in another comforting gesture.

Even through the material of his western shirt, he could feel the warmth of her hand, and that warmth moved through him, easing some of the anger and guilt and confusion he'd been grappling with. In addition to being beautiful, she was also very empathetic and sweet. And with being a doctor, she had to be smart, too. Maybe that was why she understood so well.

"You can't go by and see it again…the way it was when you grew up there," she said.

Was that why Cash might have burned down the place? Because he'd rather see it destroyed than sold? But he couldn't think about Cash now. He could only see her, only feel her. As if she'd just realized her hand was on his arm, she pulled it back, and her face flushed again.

He furrowed his brow beneath the rim of his hat and stared intently at her now. "Do you know me?" he asked. "Have we met before?" He doubted that; he definitely would have remembered her.

She shook her head. "No. I only just moved back to Willow Creek from Chicago."

"But it's like you know…" What he was going through, the secret he'd just learned. Or maybe finding that lighter had made him paranoid about everything and everybody because really, how could she know what he'd just found out himself?

"I…" She paused and drew in a deep breath, then continued, "…know the Havens."

Tension gripped him, but he reacted as he usually did in tense situations, with amusement. He grinned at her and said, "Then that makes one of us."

She grimaced. "Oh, I'm sorry. I shouldn't have said anything. It's not any of my business."

"I wish it wasn't mine either," he said with a heavy sigh. "But clearly you know what my brothers and I just found out, that we're…" He couldn't quite bring himself to say the word, to go by the name that he'd never known was actually his.

She nodded. "The Havens were here a couple of days ago when they brought their grandmother into the ER, and I overheard…" She guiltily looked away from him after the admission of eavesdropping.

"But I thought today was your first day," he recalled.

"I wasn't working," she said. "I was here because they brought Sadie in."

"So you know them." Apparently well enough

that she'd come to the hospital with them. "But didn't you just move here?"

"I just moved back," she said. "I grew up here, but I don't really know the Havens very well. But my grandfather is friends with Sadie, and I brought him to the ER to see how she was."

"The old guy..." He'd met him at Ranch Haven a couple of hours ago, but he couldn't remember his name. Going there to the ranch where his dad had grown up, from where he'd run away, had felt more like a dream than something that had actually happened. "Looks like Santa Claus?"

She smiled and nodded. "Yes, he plays Santa every holiday season in the town square. He's close to Sadie." Her mouth turned down as she said it, as if she didn't approve. "And he's the deputy mayor for Ben Haven, who is the Willow Creek mayor. And my dad works for Katie, Jake Haven's wife."

He'd met them all, but the moment had been so surreal that the names and faces were hazy. He shrugged. "Then you do have stronger ties to them than I do." He just had blood. No bonds. No memories. Like he shared with his brothers. More with Collin and Marsh than with Cash.

He hadn't seen Cash in so long. Was he back in Moss Valley? Had he come home after all this time just to burn down the place? Colton was far more concerned about his oldest brother than he was about a family he didn't even know. He was also a little concerned about Dr. Lemmon and his interest in her. Sure, she was beautiful and sympathetic and smart. But with everything going on with his family and the fire, he had no time to spare to even flirt with her. And he was never going to have a relationship and put a wife and kids through the worry he and his brothers had grown up feeling over their parents' health.

His brothers suddenly, simultaneously, appeared in the lobby: Collin down the stairs and Marsh through the automatic doors. While family had to be his focus right now, he hesitated before joining his brothers. Before leaving Dr. Lemmon, he wanted to say something to her, something to show his appreciation for her sympathy. But before he could come up with anything, Collin addressed her. "Dr. Lemmon, I'm sorry if I was rude earlier—"

"If?" Colton interjected. "You were definitely rude."

Collin ignored him as he focused on the ER attending. "I am sorry that I was short with you. I had a patient that I needed to check on right away."

"I hope everything is okay," Dr. Lemmon graciously replied.

Collin's shoulders slumped. "We'll see."

Standing behind them, Marsh muttered, "Are we talking about your patient or…"

Collin turned back and shook his head. "Let's not talk about that here."

They hadn't even talked about it on the drive between the ranch and the hospital, as if they were all floundering with how to feel about Dad's big secret. Maybe he wasn't the only one struggling with his emotions over the family revelation.

"If you're worried about airing our family's dirty laundry, it's too late. Dr. Lemmon already knows," Colton informed his twin. "Her grandfather was there today at the ranch."

"Oh…" Collin nodded. "Old Man Lemmon?"

"That's rude," Colton chastised him.

"That's what everyone calls him," Dr. Lemmon said. "Even my dad." And she smiled with such obvious warmth and affection for her family that Colton's heart flooded with warmth and affection.

For her?

He didn't even know her, and with everything going on in his life right now, he didn't have the time or the wherewithal to get to know her.

THEY WERE ALL staring at her—all three brothers who looked so much alike that they could have been triplets. But of the three, only one's gaze affected her, making her skin heat and tingle. They were all handsome, so her interest in him wasn't superficial. Maybe it was just sympathy over how lost and upset he'd looked while waiting for his brother, like he was carrying some heavy burden.

That wasn't her business, though, and she shouldn't have rushed out from behind the intake desk to check on him earlier. But when he'd closed his eyes and swayed slightly on his feet, he'd looked so shaky that she'd been worried he was about to pass out. And she hadn't been convinced that he wasn't injured in that fire despite his claims of having been prepared. Once he'd opened his eyes again, she could tell that the pain in them wasn't physical but emotional. He hadn't just lost his family home in that fire; he had also kind of lost his family as he'd known them when he'd learned about being related to the Havens.

They looked as much like the Havens as they

did each other. Standing in the ER with the Cassidy brothers was like being there two days ago with the Haven brothers and the rest of their family and her grandfather. Beneath her breath, she murmured, "This feels like déjà vu."

Colton must have heard her because he chuckled. "It was even weirder going out to Ranch Haven."

The other brother she had yet to meet grimaced, and then he must have realized he hadn't introduced himself because he held out his hand. "I'm Marsh Cassidy."

She shook it. "Nice to meet you. I'm Olivia." Steven had only ever called her that; he'd refused to use her nickname. "But here in Willow Creek, everyone calls me Livvy."

"Yeah, Marsh is what our oldest brother, Cash, called me when he was little because he couldn't say Michael March…" His voice trailed off.

"March is Sadie's maiden name," Livvy said. Her grandfather always called his former nemesis by her full name: Sadie March Haven.

"And Michael was our dad's brother," Colton added, and he reached out and clasped his older brother's shoulder. They were obviously close, like the Havens were. "Do you have any brothers or sisters?" he asked her.

He was probably just anxious to change the subject from his family and the Havens. She smiled. "Yes, I have two older brothers and a younger one. We're not very close, though." Not like they all obviously were.

"Why's that?" he asked.

And his older brother nudged him with his shoulder. "Jeez, Colton, it's not any of your business."

Hers was the face that flushed with embarrassment that she'd mentioned something so personal when he'd just asked a simple question. With her pale skin, she blushed so easily and so brightly. "I started it," she defended Colton. "I brought up the Havens, and that's not any of my business."

"Your grandpa's involved with Sadie," Colton said with a slight grin. "So it kind of is…"

She shook her head.

"They're not involved?" Colton asked, but his dark eyes held a hint of amusement.

He obviously knew that Old Man Lemmon wouldn't have been there today for that family meeting if he wasn't extremely close to Sadie. Livvy herself had seen him with Sadie the other night at the hospital. They were more than friends.

She should have been happy for him, but she couldn't help but worry. He was eighty. He'd already lost his wife, and Sadie had a heart condition. Could he survive another loss like that if something happened to her?

"Dr. Lemmon," the older nurse called out from the front desk. "We have a call for you."

She tensed, worried that it might be Steven since she hadn't answered his text, and he knew where she worked. During the four years she'd known him, he'd been impatient if she didn't respond right away even though, as a doctor himself, he should have known that it wasn't always possible for her to get to her phone. She forced a smile for the Cassidys and said to them all, "It was nice meeting you."

She was lying. The meeting had unsettled her for a couple of reasons.

Her grandfather.

Now she was worried about him.

And her interest in Colton Cassidy, in whatever burden he was carrying on those broad shoulders, whatever emotions he was dealing with after losing his family home and finding out a major secret. She shouldn't care so much, but she did. And that unsettled her most of all.

LEM JERKED AWAKE with a snort and reached for the phone vibrating in his pocket. His sudden move startled Feisty, and the long-haired Chihuahua emitted a soft growl from where she slept, curled up on his lap. He glanced over at the easy chair next to his, where Sadie had also nodded off to sleep.

Alarm sent a little jab to his heart, and he reached over to touch her hand. Without opening her eyes, she said, "I'm alive. Now answer your phone."

He'd forgotten he held the vibrating cell in his hand and glanced down at it. The screen lit up: Livvy. Smiling, he swiped to accept her video call. That was how she'd talked to him when she'd lived so far away, so they could see as well as hear each other. "Hello there, Dr. Lemmon," he greeted her.

Her laugh tinkled out of the speaker on his phone. "Hello there, Grandpa."

"How was your first day, sweetheart?"

"Would have been quite uneventful…"

"Would have been?" he prodded when she trailed off. "Did something horrible happen?"

"Not horrible," she said, but she didn't sound very convincing. And her face, on the small screen, lost its pretty smile.

"An accident?"

"No, nothing medical. Personal."

"Your ex-fiancé?" Lem had met the man only a couple of times, at Livvy's med school graduation and when she'd finished her residency in Emergency Medicine. The guy hadn't been interested in anyone but himself and *his* career. Lem was very relieved that he was her *ex*.

She hesitated for such a long time that Lem had to prod her. "Livvy? Did he show up in Willow Creek?"

She chuckled softly. "He has no interest in ever coming to Willow Creek," she said. "That won't happen."

But just because he wouldn't come in person didn't mean the man wasn't still hassling her. "Then what is the personal thing that happened?" he asked.

"Not personal to me," she said. "Personal to you. Colton, Collin and Marsh Cassidy came by the ER today."

Sadie gasped then and shot upright from her recliner chair. Before she could ask, Lem did. "Are they all right? Was anyone hurt?"

"No. Collin was checking on a patient."

Sadie waved her hand at him, urging him to ask something, and knowing her as well as he knew himself, he posed the question. "So what did you think of them?"

Sadie's dark eyes twinkled with excitement. Despite that scare with her heart a couple of days ago, she was looking like her old self again. Vital. Beautiful.

Livvy hesitated another long moment.

"What's wrong, sweetheart?" he asked. "Didn't you like them?"

"They're a lot," she conceded. "But then you know that. All the Havens are a lot."

Sadie smiled as if the comment was high praise.

But Lem was confused. "Is that a good thing?"

"Not to me," Livvy said, her usual soft voice sharp. "What about you, Grandpa? Isn't that too much turmoil for you to handle after losing Grandma like you did?"

Oh, so slowly…his sweet Mary had just slipped away from him. He felt that jab to his heart again, the old cracks from where it had broken over how much his dear wife had had to suffer. Fortunately she'd been less aware of it than he had been.

Sadie reached across the space between their chairs and covered his hand with hers. Sadie knew. She'd helped him with Mary. She'd been there through the long goodbye.

Everybody had been calling him Old Man Lemmon for so many years that Livvy must have taken it to heart. "I'm stronger than I look," Lem assured her. And younger. Or maybe he was actually the age that he'd looked for so many years since his hair and beard had turned white in his early fifties.

"I still worry about you," she said.

"And I worry about you, sweetheart." Less now that her engagement had ended and she'd come home. She already seemed more like her old self...so concerned and caring of everyone else.

Except perhaps for Sadie's family.

"Did those boys do something to upset you?"

"No," she quickly assured him. She didn't sound convinced or convincing to him.

"What happened, Livvy?"

"Nothing, Grandpa, they just have a lot going on now, and I don't want you getting stressed out over all of it," she said.

Warmth spread throughout his chest, and he smiled. "You're sweet to worry about me, honey, but I'm fine."

"Okay..." She sounded doubtful, so he must not have convinced her. "Want to meet me for dinner after I get out of here?" she asked. "My shift is over, and I'll be done with my charts in about ten minutes."

"I'm out at Ranch Haven," he said.

"You're still there?"

He smiled, feeling a bit like a kid caught out after curfew. "Yes, honey. Remember how I told you that Sadie hired the best cook in all of Willow Creek to work out here at the ranch?"

Sadie moved her hand from his, to his shoulder, smacking him lightly. Then she gestured at the phone again, and he knew.

"You're welcome to come out here for dinner, too," he said.

"No."

"Of course you are, honey."

"I meant that I don't want to," she said, then cleared her throat and added, "It's too long a drive. I'll see you another time."

"Any time," he said. "I love you."

"Love you, too, Grandpa."

The cell phone fell silent, like him and Sadie. Only Feisty murmured in her sleep as she shifted to a more comfortable position on his lap.

"She doesn't like the Havens," Sadie remarked.

Lem sighed. "That's probably my fault. I've said some things about you over the years. Called you bossy and domineering and a manipulator...you know...the truth."

She chuckled and smacked his shoulder again.

"So you warned her. No wonder she doesn't want to come out here."

"Ben warned her, too," Lem said. "Said you have plans for her."

"I do," she conceded. "But I didn't know which grandson would suit her until now."

"What do you mean?" he asked, confused.

"Well, you saw how quickly they left," she reminded him. The three Cassidy brothers had hightailed it off the ranch the minute their dad had concluded introductions.

"Yes, they didn't give you the chance to interrogate them," he said with a smile. They had obviously all inherited her shrewdness.

"At least they were telling the truth," she said. "Collin really did have to check on a patient."

"Is that the one you've picked out for my granddaughter's future husband?" he asked. "The cardiologist?"

She shook her head.

And he leaned forward in his chair, earning him another growl from Feisty. She was about as surly and demanding as her mistress could be. He ran his hand over her back, petting her. "Why not?" he asked. "It makes the most sense."

She smiled at him. "And what makes the most

sense doesn't always work. Sometimes what makes the least sense is the strongest love."

And the look in her eyes as she said it, the intensity, the warmth…sent a jolt to his heart. They didn't make sense. They never had. That was why she'd fallen for Big Jake and he for sweet petite Mary. But there was more to compatibility than size or profession or even common sense.

He smiled back at her. "So which one did you choose for my granddaughter?" he asked.

"She already chose," Sadie said.

"What? Did I miss something? She didn't sound interested in any of them."

Sadie's smile turned patronizing now; that one he recognized all too well, and when once it would have infuriated him, he just chuckled now, knowing she was about to enlighten him.

"She said they're a lot," she repeated his granddaughter's words.

He nodded. "Yeah, I'm not going senile. I remember. How does that tell you she's interested or that she chose one of them?"

"They definitely made an impression on her."

"How could they not?" Lem asked. They were all good-looking: the epitome of tall, dark and handsome like their grandfather had been.

He ignored the little twinge of jealousy as he thought of Big Jake. He'd been a good man; Sadie wouldn't have fallen for him otherwise.

"But she said his name first," Sadie replied. "Colton…"

CHAPTER FOUR

THAT LIGHTER WAS burning a hole in Colton's pocket, figuratively only, but he didn't want to share his suspicion with anyone else in the family. Especially now.

They had enough to contend with over the ranch house burning down. Even though Dusty had said he was still going to buy it, the sale hadn't closed yet, and when it did, most of that money would probably go toward the mortgage and medical bills Dad owed. The house insurance hadn't paid out much yet since they were waiting on word from the fire department. So they'd given Dad just a small draw of money for clothing and additional living expenses, but there weren't many available places in Moss Valley. Dad and Darlene had taken a suite in a motel, but the accommodations were small and rundown and the home health care nurse wasn't able to stay with them like she had at the ranch.

He gazed around the dimly lit motel room

and felt a tightening in his chest. "You can't stay here, Dad," he said. He wished he had room at his place, but he shared it with a couple of other single firefighters and they were already overcrowded.

Since Collin had finished up his cardiology fellowship in Boston and returned home, he'd been crashing at Marsh's, but the studio apartment in Moss Valley wasn't big enough for the two of them. They stood near the couch where Dad sat with Darlene, and they both nodded in agreement with Colton.

"We need to find you something nicer," Collin said.

"A place big enough that Sarah and her son can stay with you," Marsh added.

"Your grandmother wants me to move back to the ranch," Dad said.

"To Ranch Haven." It wasn't a question. There was no place to move back to at the Cassidy Ranch unless Dad and Darlene bunked in the barn with her mare.

Darlene answered it anyway, "Dusty is still buying your dad's ranch."

"Not mine," Dad corrected her before turning back toward Colton and his brothers. "That ranch was your mother's and has always belonged to you boys."

She'd actually left everything to Dad when she died, but he'd insisted on putting it in a trust for them, probably because he'd worried he would soon follow her to the grave. But knowing that Dad wasn't able to manage and finance it anymore and none of them had the time to work it, Colton, Collin and Marsh had agreed to sell it. But Cash…

Had he decided to burn it down instead? Why not just come home and help? He'd wanted so badly to help Dad all those years ago that he'd tried to give him one of his kidneys. But after that yelling match they'd had in the yard, Cash had taken off and never returned.

"Do we know what caused the fire yet?" Dad asked. "Was it the old wiring? I should have been better at keeping the place up to code."

Darlene shook her head. "You've been so sick, JJ. It wasn't your fault. I was supposed to be doing more to help."

"You couldn't have done any more," Dad assured her. "You were running yourself ragged trying to keep the ranch going."

A twinge of guilt struck Colton. He'd seen it, too, but he hadn't done enough to help. While he'd contributed money to the medical bills and ranch upkeep, he'd had to pull extra shifts to do that and hadn't had the time to physically help out.

"We all should have been doing more," Marsh said. Then he turned toward Colton. "Any word yet on what caused it? Was it the wiring?"

Colton shrugged. "I haven't heard yet, but I have a meeting with my captain tomorrow. He might have made a determination." Since their fire department was so small, the captain usually determined the cause of the fire and reported it to the insurance department. Could he have figured out what Colton took from the scene? Evidence?

"So are you going to move to Ranch Haven?" Marsh asked.

Before Dad could answer, Collin chimed in with, "I didn't think it was smart for you to be so far from town at our ranch. Ranch Haven might be even farther. You really need to be closer to a hospital."

"That's what I told your grandmother," Dad admitted.

"But we have to find you a better place to live than this," Colton said with another glance around the shabby suite.

Moss Valley didn't have a whole lot of places to rent, which was why he shared that two-bedroom with a couple of guys and Marsh had only the studio apartment.

"I would like to be closer to my mother than

Moss Valley, so I'm going to move to Willow Creek," Dad said.

Colton felt a twinge of panic about his dad moving away from him. While it was only an hour, with as busy as Colton was at the firehouse, he doubted he'd get over to see him that often. And after all the years of worrying that he would lose him, he needed to see him as often as he could. Though if he had to go to Willow Creek to see him, Colton might get a chance to see Dr. Livvy Lemmon then, too. His pulse quickened at the thought.

"What about you, Darlene?" Colton asked. "Will you be moving back to the ranch?"

She sucked in a breath as if the thought horrified her. Colton had figured her fear over returning when they'd visited a couple of days ago had been about facing her family again. But maybe being there was too painful a reminder of losing her husband in an accident on the ranch. "No," she said. "I want to stay with your father for a while and help Sarah and her son if they need it."

"Let's call Becca, then," Marsh said, referring to their realtor. "Her office is in Willow Creek. She'll know what's for sale there."

"I can't buy anything until the ranch sale goes through," Dad said. "I'm just looking for a place to stay for a bit. Old Man Lemmon called me today with a couple of options."

Livvy's grandfather. Colton's pulse quickened even more. "That was nice of him."

"Very nice," Dad said. "He and his son both have places in town, and with as little as either of them are home, they're willing to move in together and let us stay in one of their houses. Darlene and I are going to check them out tomorrow."

"What about Livvy?" Colton asked.

"Livvy?" Dad looked confused.

Marsh and Collin both chuckled and Collin added, "The pretty new ER doctor at Willow Creek Memorial Hospital."

"She's Lem's granddaughter," Colton reminded them.

"That doesn't mean she's staying with either of them," his dad pointed out, probably because none of his sons stayed with him.

Colton shrugged. "Yeah, I guess I didn't think about that. She's a doctor making the big bucks like Collin here, so she's probably got her own place."

Collin snorted. "The big bucks go towards all the student loans."

"That's why you're mooching off me," Marsh said.

"I'm going to look for a place in Willow

Creek, too," Collin said. "Now that I'll be working out of that hospital."

No doubt he wanted to be close to Dad, too. Collin probably worried the most about their dad because, as a cardiologist, he knew the most about Dad's heart transplant.

And even though Dad looked healthier than Colton ever remembered him looking, he wasn't totally out of the woods yet. His body could still reject his new heart. But he seemed good, really good and happy. And because of that, Colton couldn't tell him what he'd found in the fire. He had to keep that lighter to himself until he figured out what it meant.

"So tell me about this other doctor at Willow Creek Memorial," Dad said, and his dark eyes focused on Colton's face.

"Why ask me? Collin works with her. And Marsh met her, too."

"But you were the one talking to her," Collin said.

"Yeah, because you were rude," Colton reminded him.

"I apologized. My head was just…"

"Were you worried about your patient?" Darlene asked. "Or did you just want to get away from Ranch Haven?"

"Both," Collin admitted.

Darlene smiled. "We've been invited back to the ranch. All of us."

"More like summoned," Dad corrected her, but he was grinning.

Colton really couldn't remember the last time his dad had looked so happy. He wanted to refuse to return for another awkward visit, but seeing Dad like this...

He knew he couldn't disappoint or upset him. That was why he couldn't tell anyone about that lighter. "Let me know when," Colton said. "And I'll see if I can make it."

"Maybe Lem will bring his granddaughter along," Dad said, his grin widening.

Even as his pulse began to race, Colton shook his head. "Our new cousins warned us about Sadie. They didn't know that you're just like her."

"I must be," Dad said, "or I don't think I'd still be here."

Darlene nodded. "You are strong, like she is."

"Stubborn," Colton corrected her. They all were, but nobody more than Cash.

Where was he? Had he come home?

"You did what?" Livvy asked her dad and grandfather. She lowered her coffee cup and stared at them across the breakfast table in the eat-in kitchen of the home where she'd spent the first six, almost seven years of her life.

"*We* offered our houses to the Cassidy family," her father replied, but he shot a significant glance at her grandfather, leaving her no doubt *who* had actually made the offer.

"But where will *we* live?" she asked.

"They're just choosing one of them," Grandpa said. "Whatever one will work best for Jessup, Darlene, and the home-care nurse and her son. So we'll all move into the other house together." He grinned with delight at the idea.

Living with both her dad and her grandpa appealed to her as well, but her dad's face paled with dread. After they'd moved to Chicago, he'd kept the house where he and Mom had started their family and had rented it out. But he'd been reluctant to return to Willow Creek, worried that his widowed father might meddle in his life. Apparently he hadn't been wrong.

A smile tugged at her lips, but she suppressed it to shoot her dad a look of commiseration instead. Maybe she shouldn't have worried about Grandpa being involved with the Havens. While they were a lot, so was he. The smile slipped out and her dad glared at her before cracking a grin himself.

Grandpa narrowed his bright blue eyes and studied them. "You're both onboard with this, aren't you? It's the right thing to do after their home burned down."

"A home they were about to sell to Dusty and Melanie," Livvy's dad said. "They should have been looking for a place to stay. And now that Jessup and Darlene have reconciled with Sadie, why don't they go back to the ranch?"

"Jessup's still in early days with his heart transplant. He needs to be close to the hospital," Grandpa explained. "And they didn't already have something because they needed the money from the sale of the ranch to get out from under a mountain of debt from Jessup's medical bills. Stepping in to help with a place for them to stay in town, close to the hospital, is the least we can do."

Livvy's face got hot with a flood of shame, and her dad lowered his gaze to his breakfast plate. "It is the least we can do," she acknowledged. She hadn't even done that for her grandfather and her dad when her grandma and mom were going through their long illnesses.

"Sadie helped me with Mary," Grandpa said, his voice gruff with emotion as his eyes glistened. "She was there for me, doing what she could. I want to do this for her now."

Livvy suspected he hadn't made this magnanimous offer out of gratitude or for payback. Her grandfather had definitely fallen for Sadie Haven. Livvy really couldn't blame him; Sadie March Haven was an impressive woman. She was strong and independent: all the things Livvy wished she'd been and that she vowed she would be from now on.

While she loved reconnecting with her granddad and dad, she needed her own place. After the stagnancy and stifling of her four-year relationship with Steven, she needed to figure out how to be single, which was what she fully intended to be for a long while if not forever.

"You're both invited out to the ranch tomorrow," Lem said. "The family is having a little welcome back to the fold party for Jessup and Darlene."

"Then it should be just family there," her dad pointed out. "Why would we be included?"

Grandpa's face flushed now. "Well, you know Sadie and I have been friends for a very long time."

Her dad snorted, but now he was the one fighting a smile, his lips curving up slightly. "Friends? You haven't always spoken kindly of her and vice versa."

"We've had our differences," Grandpa admitted. "She can be bossy."

Her dad snorted again. "And you can't?"

Grandpa glared at his son. "We aren't talking about me right now."

Livvy giggled at their exchange. "I've missed you both," she said. And living with them would definitely be entertaining, but she needed to find her own place. She needed to make her own place in the world.

"So you'll come along to the ranch?" Grandpa asked, and his blue eyes brightened with something that made Livvy a little uneasy.

She suspected that Sadie Haven had roped Grandpa into helping with whatever her scheme was. "I have a shift," she said.

"You don't even know what time the party is," Grandpa pointed out.

"It's an on-call shift," she explained. "I have to be available and close in case I'm needed to come into the hospital." Given the quiet of Willow Creek, she probably wouldn't be required. But that was fine with her; after the crazy busy shifts she'd covered during her residency in a Chicago hospital, she welcomed the quiet in work and in her private life.

So no matter what Sadie Haven planned for Livvy, she wanted no part of it. No part of the chaos that seemed to be constant in the life of a Haven.

An image of Colton Cassidy sprang into her mind, with his dark hair and dark eyes, and her pulse quickened with the chaos just thinking about him caused inside her. No. She did not want a disruption like him in her life.

Not ever again…

WORRIED THAT IT might burst for all the love flooding it, Sadie pressed her hand against her heart. *They came.*

All her grandsons were here. Well, almost all. She knew there was one missing yet, one who took so much after his father that he probably wouldn't be found until he was ready to be found. She had hope now that Cash would turn up, just like Jessup had.

But while the rest of them were here, she had to figure out how to keep them here. Right now they were gathered around the long kitchen table, eating the delicious meal that Taye had prepared with the help of her seven-year-old sous chef, Sadie's great grandson Miller who had developed a sudden passion for cooking. The boy and his two-year-old and five-year-old brothers were doing so much better now that they had been getting counseling after losing their parents, but most of all because they knew they belonged here…at the ranch with all their family, especially with Taye Cooper and their uncle Baker.

Sadie had to make her older grandsons come to understand the same thing…that they were where they belonged. That they were Havens. She had already put some things in motion that would help them realize that. She peered down the table, past them, to Ben, who gave her a slight nod as their gazes met. Of all her grandchildren, he was the most like her.

As far as she knew…

She didn't know her new grandsons well enough. Not yet. While they'd showed up today, they didn't seem very willing to let her get to know them better. They answered her questions, but they didn't volunteer any more information. Especially Colton.

He was keeping something from not just her, but she suspected from the others as well. His broad shoulders bowed slightly as if he was carrying a heavy burden.

What was troubling him?

She waited until most of their family were on their way to the barn to see that bronco Dusty had sent to the ranch all those weeks ago. As Colton passed her at the table to join the others, she caught his arm and held him back. "Give me a minute."

"Is that really all you want?" he asked, and there was a spark of amusement in his dark eyes when he glanced down at her.

Even if she wasn't still sitting down, she would have had to look up to him, and Sadie was a tall woman. But her grandsons were even taller except for Dusty. And Dale.

But Dale was gone now.

Then she glanced over at Jessup heading out of the kitchen after his other sons and nephews, and she knew Dale wasn't gone. He lived on and because of him, Jessup lived. Tears stung her eyes and made her wrinkle her nose to hold them back.

Colton dropped down to his haunches and peered at her, his face full of concern. "Are you all right?" he asked, and as Baker's fingers so often did, his wrapped around her wrist.

She smiled at his inclination to check her pulse. After her recent heart scare, she often did it herself now. "I didn't ask you to stay to check on me," she told him. "I wanted to check on you."

"On me?" he asked, and he shrugged as if her concern was misplaced. But even after his shrug, his shoulders bowed yet with that burden she could tell he was carrying.

"Yes. Are *you* doing okay?"

He nodded quickly, obviously not wanting anyone to worry about him. And she realized he shared more in common with Baker than their profession. Baker's former profession. After responding to the fire at the Cassidy Ranch, he'd quit the fire department in order to take on the role of Ranch Haven foreman. That was his true calling. What was Colton's? Besides his obvious desire to make sure nobody worried about *him*.

He must have seen her skepticism because he insisted, "I'm fine."

"I hear you met Livvy Lemmon."

He laughed. "Ah, now I know why my cousins warned me about you."

My cousins.

She smiled. He'd claimed his family, so learning he was a Haven might not have been what was bothering him. What was?

"Warned you about me? I can't imagine what they would have to warn you about…" But she couldn't quite manage a straight face.

He chuckled again. "About your meddling and matchmaking."

She widened her eyes and feigned shock. "Me? They claimed I'm a meddler?"

"And a matchmaker," he added.

"They have nothing to complain about," she said because finally Michael and Darlene's sons were all happy. She wanted Jessup's sons to find that happiness as well. "So tell me what you think about Livvy Lemmon."

He chuckled and shook his head at her not-quite-subtle question. "I think Dr. Lemmon is out of my league, Grandma."

While her heart swelled with love for him, for claiming her like he had his cousins, she also felt so much concern for him. "How can you think that anyone is out of your league?" she asked. "You're a Haven."

He tensed, his shoulders stiffening while his lips slipped down at the corners.

"And a Cassidy," she added. "I wish I would have met your mother."

"Me, too," he said. "She's been gone too long. Twenty years."

Was that why he and his brothers were all still single? Were they afraid of loving and losing like their father had? Or, since Colton didn't seem to want anyone to worry about him, was he more afraid of someone loving him only to lose him?

Sadie understood that fear and loss all too well and also that reluctance to love again. But she found her gaze moving down the table to where Lem talked animatedly to Little Jake, the toddler. The boy giggled and Sadie smiled. For many long weeks after the deaths of his parents, Little Jake had stopped making any sounds except at night when he awoke screaming from nightmares.

Lem must have felt her gaze on him because he glanced over at her. He was a little tense like Colton, and she felt a twinge of regret for being snippy with him when he'd arrived without his granddaughter and his son.

How was their plan going to work if he didn't do his part in making it happen?

Hopefully Ben had followed through better than his deputy mayor had and had put everything in motion just as they'd discussed.

She turned back to Colton who intently studied her. "Why do I have a feeling that I should be very worried?" he asked.

Because he was smart.

She just smiled and reached out to pat his cheek. "Don't worry," she told him. "Everything will work out exactly as it's meant to…"

Exactly as she wanted it and she only wanted it because she knew it was what they wanted, too.

Or so she hoped…

CHAPTER FIVE

EVER SINCE THAT meeting at Ranch Haven the afternoon before, Colton had been uneasy. No. He'd been uneasy ever since he'd found *that* lighter in the fire. Knowing that he'd had this meeting scheduled with his boss had only made him *more* uneasy.

While he waited for the captain to show up, he paced the small office. Where was his boss?

He'd set the meeting time, but he wasn't here yet. What was going on?

Had he figured out that Colton had taken something from the scene? He knew what he'd done was wrong, but his first instinct had been to pick it up and to protect his brother.

Where was Cash?

If he'd come back, why hadn't anyone seen him yet?

Cash wasn't the only one missing at the moment; so was Colton's boss.

And yesterday, Livvy Lemmon had been missing. Her grandfather had said she'd had a shift, or she would have been there. But Colton wondered...

She hadn't seemed all that thrilled that her grandfather was involved with Sadie Haven. And Colton couldn't entirely blame her. Sadie Haven was one tough lady, but she'd had to be or she probably wouldn't have survived all her losses.

Now Colton understood where his dad's strength had come from, how he'd survived all his health battles and his heartbreak. But could he survive any more? That was why Colton couldn't tell anyone about the lighter, about Cash.

The door creaked open, drawing his attention around to his boss walking into the room. The blond-haired guy was just a little older than Colton and usually straightforward, but Skip Leonard didn't meet Colton's gaze as he slipped around his desk and dropped down into his chair, his head bowed. "Take a seat," he told Colton.

"I prefer to stand," he said, especially if he was on his way out the door. "Am I being fired?" Somehow Skip must have found out about the lighter.

The captain's head shot up, sending some

strands of thin blond hair across his high fore-head. "Fired? No."

His legs a little shaky now, Colton dropped into that chair. "Then what's up?"

"You are being transferred."

"Transferred? Where?" But the minute he asked, he had his answer as he remembered that look on his grandmother's gently wrinkled face. She'd meddled.

"Willow Creek," his boss—former boss—replied. "They're short-staffed, and we're actually a little overstaffed right now. And they're a bigger department, a bigger town. They need the help."

"Why me?" Colton asked, but he already had a pretty good idea why—because of Sadie Haven.

"They just had a paramedic firefighter quit."

Colton's cousin Baker. When the guy had shown them around the ranch yesterday, Baker had also shown how much he loved the place. He was definitely never going back to being a paramedic, and after having been the first on the scene of his brother's accident, Baker quitting was understandable.

"We have other paramedics on our team," Colton pointed out. "Why me?"

Skip shrugged. "I don't know. You were requested, though."

"Of course I was…" he muttered.

"They'd like you to start right away," Skip told him.

"And what about what I'd like?" Colton asked.

"You don't want to transfer?" his boss asked, his brow furrowing with confusion. Willow Creek was a bigger department; it would be busier, more exciting, so he'd probably thought Colton would jump at the chance to go there.

If there wasn't so much else going on right now, he probably would have. Even with as many shifts as Colton picked up, he was never as busy as he wanted to be. Those shifts were often uneventful. Unfortunately his life was not.

He drew in a deep breath and considered what this meant. Since his dad and Darlene were moving to Willow Creek, he'd be closer to them. And Collin was already working at the hospital. So was Livvy Lemmon.

He'd only been half-kidding when he'd told his grandmother that the beautiful ER doctor was out of his league. She was smart and driven; she had to be to have gotten through med school and her residency at such a young age. She was impressive, and Colton was impressed. But that was all. He wasn't tempted to start up a relationship with anyone. He wanted to focus on his family and his career, one that he loved. And this was a good move for him career and family wise.

"I'll accept the transfer," Colton said, but the minute the words left his mouth, a chill raced down his spine that he was falling in with Sadie Haven's plan for him.

But while he agreed to the job transfer, that was all she was going to get him to do. He had too many other things going on to start even a casual relationship with anyone. And all he would ever risk having was a casual relationship; he would never risk a serious one.

"What about the fire?" he found himself asking his now former boss.

"Fire? You'll still be working fires, too," Skip assured him. "You won't be exclusively a paramedic."

"No, at my family ranch," he said. "What about the fire? Did you figure out what caused it?"

Skip's gaze slid away from his. "I ruled it as a mechanical failure. The place was pretty rundown."

Colton grimaced with guilt that he hadn't helped out more, that he hadn't tried harder to keep the place going. But keeping Dad alive had been everyone's priority. It was why Collin had worked so hard to become a cardiologist and it was why Colton had picked up every extra shift he could, to help out financially. But it had been more important for that money to go towards Dad's medical needs than towards the ranch upkeep.

The captain's face flushed. "Sorry. I didn't mean to sound insensitive."

"You weren't," Colton assured him. "You're just being honest." And maybe now he could be the same since the cause hadn't been arson.

Skip's flush got a darker red. "I probably shouldn't do this, but I know you're honest, too, and I don't want you to be blindsided. The insurance adjuster didn't accept my determination. I think because the place was for sale, they're thinking it might have been arson. I'm sure once they find out there was already an accepted offer on it, they'll back off and pay out the rest of your dad's claim."

Colton's stomach knotted with apprehension over the other possible outcome of their investigation. That they might find out that it was arson…

LIVVY COULDN'T REMEMBER the last time she hadn't been called in on an on-call day until yesterday, in Willow Creek. But even though she'd had to stay close to the hospital, she wouldn't have gone with Grandpa to Ranch Haven. She didn't want to get close to the Havens. Any of them.

Yet she glanced up from her tablet to find one standing right in front of her. Her pulse didn't quicken, so she knew it wasn't Colton even though the brothers looked identical or nearly so. This Haven always looked so serious, with his brow furrowed and his dark gaze so intense.

"Hello…" she said uneasily.

"You don't look busy."

She tensed with the indignation she'd always felt when specialists acted as though her job wasn't as important as theirs. That just because her residency hadn't been as competitive or as long and because she hadn't had to complete a fellowship in her field, that it wasn't as deserving of respect as theirs.

But then she realized that only one doctor had truly treated her that way: Steven. And she let the indignation go with a sigh and a smile.

"Slow day?" Collin asked.

"Every day has been slow so far," she admitted.

"It's busier than Moss Valley," he said. "But

I know that you came here from Chicago, so this must seem dead to you."

She shook her head. "No. It doesn't. I haven't lost a patient yet, and I've been here a week. That's wonderful to me." While she'd wanted a change of pace, she hadn't realized how burned out she'd been getting, how broken her spirit had begun to be, until she'd returned to Willow Creek.

Alone.

Collin's brow furrowed harder, adding more lines to his face. "I hope I can say the same."

"Some tough cases?" she asked sympathetically.

He raised his bandaged hands. "This makes it tougher. If you've got a minute, can you rewrap these for me? Maybe see if they even need to be wrapped anymore?"

"I could call down a derm specialist," she offered.

He shook his head. "I trust you."

Steven wouldn't have. He would have wanted the specialist.

"Thanks," she said.

"We can do it later, if you're in the middle of something," he said, gesturing toward the tablet she held.

She sighed. "Just apartment hunting."

"Not much to choose from in Willow Creek," he said. "But still better options than Moss Valley."

"Are you staying in Moss Valley?" she asked. While she hadn't lived in the area for many years, she remembered that the other town, while in the same county, was a significant distance away.

He nodded. "For now. I'm crashing with my brother Marsh there."

Her curiosity about the firefighter compelled her to ask, "And Colton?"

Collin snorted. "There's barely enough room for me and Marsh. But I guess Colton's digs aren't much better. He's sharing a place with some other firefighters." He uttered a sigh now.

"What?" she asked with curiosity as she led him toward one of the many open treatment bays in the emergency room. "Are you worried about him?"

"I think I'm a little worried about all of us with Sadie Haven coming into our lives," he admitted.

If Collin was worried about his own grandmother, Livvy had every reason to worry about her grandfather's involvement with the strong-willed woman. Instead of sharing her concerns, she pulled on some gloves and started removing the cardiologist's bandages.

"I grew up hearing stories about Sadie Haven," she said. "And I think my grandfather mentioned her every time I've called him over the years." That hadn't been often enough, and she felt a twinge of guilt over that. "She is a force of nature."

"Looking at us from her perspective, though, I can see why she might be a little concerned about us," he said. "We're pretty old to be as unsettled as we are."

"Speak for yourself," a deep voice rumbled.

And a strange tingling sensation spread over Livvy's skin; she turned to find Colton standing behind her. "What are you doing back here?" she asked with concern. Had he been injured? Had he brought in a patient?

"Getting familiar with the place," he said. "Since I've been transferred to Willow Creek full time."

She sucked in a breath of alarm while Collin chuckled. "I'd ask how that came about, but I think I have some idea."

"Sadie," Colton said. "Skip wouldn't admit it, but it's pretty clear she arranged this somehow."

"Why?" The word slipped out of Livvy before she could stop it.

Colton met her gaze and held it for a long moment before shrugging. "I don't know. Control. She needs us close enough to be able to manipulate our lives."

"That'll only happen if you let it," Collin told him. "Why did you accept the transfer?"

Colton quickly looked away from her and focused on his brother. "You're here and Dad and Darlene will be, too. Makes sense for me to be here, too."

Livvy forced herself to focus on Colton's brother. "You need to keep the bandages on for a little while longer," she told him. "Just to keep the wounds clean until the burns heal more. But they're doing well."

She couldn't say the same for herself. Standing there with Colton so close to her had her pulse racing and her skin tingling. She couldn't let him distract her from her job or from her resolve to remain single.

Collin nodded. "Good. Thanks for your help."

She smiled at him and tried to ignore Colton's stare that she could actually feel on her. She couldn't ignore him as easily. He was so tall, the black cowboy boots and cowboy hat making him look even taller and more imposing. Why did he affect her so much, but his identical twin did not? He was more charming, sure, but there was more to Colton Cassidy than his charm. He was hiding deep emotions and some kind of burden behind that grin. She'd glimpsed that the first time they'd met, and she'd been concerned and interested and...*connected*.

"Dr. Lemmon, you have a call at the front desk," a nurse remarked; it was the older woman who always seemed to bristle with disapproval around Livvy. Nurse Sue passed her a judgmental look now as she glanced from Livvy to the Cassidy twins. "The man claims it's an emergency."

Livvy's heart rate quickened. "Is it my grandfather?" she asked with concern.

The older woman shook her head. "I don't know. He didn't identify himself, but he's been calling and insisting on speaking with you. I can finish this up for you, so he stops tying up a line."

Livvy's face heated with embarrassment, and she narrowed her eyes into a slight glare as she pointed out the obvious. "You should have asked who it was."

Now the woman had the grace to blush

slightly. But then she bristled again. "I'm a nurse. Not a secretary."

"Then why were you answering the phone?" Colton asked the question, but he softened it with a slight chuckle, as if trying to lighten the mood.

Nurse Sue was not so inclined. She glared at him with that disapproving frown on her face as well.

"I'm done changing Dr. Cassidy's bandages," Livvy said. "So I can take the call." Concerned that it was her grandfather or her dad, she turned away from the brothers. Because the nurses' station was near the bay where she'd taken Collin, she pushed through the doors that opened onto the lobby and headed to the intake desk instead.

"Nurse Sue told you a call is holding?" the attendant asked with a commiserating smile. Obviously the older woman hadn't even taken the call.

Livvy nodded. "Yeah, I'll cover the desk, too, if you want to get some coffee." And give her some privacy.

The younger woman jumped up and headed into the back. Livvy reached for the phone. Only one light flashed, so her caller wasn't exactly tying up a necessary line. She picked up the receiver and pressed the button, greeting the caller with, "Livvy here."

"Olivia," a cool male voice spoke as if correcting her on her own name.

And her skin chilled with dread. "Steven, this isn't an emergency."

"You're not returning my calls or texts," he said. "I needed to get your attention."

"You had my attention for the past four years," she reminded him. Too much of it. "We're done. That was your choice."

"You made the choice, Olivia," he said. "You chose to move to the middle of nowhere instead of continue with the plans we had made for you to stay with me until I finished my surgical residency."

"Those were your plans, Steven," she reminded him. "And you gave me the ultimatum. My job or you." It had been about even more than that, though. It had been about her family or him. He'd kept making her make impossible choices, choices she'd regretted.

"But I thought you would choose me," he said.

"I chose *me*," she said. Before he could say anything else, she hung up the phone and released a deep breath of relief. She realized now that it had really been her choice. Not between her job and Steven. Or her family and Steven. It had been between herself and Steven.

She'd lost so much of *Livvy* during their relationship. But she was beginning to find her now.

"Is everything all right?" a deep voice asked.

She glanced up to find Colton Cassidy standing on the other side of the desk, his dark eyes intense with concern. That unsettled her more than the phone call with Steven had.

She nodded. "Yes, it is." And it would be now…because that call had reminded her of how she'd lost herself once for a man. She would not do that again.

Not for anyone.

Lem walked into the ER just in time to catch the tension between the two people standing near the front desk. The way they looked at each other…

The intensity. A smile tugged at his lips.

"Sounds like some guy is hassling you," one of Sadie's grandsons said to Lem's granddaughter. "Do you need any help with that?"

Livvy bristled. "I can take care of myself," she said. "I don't need anyone to save me or protect me. All I need is someone to respect me enough not to eavesdrop on my conversations."

Colton, it must have been Colton, snapped his head back like she'd slapped him. "I'm sorry. I was just trying to be helpful."

"I don't need any help in my personal life," she told him.

He held up his hands as if letting her know he had no intention of fighting her. "I understand what you're saying. I just hope that my grandma does when I…" he trailed off as he turned his head and noticed Lem standing there.

"Grandpa!" Livvy exclaimed, and she darted around the desk and Colton to rush up to him. She hugged him tightly.

And as Lem wrapped his arms around her, he felt her tremble slightly. "Who's been giving you a hard time, Livvy?"

Was it that loser ex-fiancé of hers? He wanted to ask, but from behind her, Colton gave him a warning shake of his head before he turned and headed back inside the ER. Apparently he'd learned his lesson about eavesdropping on Livvy Lemmon.

"Don't you start now, too, Grandpa," she said. "I'm fine."

"I hope that's true," he said. "And I hope you'll be fine with moving your things over to my house. Jessup and Darlene Haven took your father up on the offer of his house."

She pulled back slightly and stared up at him, tension in her beautiful face. The smile she managed was obviously forced. "That's fine."

But he wondered if it was. After her breakup, had Livvy needed the refuge of the house where she'd spent the early years of her childhood?

"It'll be fun," he said. "Your dad and me and you all living together."

Her smile widened, and her green eyes brightened. "Yes, it'll be fun. At least for you and me."

Lem knew that his son had probably only agreed because he intended to spend a lot of time at the office, probably any time that Lem was at the house. For some reason, Bob thought Lem meddled too much.

"And Jessup said his sons will gladly help you and your father move," he added.

"That won't be necessary," she said as her smile slipped away. "I didn't bring much with me. I don't need any help."

She'd just made that clear to Colton Cassidy. Lem wondered how well his old friend's plan was going to work. Maybe Livvy could be just as stubborn as Sadie.

He felt a flash of pride and smiled. "I know you can take care of yourself, Livvy. You've been doing it a long time."

Her green eyes widened with surprise, as if she hadn't realized that until now. Her smile was genuine this time, and she leaned close and kissed his cheek. "Thank you, Grandpa."

He was glad she was happy with him. He had a feeling that Sadie would not be when he told her about this latest development, or non-development, between their grandchildren. If Sadie was going to get these two together, she had her work cut out for her.

CHAPTER SIX

"WHAT ARE YOU even doing here?" Colton asked his twin as Collin got out of his car in the driveway of Livvy Lemmon's home.

It was a big two-story brick Colonial that looked like it had come from the set of some old-time family sitcom. He could picture Livvy as a child here, learning to ride her bike up and down the sidewalk in front of it.

"It's not like you can help move anything," Colton said. "Not with your bandages."

Collin held up those bandages.

Had Livvy put these on like she had the ones a few days ago? And why did it bother him so much that his twin had sought her out to help him?

"The burns don't hurt anymore," Collin claimed. "I can help."

But Colton suspected he wasn't there to help. "Then why weren't you at the motel with me and Marsh helping load up Darlene and Dad's things?"

"Because I was working," Collin said.

With Livvy...

Colton's stomach muscles tightened with dread at the thought of his brother and the beautiful ER doctor. When he'd seen them together in the ER, Livvy holding his brother's hands, Colton had felt something he'd never felt before. Jealousy. And he didn't like it.

It had only gotten worse when he'd overheard her phone conversation with her ex. What an idiot for giving her an ultimatum. How had the guy expected her to give up everything? Her career? Her family? For him? He obviously hadn't valued Livvy at all for who she was. He'd deserved to lose her, but clearly he was regretting it now.

Like Colton regretted his eavesdropping. His face heated over how rude that had been, but he'd been worried about her emergency, worried that it might have concerned her family.

Or his...

After his own parents' illnesses, he had enormous empathy for people having to deal with those kinds of emergencies. Maybe that was why he loved being a paramedic firefighter, because in some small way he could help them.

"It's not like Darlene and Dad could have

had much stuff," Collin said. "They lost pretty much everything in the fire."

But for the lighter.

That had survived the flames. Unfortunately. Because now Colton carried it around with him…in more ways than one. What if the insurance adjuster discovered the fire had been arson?

"If you don't think they have much to move, what are you doing here?" Colton asked. At that moment Marsh backed his truck, packed with boxes of stuff Dad and Darlene had replaced since the fire, into the driveway.

Collin grinned. "Because Livvy probably has a lot of stuff she could use help moving."

Livvy.

He clenched his jaw.

Collin laughed. "Does that bother you? That we're on a first-name basis?"

Colton shrugged. "Of course you're on a first-name basis. You work together." Over the past few days, since assuming his new position in Willow Creek, Colton had worked with her, too. And work was definitely all they'd done. She'd only talked to him about patients, nothing else since she'd gotten mad at him for eavesdropping on her.

"Yes, we work together," Collin said, and his

grin widened as his eyes glinted with humor, like he was somehow implying they were more than friends.

And Colton nearly reached out to smack the grin off his face. Marsh must have noticed how tempted Colton was because he jumped out of his truck and asked, "What's going on? You two look like you're about to get into a brawl."

"I'm fine," Collin said. "Your brother is the one who has the problem."

Colton couldn't deny that. "Yeah, you."

Marsh chuckled. "Don't make me call the sheriff on you two. Oh, that's right…I am the sheriff."

"What?" Collin asked.

Marsh grinned. "You're looking at the new interim sheriff of Willow Creek. I've been asked to step into the job until the next election." He gestured toward the boxes. "Some of this stuff is mine. I'm going to be staying here, too."

"You're the Willow Creek sheriff?" Colton asked, and he furrowed his brow with suspicion over it all. "How did that happen? What happened to the current sheriff?"

"He suddenly decided to retire," Marsh said. "Leaving our cousin Ben, the mayor, in a terrible lurch as well as the entire town of Willow Creek."

"So Sadie…" Colton murmured, and that sick feeling churned in his stomach again. This time it wasn't jealousy but dread.

But then a small SUV pulled up to the curb outside the house, and when Livvy stepped out, both his brothers stared at her. And that jealousy returned.

He could understand why they were staring. Her hair was down, the long strawberry blond curls spiraling down her back, and the scrubs brought out the vivid green of her eyes. She was so beautiful…even with dark circles beneath her eyes. Her steps slowed as she approached them. "I forgot today was moving day."

"We're here to help," Collin assured her.

Colton's stomach muscles tightened even more.

"Yes, whatever you need," Marsh told her.

She smiled at his older brother. "Thank you, but I just have a few things. It won't take me long to pack them up and put them in my vehicle. I would have already done it…"

"But you've been pulling doubles at the hospital," Collin finished for her.

Colton knew that. He'd been pulling doubles, too, since his transfer. He'd probably spent more time with her over the past few days than his brother had, so he had no reason to be jealous of his twin. Or of Marsh, but when both men kept grinning at her like they were idiots, his irritation increased. "You two going to stand around like a couple of morons or help unpack this truck?" he asked them.

"Don't let me keep you," she said, and she hurried off toward the house.

Collin and Marsh laughed. Not at her. They were both laughing at him.

"What?" he asked.

"You've got it bad," Marsh said. "I don't think I've ever seen you like this."

"Like what?" he asked. But he knew. He was acting like a fool. He had no reason to be jealous of Livvy because he didn't want a relationship any more than he suspected she wanted one. She'd just gotten out of a bad one. And he had no interest in ever getting into one.

He was interested in Livvy, though. She was so smart and strong but also soft and caring. She'd offered him so much sympathy during their first meeting, and he was a stranger to her.

He shook his head at his brothers, ignoring them, as he often had growing up. And he carried in an armload of boxes. But the house drew his interest like Livvy did. It was big with a lot of rooms but not much clutter. Contained yet comfortable. He looked around, imagining Livvy here as a child, and then he found her in a back bedroom on the second story. He knocked on the door she'd left partially open.

She glanced up from staring at a picture she held, and her lashes blinked furiously as if she was fighting back the tears glistening in her eyes.

"Are you okay?" he asked with concern. He could still remember his mother's tears; she'd cried often with worry over his father. And she should have been worrying about herself instead.

Livvy nodded, but her lips were pursed. She obviously wasn't any more inclined to speak to him now than she'd been at the hospital.

"I'm sorry," he said, and he took a step back into the hall. "I didn't mean to intrude, today or the other day, when I overheard your phone conversation."

She released a shaky sigh. "I know. I'm sure you have enough going on yourself without getting caught up in my drama. I overreacted."

The tightness of his stomach muscles eased. "Not at all. I understand."

"You have an overbearing ex-fiancée, too?" she asked, and her lips curved into a slight smile.

He shuddered at the thought of being engaged to someone like that or to anyone for that matter. It wouldn't have been fair to them, not with the unhealthy genes he'd inherited and the dangerous job he'd chosen.

"Nope. The only thing I've ever proposed was getting a drink after work." Casual dating was all he'd ever done and all he would ever do. "And I don't even have time for one of those right now."

"Then don't let me keep you," she said. "I really don't need any help."

He held up his hands as he had that day in the ER, letting her know that he wasn't trying to control her like her ex had. "I wasn't offering. I was just being nosy again. I thought you looked upset." He gestured toward the picture frame. "Is that a picture of the ex?" Maybe their engagement photo?

She stared down at it again, and those tears rushed back into her eyes. Then she turned the picture toward him. It looked like a family portrait. The man he assumed was Livvy's dad, with salt and pepper hair, stood in the middle, next to a frail-looking, dark-haired woman. Livvy stood next to her, her arm around the woman's waist.

"That's my mom," she said. "The last picture that was taken of her before she died."

He sucked in a breath and took the photo from her hands. "She was beautiful."

"Yes..." Her voice caught. "Even as sick as she was then, from the breast cancer, she wanted that picture taken, wanted us all together as a family for it."

"I lost my mom to breast cancer, too," he said.

"I'm sorry."

He shrugged. "It was a long time ago. Nearly twenty years." Eighteen to be exact, while Livvy's family portrait seemed pretty recent. She looked exactly the same. A dark-haired man stood next to her while two other men, both with auburn hair, stood beside her father. He pointed toward the man next to her. "Is this your ex?"

She laughed. "No, that's my younger brother. Liam." She indicated the two men next to her father. "They're my older brothers. Brett and Blake."

"You said you're not close to them." He remembered that first conversation they'd had, just as vividly as he remembered their last even though it was just an exchange of a patient's vitals. "You told us that when Collin and I met you at the hospital."

She shrugged. "I don't really know. I guess it's because I was always very interested in school, in studying and learning." She smiled sadly. "And they weren't. They couldn't wait to move back out here."

Colton had been like her brothers, and his brothers had been like her, very interested in school and always studying. Even Cash, before he'd run off, had graduated with a full scholarship to a college with a program that combined undergrad and veterinarian school. And Marsh had his criminal justice degree, which was probably why Sadie had been able to convince her grandson the mayor to appoint him as interim sheriff even though he'd only been a deputy in Moss Valley.

Colton had no regrets over the path he'd chosen. He loved his job, too much to give it up for anyone. Just as Livvy had chosen not to give up hers for her fiancé. But finding out about her brothers confirmed how different Colton was from Livvy, who wasn't close to her brothers because they were too different from her, too much like he was.

"They live in Willow Creek?"

She shook her head. "Back out west, I should

have said. After living in the city, they wanted even wider and more open spaces than Willow Creek, Wyoming."

He chuckled softly. "Willow Creek seems big compared to Moss Valley." She'd spent most of her life in Chicago. They definitely had nothing in common. "Why did *you* decide to come back here?" It sounded like that decision was what had ended her engagement.

"Because *I* wanted to," she said. "And I should have done it long ago."

Broken the engagement? He wanted to ask, but he'd already pried too much. And he was worried that getting to know Livvy any better might tempt him to break his own rule regarding relationships. "I should leave you to your packing..." he said as he turned for the door.

She should have let him walk away. But while he'd apologized to her, he wasn't the only one who needed to apologize. "I'm sorry, too," she said.

"I told you my mom died a long time ago," he said.

He'd misconstrued the reason for her apology. She was sorry about getting so defensive at the hospital that day, but because she was curious, she prodded a bit. "You said twenty years ago?"

He uttered a heavy sigh. "Eighteen, actually."

"But you were just a kid."

He shrugged those broad shoulders of his. "Fourteen."

"Just a kid," she said. "I was twenty-six, and it was still hard on me."

"We grew up with my dad always being sick," he said, "with lupus. He had to have a kidney transplant a couple years before she got sick. The kidney failed after she died, and he had to have another one." He drew in a shaky breath; maybe he was worried the new heart would fail his father, too. "Dad was in and out of the hospital so many times all our lives. Maybe that was why it was such a shock that she was the one who died."

Livvy nodded. "It was a shock with Mom, too. She had cancer the first time when I was young, but she and Dad didn't tell us. They wanted to shield us. I didn't find out she'd had it before until it came back. And then... I was busy with med school and my residency..."

Now she was busy with the burden of guilt she carried over not being there for her mom and her dad. Or for Grandpa either. The tears rushed up again, and she closed her eyes to hold them back. Then suddenly strong arms closed around her, and while she wanted to pull away, she was also tempted to lean in, to lay her head on his big chest.

"You have nothing to feel guilty about," he told her.

She did pull back then, opened her eyes and stared up at his face. "How did you know...?"

"I've been there," he said. "I *am* there."

"I wasn't," she said. "I wasn't around to help Dad with Mom or be there for her. Or for Grandpa when he was dealing with Grandma Mary's Alzheimer's."

"You had a life, too," he said. "You couldn't stop living because of what was going on. And your grandpa and your dad managed."

"I still should have been there," she said. And she would have been if not for Steven convincing her that her going home would have upset them, because her family had insisted that she stay in her residency program. "You don't have any reason to feel guilty either," she said. "You're here. You're helping your dad and..."

"Darlene," he said. "Aunt Darlene..." He shrugged. "So weird that we never knew that. We always thought she was my mother's best friend. That they'd been barrel riders in the rodeo together."

"That wasn't true?" she asked.

"They were both barrel racers, but Mom was older than Darlene. They were with the rodeo at different times. Their paths never really crossed. Darlene turned up at the ranch not because my mom died but because she was looking for my dad, wanting to bring him home to Sadie after Sadie lost her youngest son, Michael, Darlene's husband. That was a long time ago, though, and Dad was so sick." He sighed now, stirring the wispy strands of hair that framed her face so that they tangled in her lashes.

Before she could reach up to push back the strands, his fingers were there, brushing them across her cheek, tucking them behind her ear. She shivered at the sensation of his fingertips gliding across her skin, and then she stepped back and pulled fully away until his long arms fell back to his sides.

"He's better now?" she asked about his dad, concerned for him and for his family.

Colton nodded. "Yes. So far. His body isn't rejecting his new heart."

His nephew's heart. That was the speculation around the hospital, around town, though Livvy tried hard to ignore the gossip. She didn't want to take part in it, didn't want to get wrapped up in any drama.

Not anymore. She'd had enough drama with Steven. Still had too much with his constant texts and attempts to call her.

"It's still good for him to be close to the hospital," she said. "I'm glad he's staying here."

"Are you?" he asked. "You don't feel displaced from your home?"

She sighed now. "This hasn't been my home for a long time. I haven't lived here since I was a little girl."

"Until now."

"I've only been back a little over a week."

"A little over a week…" Colton echoed the words with a strange expression on his face.

"What?"

"That's when I found out how much I didn't know."

He must have been talking about his family, that he was a Haven, but he was staring at her with a strange expression on his face. He'd known her just a little over a week as well.

"I stopped you to apologize," she reminded herself and him. "I owe you one for how I reacted to your overhearing that phone conversation with Steven."

"Steven…" There was a trace of humor and bitterness in his deep voice when he repeated the name. Then he sighed and continued, "You don't owe me an apology. I was out of line. None of my business."

And it really wasn't. Colton clearly didn't want to learn any more about her broken engagement, and she didn't want to talk about it anymore either. All she added was, "You have a habit of catching me at my most vulnerable."

"Ditto." His mouth curved into a grin.

She smiled back at him.

"Colton!"

"Where are you?"

As his brothers shouted for him, his grin widened. "Let me know if you need any help moving anything," he said. Then he turned and walked away from her.

And she almost called him back again. Not to help her. But to talk some more…

He actually understood her, how she felt… the guilt, the loss. He'd dealt with it all, too.

The only thing Steven had ever lost in his life was her. And that had been his choice. She'd been willing to do the long-distance thing. They hadn't lived together anyway, hadn't even set a date for the wedding. She'd believed that they could keep the relationship going with calls and texts and the occasional dinner out when their schedules matched up. She would have flown back to see him, as she had when he'd switched residencies a couple of times.

But he'd wanted more. He'd wanted all of her time.

And she'd already given up too much of herself to him. She had to keep what she had left for herself. To build her life into what she wanted, not into what someone else wanted from her.

HE WASN'T COMING over tonight. Sadie should have been relieved that she had a night to herself, that Lem wasn't going to fall asleep in the easy chair next to hers and snore so loud she had to increase the volume on the television to hear her show.

But once she clicked off the cell and sat in the silence of her suite, an odd sensation settled over her. Loss. She hated this feeling but had experienced it entirely too often. But not over Lem.

Well, when they'd had that big fight a few weeks ago, but that had been her fault, getting mad at him when he'd just been telling her the truth. The truth she hadn't wanted to hear, and she'd thrown him out for saying it.

He hadn't wanted to leave. Or so she hoped.

They weren't fighting now. In fact, they should have been celebrating that things were going according to her plan. Jessup and Darlene and even Marsh and Collin were going to stay at Lem's son's house since it was the bigger one, and Livvy and Bob had moved in with Lem.

That was why he was staying home tonight, helping them unpack and settle in…and sharing dinner with them instead of coming out here to mooch meals like he usually did. She should have been relieved, but…

The chimes of the ringing doorbell whipped Feisty into a frenzy. She jumped down from Sadie's lap and ran out the open door and into the hall. Her barking turned to growls at the giggles from little boys and the deep rumble of male voices.

Those were the usual sounds around the house but for the doorbell. Very few people ever rang the bell. The last one had probably been Beth Lancaster, the school psychologist who was working with the boys and Baker. But she hadn't been scheduled to come tonight.

So who…?

Then there was a knock against her open door and long shadows spilled into her room, across the hardwood floor. Her grandsons often popped in and out of her suite, but they rarely knocked. But these weren't Michael's boys standing in her doorway; Jessup's sons had come to visit.

Without her requesting a meeting.

Without calling ahead to schedule something.

They'd just stopped by the ranch and come to see her. Warmth flooded her heart, and she smiled up at them. They did not smile back. Maybe that was because Feisty was tugging at the bottom of Marsh's jeans. Marsh.

Michael March. No matter how much Jessup must have wanted to escape her and her overbearing protectiveness, he'd honored his family with the name of this son. The new sheriff of Willow Creek crouched down and plucked up the little ball of black fluff that then began licking and kissing him. He stared down at it with a look of confusion and almost of horror. "What's with this thing?"

"That's her ploy," Jake said as he walked up behind his cousins. "She'll bug you until she gets your attention."

"But I'm not an animal person, not like my brother Cash was…" When his voice trailed off, his brow furrowed beneath the brim of his white Stetson. The lawman wore a white hat while his younger brother the firefighter wore a black Resistol. And the doctor wore no hat, just a slight grin.

"Feisty is like a cat," Jake said. "She likes the people the most that like her the least, like me."

"Liar," Sadie accused him. She knew he secretly loved her little dog as much as she did.

"Did you really break the window of a Caddy to rescue this thing?" Marsh asked as he handed off the little Chihuahua to her.

"Your predecessor telling stories about me?"

"Funny that you knew your old friend was retiring, apparently before he knew…" Marsh said, his dark eyes focused intently on her face.

She faked a shiver. "You must be great at interrogating suspects."

His mouth started to curve up before he managed to pull it back into a frown. "Have you done something wrong?" he asked her.

She shook her head. "Not at all. I'm doing everything right."

"Meddling in our lives?" Colton asked the question, and his dark eyes were intense, too, as he stared at her. They all looked so alike, but they were so different, too. Their interests all so diverse.

Except for, perhaps, Livvy. Lem had texted a tidbit of gossip that when he'd showed up at Bob's house, her grandsons had been squabbling with each other over helping her load her things into her SUV.

"It's not right to meddle like that," Colton added.

"I warned you," Baker said as he joined his brother Jake and his cousins in her suite. "I told you to watch out, that she was going to play her matchmaking games."

"What matchmaking?" she asked, feigning innocence now.

Baker snorted.

"Well, I liked the former sheriff," Marsh said, "but he's happily married so I don't see a future there."

Sadie laughed over his teasing her. "What about the job?"

He couldn't fight his grin this time; it spread across his face. "That I am going to enjoy."

"And you?" Sadie turned toward Colton. "You don't like working for a bigger, busier fire department?"

A muscle twitched along his tightly clenched jaw before his grin slipped out along with, "There have been a lot of calls. A lot of fires. A lot of action." And from the excitement vibrating in his voice, he enjoyed that; he loved his job.

She smiled.

Collin held up his bandaged hands. "I'm not complaining about anything. I already had my job."

"You were my cardiologist," she said. "But we hadn't met." He'd given orders over the phone when she'd had her attack, but he hadn't been there to treat her.

He wiggled his hands. "I was a little tied up then."

She'd been so worried about them, so worried when she'd heard about the fire at the Cassidy Ranch and that there had been injuries.

"You should be relieved she's just messing with your careers and not your love lives," Jake told his cousins.

Marsh snorted. "What love lives?"

Collin glanced at Colton, who was curiously quiet with that intense look back in his dark eyes. But he wasn't staring at her now, instead he seemed entirely focused on whatever was on his mind. Livvy Lemmon?

Sadie fought her smile.

Her plan was working out just fine.

CHAPTER SEVEN

THE APARTMENT AVAILABLE for sublease was in one of those old factories that had been converted into residential spaces. It was close to the firehouse and the hospital, so it was perfect.

Colton had suspected as much when Baker had mentioned it a couple of nights ago when he and his brothers had gone out to confront their grandmother over her meddling in their lives.

Instead of being ashamed or apologetic, she'd been elated, and the impromptu visit to confront her had become a party to celebrate their new jobs. They'd all gathered in that enormous kitchen with the kids and the dog, eating cookies and drinking punch. And Sadie had been so happy that staying mad at her had been too hard.

She really was something else.

His lips twitched, and since she wasn't here, he let himself smile as he thought of her. He couldn't remember his maternal grandparents who'd died when he was a toddler. And his dad had claimed that his were already gone, too.

Thinking of all the years he'd lost out on with his grandmother had Colton's anger with his dad flaring up again. But then he had to remind himself that his dad was alive against all odds. Because of that, Colton wanted to spend as much time with him as he could, but he didn't want to move into Livvy's old house. It was already fully occupied with the nurse and her son staying there, and Marsh and Collin were both crashing there, too. Fortunately the house had five bedrooms and an office where Collin was sleeping, so it wasn't over-crowded with them.

Colton had been staying in the bunkroom at the firehouse; with all the shifts he'd worked, it had made sense. But it was time, past time actually, that he got a place of his own and some space.

Ever since he'd found that lighter, he hadn't felt as close to his family—not with this secret he had to keep from them. But with the insurance company investigating, he couldn't let it get out about the lighter. They would think for sure that it was arson then. He sure hoped it wasn't, though. But carrying that secret, that burden, had disconnected him from his immediate family even as he was connecting with his extended family.

He liked Baker. A lot. Maybe it was because they'd had the same job or were the youngest ones in their family, although with Colton it was only by ten minutes. Collin always lorded those ten minutes over him, though. But now, with these new cousins, Colton wasn't the youngest anymore. Baker technically was, of the grandchildren, but he was one of those people who had an old soul. Or maybe it was just all the things he'd seen as an Army medic and a first responder that had aged him.

Colton hadn't felt old himself until he'd found that lighter. But he hadn't found Cash. He wasn't even certain where to look for him. Or if he really wanted to find him. If he'd started that fire… If he'd risked the lives of people Colton loved…

No. Maybe it was better not to find him.

He'd arrived at the apartment, or at least the parking lot, but Baker's truck wasn't here yet. He was supposed to meet Colton to let him in and show him the place. While he watched out his windows for the truck to appear, he noticed another vehicle pulling into an open space. A familiar-looking little SUV, and the woman

who stepped out of it was even more familiar…
since he couldn't get her out of his mind.

She was so beautiful. Her long hair fluttered
around her slim shoulders as she started across
the lot toward the brick building. He couldn't
see her eyes since she wore sunglasses, but
she must have seen him sitting in his truck
because she froze.

He pushed open the door and stepped out
onto the asphalt. Heat shimmered off it from
the hot July day.

"I thought Baker was going to meet me…"
she said.

"I thought he was going to meet me," he said.
He sighed. "I wonder if my grandmother enlisted him in her plot like she did Ben."

Instead of being annoyed like he was, she
smiled.

"That doesn't bother you?"

She shook her head. "I wouldn't say that.
It was just that…you called her your grandmother."

He heaved a heavy sigh. "She is. Even though
I haven't known her long, it's like I've known
her forever. She and my dad are very much
alike, which maybe was why he ran away like
he did. Like…"

"Like what? Or who?" she asked after he trailed off.

He shook his head now. Like Cash. But he didn't want to bring up his brother to her, not yet…not with that lighter in his pocket. Not with the suspicions and the secret he was harboring.

An SUV pulling into the lot kept him from having to answer her. He'd thought Baker drove a truck, but he unfolded himself from the small vehicle before opening the back door and helping the toddler out of his car seat. The little boy clutched at Baker's shirt as he roped his other arm around his neck. Little Jake, as he was called, looked exactly like a miniature version of his namesake Big Jake Haven.

"He looks like you," Livvy said, and she smiled and waved at the little boy who offered her a slobbery smile.

Another little boy spilled out of the SUV, his sandy brown hair tousled and his hazel eyes bright as he stared up at Colton. The kid's intensity made him a little uneasy. He'd met the youngest Havens at the ranch a few times now, but he still wasn't comfortable with them. He wasn't much of a kid person. Until the nurse had moved to Cassidy Ranch with her little boy, he'd never been around kids unless it had been on a firehouse call. He'd met these little guys for the first time on one of those calls; he just hadn't known he was related to them at the time.

Maybe that was a good thing. The car crash had been so tragic. He couldn't imagine the nightmares Baker must have about it. Because Colton only saw kids at accidents and in fires, he wasn't seeing them at their best, so deciding not to have any had never seemed that great a sacrifice for him. Giving up on a future family had felt like the smart thing to do, so that he wouldn't put anyone through what he'd gone through as a kid, that constant worry and uncertainty.

Even now that Dad was doing better, Colton wasn't going to change his mind about never getting married or having kids, especially now that he was working for a busier fire department. There had been a few fires over the past week on some old industrial buildings being remodeled. It would have been easy to get trapped in one of them, easy for someone to worry about him if they'd known how hot the fire had been, how close a call he'd had getting out.

He glanced over at Livvy who was still making faces at the toddler. But even with sunglasses on her forehead, her eyes crossed and her lips pursed, she was beautiful. Funny. But beautiful.

Little Jake giggled, and even the older boy, Ian, laughed. "Who are you?" he asked her.

"I'm Livvy Lemmon," she replied.

"You met her at the hospital when Grandma was there. She's Old Man Lemmon's granddaughter," Baker reminded them. "Hi, Livvy. This is Ian. And Little Jake…" He jostled the little boy on his hip. "And climbing out now is Miller."

The oldest boy had a slight stiffness to his leg. Colton knew why since he'd responded to the crash. He was actually doing better than Colton would have expected, but Sadie had hired a physical therapist to move out to the ranch to aid his recovery.

Despite her meddling, the old woman really wanted what was best for her family. He glanced over at Livvy again who was greeting Miller with a bright smile. The little boy gave her a shy one in return. He was probably as dazzled by her beauty as Colton was. But then there were a lot of pretty women at Ranch Haven: the cook, Taye Cooper, who was engaged to Baker, the schoolteacher who was engaged to Ben, and Jake's wife, Katie, and Dusty's wife, Melanie.

But, like Sadie, they already felt like family to Colton. Livvy wasn't family. And despite his grandmother's matchmaking, he doubted she would wind up as a Haven or as anyone's wife.

"So why are we both here?" Colton asked, gesturing at himself and Livvy. "You only have one apartment you need to sublet, right?"

Baker grinned and shrugged. "Grandma heard me mention it to you and…"

"Grandpa Lem told me," Livvy said. "He said you were expecting me."

Baker chuckled. "He's been spending too much time with my grandma."

From the way Livvy's lips pursed with displeasure, in a gesture—he wanted to tease her—that reminded him of Nurse Sue, it was obvious she thought her grandfather spent too much time with Sadie, too.

"This is awkward…" Colton began.

For a few reasons.

"The guys and I are happy to show you both the place," Baker said, "and you can figure out if either of you wants it."

Colton glanced back at his truck, tempted to crawl inside. He shrugged. "Well, the doctor will definitely be able to pay you more than I will." Especially since he was helping his brothers pay some of Dad's medical bills and Sarah's wages.

She gave him an irritated glance.

"I'm only stating a fact," he said.

"You don't know me," she reminded him. And from the sudden chill in her tone, it didn't sound like she was going to let him either.

But Colton already knew a lot about her, about her family, about her job, about her insistence on taking care of herself.

Baker handed his keys to Miller. "Why don't you let Miss Livvy into my place and we'll join you in a minute?"

Miller scampered toward the building, the keys dangling from his hand. Livvy hesitated a moment before telling them, "I'm the one who doesn't have a chance since you two are family."

Before Baker could confirm or deny her suspicion, she headed after the seven-year-old to the door he was unlocking.

"Is that true?" Colton wondered. But if he took the place away from her and she was willing to pay a higher sublease, he would feel bad for Baker.

"What's true is that you won't have a chance with her if you're not careful."

Colton shook his head. "I don't have a chance with her. She's as determined to stay single as I am."

Baker smiled. "I used to feel that way, too, but then I fell for Taye and the instant family we have with these guys." He hugged Little Jake closer and dropped a kiss on the top of the toddler's head.

"And gave up your job," Colton said. "I'm not willing to do that. I love being a firefighter."

"I want to be a firefighter, too!" Ian chimed into the conversation.

"You're his new hero now," Baker told him.

"Do you like being a firefighter?" Ian asked.

"Yes," Colton told him. "It's all I ever wanted to be." A first responder. And while that might make him a hero for a five-year-old, he didn't want that five-year-old to be his kid, lying awake worrying that he wasn't going to come home from a fire.

He wouldn't put anyone through that. It was better to stay single just like Livvy seemed resolved to do, so no matter how hard his grandmother and her grandfather tried to matchmake the two of them, it wasn't going to happen. He ignored the little twinge of regret that struck his heart.

THE MINUTE MILLER opened the door, Livvy fell in love with the apartment. She was also a little bit in love with the boys, too. She had been so focused on becoming a doctor for so long that she'd never considered having a family.

Steven hadn't wanted any children; she realized now that was probably because he hadn't wanted to share her attention with anyone else. She suspected that was his real reason for not wanting her to move to Willow Creek, because he hadn't wanted her to be close to her family. While they'd been going out, she'd spent less and less time with her friends because she'd stayed home, waiting for his scheduled call.

Nobody would ever consume her time— her life—like that again. But then she heard giggling and she turned to find Colton ducking low as he walked through the door, so the boy riding on his shoulders didn't hit his head. The boy grasped Colton's hat, pushing it low over his eyes, and Colton stumbled a bit on the throw rug. She reached out and grasped his arm. "Whoa, there, horsey," she said. "Don't fall."

But she wondered if she was talking to him or to herself. She couldn't fall for him. Or for anyone. Not until she was strong enough that she wouldn't lose herself again.

Baker ducked in behind his cousin with the toddler on his shoulders, Little Jake giggling wildly now. And Livvy couldn't stop herself from smiling. These big guys were so great with the kids, so sweet. She wasn't surprised that Baker was, they were his nephews. They'd forged a bond during that accident as well. But Colton...

He'd only just met them, but the kids were drawn to him, too. Maybe just because he looked like their uncles or maybe for the same reason that she was drawn to him.

There was just something about Colton Cassidy.

Something that attracted people, even her.

And that scared her.

"I need to leave," she said to no one in particular. No one was paying attention to her as they toured the small apartment. The little boy on Colton's back fired questions at him and even the older, quiet child listened to his answers while Little Jake giggled and cooed at the faces Colton was making. Faces like she'd made at him earlier.

But she couldn't play anymore. "I have to go to work," she said, and she was a bit surprised she didn't choke on the lie. It would probably come back to bite her because Colton might learn from his twin that she was lying.

But before anyone could stop her, she rushed back out to her SUV and sped off, not toward the hospital but toward home. Or Grandpa's home, where she would probably be staying for a while.

With the family connection to Baker, Colton definitely had first dibs on subleasing the apartment. The small and practical one bedroom, with the exposed brick that reminded her of Chicago, would have been perfect, and more affordable than trying to buy something. Colton could probably afford to pay more than she could. She had student loans and a car payment that would affect her mortgage qualification.

She parked the SUV on the street in front of Grandpa's stone Cape Cod house, just in case she did get called into work. She walked past the stone fence that encircled the flower gardens on either side of the walk and stalked into the house to find Grandpa at the stove, stirring something in a pot. The kitchen was bright with deep blue cabinets and sunny yellow walls. Grandma Mary had loved color, in her house as well as in her flowers.

"That was fast," he said. "What did you think?"

"I think you and Sadie better give up your matchmaking. Neither Colton nor I are interested in your scheme or each other. The only thing we were both interested in was that apartment. But you wasted my time going there."

"Why? Didn't Baker give you a chance to sublease it?"

She snorted. "Like that is going to happen…"

"Why wouldn't it?" he asked, arching his white brows about those bright blue eyes of his.

He was so cute that it wasn't fair. She couldn't stay mad at him. So she sighed. "He won't choose me over his cousin."

"They've only just met," Grandpa reminded her.

She shook her head. "It doesn't seem like that. They all are getting really close already." And she'd felt like an outsider to that family, just as she'd felt like an outsider to her own when she'd left for college.

But that was her fault…even more than Steven's. She should have come home more; she should have been there for her family. But here she was, living with her dad and her grandpa, and she wanted her own space.

"Does that bother you?" Grandpa asked her. "That Colton's getting close to the Havens or that he's getting close to you?"

She was wrong; she could stay mad at him, no matter how cute he was. "Stop scheming with Sadie. I am not interested in Colton Cassidy." But she was or she wouldn't have asked him so many questions about his family, about his life. She just didn't want to be interested and distracted from the plan she had for her return to Willow Creek; he wasn't part of it.

Maybe she should buy something even if a down payment and a mortgage might be a bit of a financial struggle right now. She needed to put down roots, to prove she was staying, to herself if not to Steven. She needed to make her own long-term plans and commitments, her own choices without anyone else's input.

Grandpa Lem laughed. "You two remind me of me and Sadie."

"Which one of us is Sadie?" she asked, narrowing her eyes in warning as she met his gaze.

He chuckled again. "You're more like her than you know."

"I don't know whether to be offended or flattered," she admitted.

"Flattered. Sadie March Haven is a strong and fiercely loving woman."

Fiercely loving. Livvy hadn't loved Steven like that, so it was good that she'd returned his ring. But she remembered when she'd peeked through the door into Sadie's hospital room, the way the two octogenarians had been staring at each other. With love…

No. She and Colton were nothing like them. Nothing at all.

LEM WAS NO Taye Cooper, but he'd managed to heat a can of soup for dinner with Livvy. Bob was eating at the office, or so he claimed.

And Lem was spending another night away from the ranch. It was a long drive; he should have been relieved to stay home. He should have been happy to get to spend time with his granddaughter.

But she wasn't happy with him, and that stung his heart and it had already been aching from going two days without seeing Sadie.

How had that happened? How had he come to count on seeing her every day? Why did it bother him so much when he didn't?

He used to dread her coming by the mayor's office, lodging complaints, making demands, telling him everything that he was doing wrong.

Maybe it was time that someone told her what she was doing wrong. He waited until Livvy went up to her bedroom. Then he called Sadie's cell.

"You're pushing too hard."

"What? I didn't ask you to come out here tonight," she said.

And he wondered if she had wanted him to. Was she missing him, too?

"With Colton and Livvy," he said. "She's irritated."

"With him?"

"With me," Lem said. And he hated that he'd upset his granddaughter. She'd come back to Willow Creek so quiet, so broken...and it wasn't heartbreak. It was something more.

Something deeper. Something that reminded him of Mary when she'd forgotten who she was. So maybe Livvy getting so angry was a good thing, but he wasn't about to admit that to Sadie.

He wasn't about to admit that she was right about putting Livvy and Colton together. It had brought his granddaughter back to the feisty girl she'd once been.

"Then she's feeling something," Sadie pointed out. "She's healing her heart from that unhealthy relationship with the brain surgeon. She made the right choice ending that engagement and she'll make the right choices for herself now...with a little help from us."

Lem had told her how worried he'd been about his only granddaughter dating such an obnoxious, condescending man. "I don't want her to be mad at me," he said.

"She'll get over it," Sadie said. "I always do."

Would Sadie get over him? Or was she even, as the kids nowadays put it, *into* him? Or maybe it was her late husband she couldn't get over? Sadie had certainly been alone longer than he had. But then Lem had been alone even when Mary was alive.

He sighed.

"You sound tired," Sadie said. "Aren't you sleeping well unless you're snoring in the chair next to me keeping me awake?"

"Something like that," he admitted. He was missing her too much. And maybe it was time he did some matchmaking of his own for himself. He'd said things that night in the hospital, alluded to things, but she'd been sick and vulnerable. And he didn't even know if she remembered what he'd said…about making an honest woman out of her.

Did she have any idea how he felt about her?

Or maybe she knew and just didn't want to acknowledge it because she didn't return his feelings. Maybe she'd been right all the times she told him there was no fool like an old fool because Lem felt very much like a fool right now, for so many reasons.

CHAPTER EIGHT

EVEN THOUGH COLTON had found the place he'd like to stay, a few days after his visit to the apartment, he walked down Main Street in Willow Creek and pushed open the door to a realtor's office. He wasn't here house hunting; he was here *Cash* hunting. If anyone would know if his brother was back in town, it was Becca Calder.

Becca had been Cash's best friend all through school. If he'd kept in touch with anyone after he'd run away, it would have been her. Because Becca had been like a sister to Cash, she'd been like a sister to Colton, Marsh and Collin as well.

And she'd been like a daughter to Dad; that was why he and Darlene had had her list the ranch for sale. Would she have done that without letting Cash know? Was she the reason he'd showed up at the ranch again?

He should have sought her out earlier to ask, but he struggled between wanting to know the truth and just keeping his suspicions a secret for everyone's sakes…even his own.

An older woman glanced up from the reception desk and greeted him with a welcoming smile. "Collin—"

"Colton, Mrs. Calder," he corrected Becca's mom.

"I'm sorry," she said, her face flushing slightly with embarrassment.

He waved away her apology. "Very few people can tell us apart," he assured her. "Even though I am by far the better-looking twin."

A laugh drew his attention to the doorway of one of the offices that opened off the reception area. Becca leaned against the jamb, her neck tilted as if she was assessing him.

He assessed her right back. In a sleek gray suit and heels, she looked nothing like the girl who used to hang out with Cash in the barn, getting manure smeared on her ragged jeans from playing with the animals. Her once long hair just skimmed her chin now. It was dark, like her eyes, and she was tall, too, even without the heels. With her coloring and height, she could have been his biological sister. Maybe that was why she and Cash had only ever been friends.

She shook her head.

"Really?" Colton asked. "What is it? The white coat? That doctor thing definitely gets Collin attention. Must be why he did it." He did it for Dad; they were all well-aware of that. But he liked teasing about his twin even when Collin wasn't around to hear it.

"It's the black hat," she said, pointing toward his head. "Makes you look like the bad guy."

"I thought ladies always went for the bad boys."

She shuddered. "Not the smart ladies."

"Is that why you and Cash were only ever friends?" he asked.

"We were only ever friends because he's like a brother to me."

Colton noted the present tense and knew he'd come to the right place for information. "When's the last time you talked to him?" he asked.

She narrowed her eyes and shook her head. "Not going there, Colton. Now, if you're here to discuss the ranch or to look for a house…?"

"I do need a place in Willow Creek," he said. "I'm working at the firehouse here now."

She didn't seem surprised. Even though Willow Creek was bigger than Moss Valley, it still had that small town feel where everyone knew everyone and therefore knew each other's personal business.

She glanced at her wristwatch. "I only have a few minutes before my new client arrives. We'll have to set something up for another time."

"Can we talk about Cash then?" he asked.

She shook her head again.

"Why aren't you going there? Why doesn't Cash want to talk to any of us?"

"Colton..."

When she trailed off without answering him, he wondered if she even knew. "At least tell me the last time you've talked to him and if he knows that Dad put the ranch up for sale?"

"I really don't have time for this right now," she said with another pointed glance at her watch.

Frustration wound up his tension, and he thrust his hand into his pocket, sliding his fingers over that lighter. Should he pull it out? Should he show it to her? Prove to her that he knew Cash was back?

But the outside door dinged as it opened behind him.

"Hello," Mrs. Calder greeted the newcomer.

The person replied with a slight gasp, and he turned around to find Livvy Lemmon standing behind him. "What are you doing here?" she asked. "I thought you were subletting Baker's place."

"I thought you would," he said.

"You're his cousin," she said. "He offered it to you first."

He had. And Colton knew he should take it, but if Livvy wanted it…

Colton wanted her to have what she wanted. He wasn't sure why. He barely knew her. But what he knew of her, he respected. She was a good doctor; he'd already seen that firsthand in the ER. She was overqualified for Willow Creek. But she was here because of her family, because she wanted to be close to them. And he liked that about her.

He liked everything about her. It didn't matter if her hair was up and she was wearing scrubs and a face mask, or if she looked like she did now, in a jean skirt and white blouse. She was always beautiful but he suspected a lot of that came from the inside and radiated out.

But he was determined to ignore this attraction he felt. He had more than enough to deal with right now, and clutching that lighter reminded him of all his concerns. He turned back to Becca. "Can we talk later?" he asked her. "Please?"

She sighed but nodded.

And he had hope that maybe he could get through to her, that he could get her to give him Cash's contact information. They must have stayed in touch; they'd been so close in high school. But that had been a long time ago.

Becca had married and divorced since then. She had a young daughter she was raising alone while running her own business.

And Cash...

Could be anywhere.

But Colton had a pretty strong reason to believe that he was back. Or at least he'd been back the day the ranch had burned down. And maybe it was better that Colton find out why before the insurance adjuster did and brought his findings to the authorities.

LIVVY HELD HER breath until Colton stepped around her, opened the door and walked out of the realtor's office. Then she released that breath in a slightly shaky sigh. It really wasn't fair that she kept seeing him everywhere. At work.

At her dad's house.

At Baker's apartment.

And now here.

Had Sadie Haven orchestrated this meeting, too?

Livvy's dad had been the one who'd told her about this real estate company, which was next door to the accounting office he ran in town for Katie Morris-Haven. Had Sadie recruited him in her matchmaking scheme like she had Grandpa?

And what about the realtor?

"Dr. Lemmon," the woman who'd been talking to Colton greeted her. "I'm Becca Calder. It's wonderful to meet you. I would have introduced you to Colton, but it's obvious you two already know each other. From the hospital?"

Livvy nodded. That had been where she'd met him first. "My grandfather is also... friends...with his grandmother."

The woman's smooth brow furrowed for a moment, with confusion probably, then she nodded. "That was a shock, I'm sure, to find out that he's Sadie Haven's grandson."

Livvy wanted to ask how Becca Calder knew Colton, but it wasn't any of her business. And she didn't want it to be.

Didn't want to wonder and worry about why Colton had seemed almost desperate to talk to Becca Calder. The woman was beautiful and, according to Livvy's dad, very hardworking and successful. Livvy respected hard work. And she would love to make a friend in

Willow Creek who wasn't part of the medical field so that every conversation they had wasn't about work.

Not that she'd made any friends at the hospital yet either. But that was because she didn't want to participate in the gossip or become the subject of it. She suspected it was too late for the last part, though. Every time she and Colton worked a case together, Nurse Sue wore her look of disapproval while the younger ones smiled.

Like they all knew how interesting Livvy really found him. Fortunately he seemed to have no idea, and she wanted to keep it that way.

"Would you like anything? Water? Coffee?" the receptionist asked Livvy before shooting a pointed look at her boss.

The boss smiled. "Dr. Lemmon, this is my mother, Phyllis Calder."

Livvy noticed the resemblance between them. And she felt a pang of envy that she wasn't able to even see her mother anymore let alone work with her. She'd rather that was the only reason she was envious of the beautiful realtor, though.

Livvy smiled at Mrs. Calder and shook her head. "No, thank you. I'm fine."

"Come into my office," Becca said and stepped back from the doorway to gesture her inside. Once Livvy walked into the sun-filled space, Becca closed the door and asked, "Really?"

"What?"

"Are you fine?" she asked. "You seemed a little upset with Colton...over an apartment?"

She met the woman's gaze and saw only curiosity, not jealousy. "It was a real nice apartment," she said.

Becca laughed. "Colton's a real nice guy. If you asked, he'd probably give it up to you."

Livvy's own curiosity overwhelmed her. "How do you know him so well?"

"His oldest brother, Cash, and I are best friends."

"Cash? I haven't met him. Just Marsh and Collin and...Colton..."

"Cash hasn't been around for a long time," Becca said, and now she released a shaky sigh. Then she forced a smile. "So what are you looking for, Dr. Lemmon—"

"Livvy, please call me Livvy," she interjected. She wished she knew what she was looking for, and why. Even though she wasn't looking for him, Colton Cassidy kept turning up.

Distracting her. Irritating her. Scaring her.

She had to focus on herself now, finally. "I

decided I don't want to rent after all," she said. "I want to buy."

"A house? A condo?" Becca asked.

Livvy hadn't really thought about it yet, hadn't envisioned how her life would be in Willow Creek. She'd only been able to remember the nostalgia of how it had been when she was little and on her visits home for the holidays.

What did she want? Not a big place like her dad's house. Maybe a small Cape Cod like Grandpa's with a yard where she could tend the flowers? Or a condo where she had nothing to do but relax?

For the first time ever, she could focus only on what she wanted, not on anyone else. A heady rush of freedom overwhelmed her, making her feel lighter and happier than she remembered feeling in a long time. She was in charge of her own life now. And she was not about to let another man distract or influence her.

EVEN THOUGH THE house was full of people laughing and talking and eating, Sadie felt alone. She sat at the end of the table, in her usual place, with her back to the fireplace hearth. It was too warm for a fire now; the

July sun pouring through the French doors that opened onto the patio.

But when she looked out the doors, she looked over at the empty spot where Lem usually sat on her left, next to one of the little boys that always lined up on the long bench. Lem was missing another dinner.

She'd once complained about his mooching meals, but that had been a while ago, when she'd been irritated with her grandson Ben for turning the tables on her and meddling in her life when he'd invited his deputy mayor to dinner. Now she missed Lem.

Which was crazy…but also proved to her that even when part of a big family, someone could feel alone. She'd felt alone for so long after her husband, Jake, had passed away despite her grandsons gathering around her then like they were now. Michael's sons.

She hadn't known about Jessup's. And now that she knew, she couldn't stop thinking about them. Worrying about them.

"You okay, Grandma?" Baker asked as he crouched next to her chair. And just as Colton had, he reached for her wrist, checking her pulse.

She smiled. "My ticker's still ticking," she

assured him. Then she wondered aloud, "Do you miss it? Being a paramedic?"

He shuddered and shook his head. "No. I'm where I belong. I love the ranch."

Her smile widened that he so easily admitted what he'd denied for so long. "I'm so glad you took the position as ranch foreman."

"Me, too," Jake heartily agreed. He oversaw the entire operation, but Dale had been his ranch foreman…before they'd lost him.

But, thanks to Jessup, he wasn't entirely gone anymore. And thanks to Dale's sons: Little Jake, and Ian and Miller who both looked so much like him.

Baker was staring at the boys, too. "I want to make it official, Grandma," he said.

He was already ranch foreman. "Marrying Taye? Have you set a date?" she eagerly asked.

"I want to officially adopt the boys," he said. He'd already claimed primary guardianship. "You think anyone will object to that?"

Jake shook his head. "You made your case. And I think you're right. I think it's what Dale wanted."

"What about Jenny's family?" Baker asked.

Sadie sighed. "They disowned her when she married Dale right out of high school instead of going to college. Then they moved away just a year or so later. I didn't even know how to contact them when she died. Poor Jenny…"

"She had us," Baker said. "She had *you*."

"Not everybody is as happy about having me as you are," she said. "Sometimes you're not even that happy about it."

"Did something happen between you and Lem?" Baker asked with a glance at that empty space on the bench. Nobody else had taken it.

Maybe she wasn't the only one missing him.

"No, he's just spending some time with his granddaughter," she replied. At least she hoped that was the reason he was staying away.

Baker chuckled. "I think someone else would like to spend some time with her, too."

She smiled. "Colton?"

Baker nodded. "Your little plan to throw them together at my place didn't work, though. She took off, and neither of them has asked to sublet it yet."

Because they didn't want to upset the other? Lem was wrong. Her plan was going to work out just fine.

"I think Colton has something else weighing on him," Baker added.

And for a man who'd carried more than his share of guilt over not saving his brother and sister-in-law after the crash, he would easily recognize when someone else was shouldering a load of it. But why? What did Colton have to feel guilty about? He'd clearly done all he could to help with his dad and with the ranch. He had to see that having a steady paycheck, from a job that helped other people, had helped his family the most. Colton was a good man.

Sadie needed to talk to him and find out what was going on with her grandson. She didn't want any more secrets being kept in her family.

CHAPTER NINE

COLTON HAD BEEN summoned to Ranch Haven.

A Sadie summons that he hadn't been able to turn down although he'd tried. There was just something about her. Despite all her toughness and her manipulations, there was also a vulnerability about his grandmother. She'd suffered a lot of losses, a lot of pain, throughout her life.

He didn't want to add to that, but he also needed to make it clear to her that she couldn't meddle in his love life because he didn't have the time or the stomach to have one.

And even if he did, Livvy Lemmon clearly wasn't interested in having a love life either. But after he told Sadie all that the next day in her suite, she just smiled at him.

And his heart beat a little harder. A little faster. Had her friend Lem told her something that his granddaughter had shared with him? Could he have a chance with the beautiful ER doctor?

He snorted in derision. "I'm not kidding,

Grandma—" Tears suddenly welled in her dark eyes, and he dropped to his knees next to her easy chair. "What is it? What…"

She reached up and cupped his cheek in her big hand. "I love it when you call me Grandma…" She drew a shaky breath and released it, and she must have willed the tears away because her eyes cleared. A bit. "I didn't know if you and your brothers would ever think of me that way. Or if because of all the years we lost, you'd always think of me as a stranger."

"Strange, maybe," he teased. "But never a stranger. The first moment I met you, it was like I've always known you. And that's not just because of all the rumors about you I've heard over the years…"

"Where did you hear those?" She sounded hopeful.

She probably wanted to know if Dad had talked about her, but he hadn't. He hadn't had to, though. He had *been* her in so many ways. So strong. So stoic. So loving.

He shrugged. "Around. You're kind of a legend, you know."

She shrugged now, but a smile tugged at her mouth.

She wasn't the only impressive Haven. Her

husband and his namesake Jake were revered for how well they ran their ranch. And Dusty. While he hadn't ridden as a Haven, he was a famous rodeo rider.

"You're a lot to live up to," he admitted. All of them were. And he'd already been a bit in his twin brother's shadow and Marsh's. But like Baker, he'd learned not to compare himself to them. They were different. With different interests and talents.

"What's going on with you?" she asked. "Is something bothering you, Colton?"

He shoved his hand in the pocket that held the lighter. And he considered showing it to her, telling her about it, about Cash. But what if she shared Colton's revelation with Dad? Or, maybe worse yet, Marsh?

While he felt like he'd always known her, he couldn't entirely trust her. If his brother had burned down the ranch, he wasn't sure who he could trust. Certainly not Cash.

"You're here! You're here!" a little boy exclaimed as he ran into the room. He had no limp, so this was the middle one. Ian.

Colton glanced around him for a second but realized the kid was talking to him. Was excited to see him...and warmth flooded his chest. When the little boy threw his arms around Colton's neck, that warmth nearly suf-focated him for a moment. He drew in a breath that smelled like hay and horse, patted the lit-tle boy's back and eased away to stare down at him. "Hey, Ian, what's up?"

"We're going on a ride. Do you want to go with us? I saw you drive up, and I told the oth-ers to wait, that I would ask you. I don't think they're waiting, though."

"I'm sure they didn't leave you behind," Colton said soothingly. He knew how it felt to be the odd man out. Like when everybody else had left the ranch before him. Marsh and Collin for college and Cash...

Who knew where Cash had gone?

Becca. She probably knew, but for some rea-son she was still loyal to her old friend. Maybe if Colton showed her the lighter, she would understand why he had to talk to his oldest brother. He wanted to know the truth before they heard back from the insurance adjuster.

"Will you come? Will you?" Ian prodded. "Or do you have to go to work? Can I go to work with you?"

Sadie chuckled. "Slow down," she advised him. "Colton isn't used to being around kids."

Had she figured that out on her own because

he had no nieces or nephews? Or because of how awkward he was with them?

He chuckled now. "I'm keeping up," he told her. "I don't have to work today." Which was his first day off in a while, but Sadie had probably had something to do with that, too, since she'd summoned him to the ranch.

"Do you wanna ride around the ranch?" Ian asked with all his breathless eagerness.

And because of that, Colton couldn't turn him down. It was probably also safer than staying with Sadie and letting her interrogate him. She was so fierce that she would undoubtedly make him crack faster than Marsh had ever cracked a suspect. Fortunately Marsh was too busy with his new duties as sheriff of Willow Creek to worry about the fire at the ranch, or he might have already interrogated Colton. He'd always been able to tell when Colton was keeping a secret, or when he was pretending to be Collin.

"I'll go," he told his young cousin.

"Do you wanna go, too, Grandma?" Ian asked Sadie.

She looked at Colton, and there was a glint of mischief in her dark eyes. She must have figured out that he'd leapt at the chance to get away from her. And to thwart his effort, she must have been tempted to join them. But then she shook her head. "No. Feisty and I are going to take a little nap. You'll have to come back before you leave for town and tell me what you think about the ranch, Colton."

And so he'd been summoned again. He smiled and nodded and hoped that he would be able to sneak away without seeing her again.

Ian talked nonstop as he led the way to the barn. He held Colton's hand, tugging him along behind him as if Colton might have gotten lost without him. He might have.

The place was big, and Colton had been so dumbstruck during his first tour that he hadn't paid much attention. It had hurt a bit to see the prosperity of the ranch and know that his cousins had managed not just to keep it going but to make it thrive...while he and his brothers had let the Cassidy Ranch go. But then nothing had mattered as much as keeping Dad alive.

In the end, one of his cousins had been responsible for that as well, but he'd given up his life to do it. Colton could have resented them, but he appreciated them too much, appreciated that his dad finally had a shot at a normal life.

But Dale's poor kids wouldn't have a normal life now, not after all they'd lost. He squeezed the little boy's hand and blinked back the moisture that suddenly welled in his eyes.

"What horse do you want to ride?" Ian asked as he led him into the barn. "Do you want to ride Midnight?"

Colton couldn't remember which horse was Midnight. This barn wasn't like the rundown one at Cassidy Ranch that just held the mare. When he'd toured the place with his brothers, he'd seen that this barn had a horse in every stall, and there were a lot of them. But that had been a quick tour, after he'd caught up with them. Sadie had pulled him aside that day, too.

"Which ones are left?" he asked as he followed Ian down the wide aisle. The others must have started their ride, or they were outside somewhere, waiting for Ian to join them. Only a couple of grooms were in the barn, cleaning empty stalls. They didn't look up from their tasks as he and Ian passed them.

"I'm sure you can ride him," Ian said. "You can do anything."

Colton chuckled. "I wouldn't be so sure about that." He couldn't get Livvy Lemmon off his mind. Even with everything else weighing on him, he thought of her constantly. She totally distracted him.

Even now he was barely listening as Ian chattered away to him. He stopped behind the little boy outside a stall. A bucket was already turned upside down next to it, and Ian hopped onto that bucket to open the stall door. When the door creaked open, a black horse flew out, all flailing hooves and loud cries.

Colton froze with shock for a moment, stumbling back. But he wasn't the one in danger. The boy was. Colton grabbed for the horse, pulling it away, letting it tear through the barn as it sought to escape from him. His heart pounded in his ears, deafening him. He couldn't hear anything now. He could only feel. Fear...

Such fear.

For Ian...

He whirled back to where the five-year-old had been precariously balanced on that bucket. He wasn't there now. He was lying on the barn floor next to the crumpled bucket. His eyes closed. His consciousness lost.

This was Colton's fault. All his fault. He dropped to his knees beside the boy and felt for a pulse. It was there but it wasn't strong.

And neither was the child.

He'd already been through so much.

Had already survived so much.

He had to be okay.

Colton had to make sure he was okay.

LIVVY WAS SCARED. She was scared because she'd heard the fear in his voice when Colton had called in about a patient. It was supposed to be his day off, but he was on his way here with the victim of a ranch accident.

With one of those sweet little Haven boys.

Those poor kids had already been through so much; he had to be all right. According to Colton, the five-year-old had lost consciousness for just a few minutes before coming around, but the paramedic was worried.

She knew why; Grandpa had told her about the severity of the concussion the boy had sustained in the crash that killed his parents. His short-term memory had been so affected that he'd kept forgetting that they'd died, and every time he'd asked where they were, he'd had to learn again and again what had happened to them. That they weren't ever coming home, and he'd had to grieve them over and over again.

A sob of sympathy stuck in the back of her throat, but she swallowed it down, determined to act professionally. Nurse Sue already scrutinized her every move, as if just waiting for an opportunity to report her for something. She suspected her only real issue with Livvy was her age.

The other ER doctors were older than she was. So much so that many of them had partially retired and only picked up the occasional shift. And the ones with whom Livvy had worked had been quick to point out that she knew more than they did.

She hoped that was true right now. She hoped she was the best physician to treat the little Haven boy. But because she wanted to make sure all her bases were covered, she also called the neurologist. Willow Creek didn't have a pediatric one on staff.

But she knew a pediatric neurosurgeon. Or she would once Steven finished his fellowship. While he didn't like kids, for some reason he wanted to treat them. He'd said before it was more of a challenge than treating an adult.

Maybe it was also because he thought he could fool children easier into thinking he was a better person than he was. She suspected he was going to be disappointed about that like he'd been disappointed in her. Children were sometimes more perceptive than adults. She certainly hadn't been very perceptive when it had come to Steven.

If she wanted another consultation for Ian, she would call the pediatric neurologist on staff at the children's hospital in Sheridan. She already had the number handy and just hoped that Ian wouldn't need it, that he would be all right.

For the little boy's sake and for Colton's.

He'd sounded so upset when he'd called into the ER. Then when he'd heard her voice, his had gotten steadier. With relief? Did he trust her?

The doors to the ambulance bay opened, but it was a truck that pulled up. Not an ambulance. Colton had strapped the kid to a board, though, and buckled him onto the backseat of the truck. "I stabilized his neck and back," he told her.

"Does he have any pain? Any numbness?" she asked.

"His ankle hurts and his arm, but he has feeling in all his extremities."

"We'll get an MRI," she assured him. "And a CT scan. We'll take care of him."

But even after laying the boy on a gurney, he followed beside it as she pushed it down the hall. The little boy clutched his hand tightly.

"It's going to be okay," Colton assured him. "Dr. Livvy is going to take good care of you. And your uncle Baker and Taye are right behind me with Little Jake and Miller." And then they were in the ER, too, coming through the ambulance bay just like he had.

Baker had once been a paramedic firefighter with the Willow Creek Fire Department, too, so it had probably been instinct for him to come through that way.

Instinct and anxiety. He rushed toward the gurney. A tall blonde woman, Taye Cooper, followed close behind him, the toddler clinging to her, his chubby hand wrapped tightly around her thick braid. Miller limped along beside Baker, holding his hand like a lifeline.

"I know you all want to help," she said. "But you have to go into the waiting room and let me examine Ian. I'll take good care of him."

The entire group stared at her for a long moment, as if assessing her, as if they wondered if they should believe her.

"She's the best doctor here," Colton said. "And that's counting my brother. Let's back off and let her do her job."

His words answered the question she'd mentally asked herself just moments ago. He trusted her.

She had to make certain to validate his trust in her by taking good care of his little cousin. "Let's go for a ride," she told Ian, who grimaced as he stared up at her. "What? Are you in pain? What hurts?"

He shook his head and grimaced again. "No. We were going for a ride when Midnight knocked me down."

"Well, I promise not to knock you down," she assured him. "I will take very good care of you."

He let go of Colton's hand then and reached for hers. "Okay," he said trustingly. "I believe you. Colton said you would."

She squeezed his hand in hers. "Okay then, let's go take pictures of all your insides."

"Can I see them?" he asked.

She nodded. "Yes. Maybe we'll even be able to tell what you had for lunch." She started to move the gurney, but a big hand on the other side held it for a second. She looked up and met Colton's gaze.

"Thank you…" he murmured, his dark eyes full of all the emotion he couldn't quite contain.

She couldn't quite contain hers either at the moment, so she could only nod. Then he released the gurney, and she whisked her patient away. While she focused on treating Ian, she couldn't get Colton entirely out of her mind. She was nearly as worried about him as she was the little boy.

But Ian's vitals were strong and while he had some contusions, she detected no broken bones, and he didn't appear to be in any pain, just very curious about all the equipment. Instead of having a nurse take him to Radiology, she personally rolled his gurney into the elevator and took him up herself. She was reluctant to leave him. She'd already started falling for the little guy.

Maybe that was why she was reluctant to return to the ER. She didn't want to start falling for Colton, too.

BAKER COULDN'T STOP SHAKING, not even when Taye closed her arms around him and held him close. She'd just handed off Little Jake to Colton while Miller had taken Livvy Lemmon's free hand; his cousin and the ER doctor were giving the boys a tour of the emergency room. Ian held Livvy's other hand, beaming up at her as he peppered her with questions. He was fine.

He just had some bumps and bruises. But tears stung Baker's eyes. Tears of relief.

"He's okay," Taye said. But she trembled against Baker and a tear streaked down her cheek from the corner of her eye.

He wiped it away with his thumb and softly kissed her lips. "Thank you."

"I didn't do anything," she said, her voice gruff with guilt.

"Neither did I," Baker admitted. He hadn't been given the chance. Colton had snapped into action as the first responder, and he had been first at the scene.

As his cousin walked away with the boys and Livvy, Colton's broad shoulders slumped and it wasn't just from the burden of carrying Little Jake. He felt guilty about Ian getting hurt. But accidents happened. Baker knew that all too well.

"We definitely need to meet with that lawyer and get the adoptions started." As one of the named guardians with his brothers and grandmother, he was able to authorize medical treatment for the boys. Maybe it was good that so many of them were listed as guardians. But he wanted him and Taye to be primary. To be parents even though nobody would ever forget Dale and Jenny.

"Do you think there will be any issues?" she asked, looking concerned.

He shook his head. "Grandma and I talked about it. Jenny's family all disowned her years ago."

Taye sighed. "I can't imagine…" But they both knew she could; her family had never been there for her. Not like the Havens were for each other.

"Jenny's family wanted her to go to college, to be more than the wife of a rancher." He stared into her eyes. "Do you want more, Taye? Will that be enough for you?"

"Did Midnight kick you in the head?" she asked. "You and the boys—our family—are so much more than I ever thought I would have. So much love. Jenny's family has no idea how much she had and how much they lost."

Baker had a faint inkling of unease then. What if they realized that? He tightened his arms around Taye. "Yes, let's make it official as soon as possible."

She nodded.

"And us," he said. "Let's make *us* official, too. Let's get married right now."

"But Ben and Emily—"

"They set a date," he reminded her. They'd decided to get married over the holidays and go someplace warm for their honeymoon.

"So we should wait until after their wedding."

He shook his head. "I don't want to." A horrible thought occurred to him, gripped him. "Unless… Do you want to wait? Is it too soon for you? I know I'm still a work in progress, but I haven't had a nightmare in weeks—"

She kissed him then pulled back. "You're perfect, just the way you are. And I do want to get married right away. Let me just make sure Emily will be okay with it."

She was friends with Ben's fiancée and his other brothers' wives. No. They were closer than friends; they were already like sisters. Sadie had done good when she'd hired them all to help out with the boys. When once he'd resented her meddling, Baker couldn't thank her enough for it now. Would Colton thank her some day?

Because he was sure she was already meddling in his cousins' lives, bringing them all to Willow Creek and Colton here to Livvy Lemmon. The two of them walked back with the boys then, acting as if they were totally focused on the kids while they sent each other furtive glances.

"Oh, Grandma…" he murmured.

Taye smiled. "Sadie strikes again."

"Maybe," he agreed. "But one of these times she's destined to strike out."

Colton was stubborn, every bit as stubborn as Baker and his brothers. But Baker was pretty sure Colton had something else going on, something weighing on him. And if he didn't find a way to deal with it, like Baker had, he wouldn't be ready for a relationship with anyone.

CHAPTER TEN

A FEW DAYS LATER, standing on the doorstep of Livvy Lemmon's childhood home, Colton was still shaken over the incident at the ranch with the bronco and Ian getting hurt. The child was fine, though. An MRI and CT scan had confirmed that Ian had no broken bones and no current concussion. Livvy suspected he'd probably fainted with fear or lost his breath and that he hadn't actually lost consciousness due to a head injury.

It would have been cruel had the kid had another concussion. Miller had told Colton about how his younger brother kept forgetting stuff for weeks after the crash, like the fact their parents had died. Colton pressed a hand over his heart as a twinge of pain struck it when he thought of all those poor kids had endured. He didn't want to have any kids, didn't want to put them through pain like that. His dad opened the door just in time to catch him with his hand still on his chest.

"Are you okay?" Dad asked, and he reached out to grasp his shoulders. "Is everything all right?"

"I'm fine," Colton said. But it was a lie and clearly his dad knew it.

His dark eyes narrowed with skepticism. "Then why are you ringing the doorbell? You should have just come in." He stepped back so Colton could join him in the foyer.

"It's not our house," Colton reminded him.

"It will be," Dad said. "Once the insurance company finishes their investigation and pays out for the house."

But would they pay out if it was arson? Would it matter since the place was selling? It would matter if the insurance company accused Dad of starting it.

"They need to settle the case before the ranch sale can close," Dad continued. "Something about liens and escrows and such. But once that's done, I want to buy this house from Bob. He had offered to sell it to Katie O'Brien a while ago, but then she married Jake and moved to the ranch."

What about Livvy? How did she feel about her dad selling her childhood home?

Colton kept those questions to himself, worried that his father would misconstrue his concern for her as something more personal. He stepped inside the house's wide hall entrance. The formal living room was on one side and formal dining room on the other. "It's a pretty big place. A family house."

"A lot of family is staying here right now," Dad said with a smile. "You could, too. There's room. You don't have to keep crashing at the firehouse, you know."

He shrugged. "I've been working a lot, so it makes sense to stay there." It would have made more sense to sublease Baker's apartment from him, but Colton wanted to make sure that Livvy didn't want it. He hadn't had a chance to talk to her about it. They hadn't actually talked about anything but patients, first Ian and then the other ones he'd brought into the ER over the past few days. He'd only had a couple shifts as a paramedic, though; mostly he'd been focused on fighting fires. There'd been a lot of brushfires, thanks to the heat and dryness and teenagers partying on their summer break.

Even though he'd been busy, he hadn't been busy enough to stop worrying about Cash and his dad. He studied his dad's face. His skin had color for once instead of the sickly pallor he used to have, and there was a fullness to his face. Not the fullness he had when he was accumulating fluid on his failing heart either, but a healthy fullness, like he was eating and getting outside. That was where he led Colton down the hall, through the big eat-in kitchen toward the slider that opened onto the back-yard.

"This is my favorite place," Dad said as he drew in a deep breath. "Isn't it beautiful?"

Colton breathed deep, too, smelling the flowers and fresh-cut grass. "It is nice," he agreed. Farther back in the yard was a play-set where Sarah's son, Mikey, was swinging until he saw Colton; then he stopped and his eyes got wide. He was a cute little kid, prob-ably around Ian and Jake's son Caleb's age with curly reddish-blond hair. He looked like he could have been Livvy's kid with that hair.

The thought of her having a child had some-thing tightening in his stomach, and he gri-maced.

The little boy jumped up from the swing.

"It's okay," Colton assured him. "Don't let us stop you. Have fun."

"He loves that swing," the boy's mother said. Sarah stepped through the slider and joined them on the deck, carrying a tray with glasses and a pitcher of lemonade. Colton quickly took the tray from her to settle onto the patio table. "Come get a drink," she called out to her son.

Mikey shook his head.

Colton felt a little uneasy with how intently the child was staring at him. "Is he afraid of me?" he asked Sarah, lowering his voice to a whisper.

"No..." she said, and her brow puckered with concern. Her hair was blond but a lighter shade than her son's, and it was straight. "I think he thinks you're your brother Marsh."

"He's afraid of Marsh?" he asked, but he wasn't totally surprised. His older brother could be intimidating when he wanted to be. Maybe he was so used to scaring adolescents away from lives of crime that he didn't know how to act around young children.

Colton wasn't sure that he knew either, but since recently hanging out with his young cousins, he was getting better. "Hey, Mikey," he called out to the boy. "I met some kids about your age. They live out on this big ranch. They have lots of horses."

Colton remembered how much the boy had liked Darlene's mare. He'd been nearly as obsessed with it as little Caleb was with Midnight. Colton could certainly understand Mikey's obsession more than Caleb's. That bronco was a scary beast, but Caleb had kept insisting that he wouldn't hurt anyone and that Ian's injuries were from falling off the bucket.

But Colton remembered how that bucket had been smashed. Ian hadn't done that; Midnight had. That bucket could easily have been the little boy instead.

"What kind of horses?" Mikey asked softly as he approached the deck.

"Mostly work horses like quarter horses. But there are some Appaloosas, too, with the spots all over them, and they have this big, scary black bronco." He gave an exaggerated shudder that wasn't actually all that exaggerated. That thing had taken him by such surprise when it had barreled out of its stall.

"*You* get scared?" the boy asked, his blue eyes widening with surprise.

Colton nodded. "All the time…" For so much of his life, he'd been scared.

"Mr. Colton is the firefighter," Sarah said, probably to point out that he wasn't Marsh.

But the boy's face lost all its color then, and his mouth dropped open in shock or fear.

"It's okay," Colton assured him. The kid had probably been traumatized over the fire at the ranch. He'd been so scared that he'd hidden in the barn so well that it had taken Sarah and

Darlene quite a while to find him behind molding piles of hay way in the back of the loft. "I'm just here to see my dad. There's no fire here. And I checked out the place before you moved in, there is no chance of a fire happening here. The alarms are all up-to-date and I replaced all the batteries myself the day my dad moved in. It's okay."

But the little guy didn't look reassured; he looked shaken. "It really is," Colton promised. "Nothing bad is going to happen here."

The kid released a shaky breath and nodded. "Okay. And just in case, I got a lucky charm. A whole bunch of them on this bracelet I found." He reached into his pocket and pulled out a silver bracelet. An assortment of charms dangled from the delicate chain.

"Where did you find that?" Sarah asked.

"In my room."

"Is it yours?" Colton asked Sarah. A couple of those dangling charms reminded him of someone else. The mini stethoscope. The bracelet could also belong to a nurse, though.

But Sarah shook her head.

There was also a mini scalpel and a tiny needle with thread.

"Livvy's," he said. "It must belong to Livvy." He smiled at the boy. "Which room is yours?"

Mikey didn't answer.

"The one at the back of the house, end of the hall," Sarah answered for him.

"That was Livvy's room."

Sarah told her son, "We need to return that to her. I'm sure it's very special to her. Each of these charms was probably to celebrate something she accomplished."

"There are a lot of them," Mikey said with awe.

"There are," Colton agreed. That was how hard Livvy had worked, how driven she was. "She's a special lady."

"You know her well?" Dad asked the question, his dark eyes gleaming.

Colton groaned. "You are so much like your mother."

Dad groaned but then he laughed. "I should take that as a compliment. She's tough and smart."

"Yes, she is," Colton agreed. "But she's wrong about me and her matchmaking plan."

"But you'll return that to Livvy?" Dad asked. "You must see her all the time."

"Just when I'm at the hospital," Colton said. "We just work together."

But Dad chuckled as if he didn't believe him. With his mother gently prodding him, Mikey handed the bracelet to Colton. Before he could close his hand around it, his dad pointed at it.

"That bracelet reminds me of something that was found in the remains of the house," he said.

Colton froze with shock. How had Dad found out about the lighter?

"Your mother's rings," he said with a smile. "They survived the fire. I'm going to bring them to the jeweler's to be cleaned and restored."

"That's good," Colton said. He was glad something more than just memories of his mother had survived the house fire. All the pictures of her had gone up in flames.

"Yes, because with my mother's track record for matchmaking, one of you boys will probably need those rings pretty soon."

Colton snorted. "We've all been single a long time," he said. "She's not going to have luck with any of us."

"Maybe she will with you now," Dad said, and he pointed to the bracelet. "You're the one with all the charms."

Colton chuckled. "They're not mine. I'm going to give this back to its rightful owner." She was the one with all the charms, but she and those charms weren't going to tempt him to change his mind about marriage, especially after that incident with Ian.

"YOU'RE CERTAINLY HERE a lot," a deep voice remarked, and Livvy turned to find Collin approaching her. She knew it was Collin because her pulse didn't quicken, her skin didn't flush with heat.

Why couldn't she have this non-reaction to his twin? Why was it that she had to fight to focus on her job every time Colton brought a patient into the ER? Why did he affect her so much, but the man who looked identical to him didn't affect her at all? But then her attraction to Colton wasn't about the way he looked; it was about the way he felt, with all those emotions in his dark eyes. He cared so much, carried so much on his broad shoulders. He was such a contrast to Steven who'd only really cared about himself.

She emitted a soft sigh and forced a smile for Collin. "Lowest in seniority gets the most on-call shifts." And Willow Creek was such a small hospital that they didn't get interns and residents; it wasn't a teaching hospital like the one where she'd done her residency. "And everybody has more seniority than I do."

Nurse Sue, and her pursed lips of disapproval, never failed to remind her of that. She sighed again.

"Hey, I think I only have a week on you," he said with a grin.

"Yes, but you're not in the same department I am. You are here a lot, too, though." Not that she saw much of him. He only occasionally came down to the ER for a consult.

His face flushed and he glanced away for a moment. "Well, I'm not always working when I'm here."

"Oh…" she said with sudden understanding. "Are you seeing someone at the hospital?" Maybe she should start listening to gossip, but she was worried if she did that it might be about her. With the way everybody watched her, they'd probably noticed her reaction to Colton, how he affected her.

Collin smiled. "I am seeing someone," he said. "A patient."

"Oh." Not liking how unethical that was, she regretted her question.

"You don't need to report me," he said. "She's just seven years old. She had a heart transplant months ago at the children's hospital in Sheridan but has been having some complications."

"Oh, no," Livvy said with concern.

"They're minor, but she's here because social services haven't been able to find her a good foster home placement."

"What happened to her parents?"

He shrugged. "She had a lot of health issues. It was too much for them, just like it is for foster families apparently. No one wants to deal with all her doctor's appointments and anti-rejection medications."

"So she can't go home." Sympathy gripped Livvy's heart. "Poor girl…"

"She doesn't have a home," Collin said. "Just an overworked social worker."

"And you," she said. "Now I know why you're at the hospital so much."

He smiled again. "She's so sweet. She's charmed everyone on her floor. But she needs a family, people who won't just keep coming and going in her life. She needs permanence."

"Sometimes family comes and goes in our lives," Livvy remarked, thinking of how she'd done that with hers. That she hadn't been there for them when they'd needed her.

"And sometimes they're gone forever…" Collin said, his eyes even darker with emotion.

Knowing he'd lost his mom like she had, she reached out and clasped his forearm through his white coat. "I know. It's hard to let them go."

She was actually relieved that she'd had to

move from Dad's house to Grandpa's. Being in the house where she'd been a child had been hard because all her memories there included her mom. She'd kept expecting to find Mom in the kitchen cooking or on the back deck with a book and a cup of tea. Not that she didn't want to remember her mother...but along with the memories came so much grief.

Maybe it was good that she couldn't find the charm bracelet her mother had given her. But tears prickled the back of her eyes as she lamented the loss of what was her most treasured possession.

"I don't want to let Bailey Ann go," Collin said.

Livvy frowned in confusion. "I don't understand..."

"I know it's a rookie move, getting attached to a patient like this, but I am." He shook his head in disparagement of himself.

Livvy smiled. "My patients come and go. I have no chance of getting attached to them." And she liked that. She liked treating and releasing them. Though, there were the repeat visitors, the ones who treated the ER like a doctor's office where they didn't have to make an appointment, where they just showed up with their sniffles or their indigestion. "But with her ongoing heart condition, you'll be seeing her for a long time."

"Would you like to see her?" Collin asked.

"I'm not a cardiologist," she said. That had been her toughest rotation in med school; looking at EKGs had been like trying to decipher hieroglyphics on a cave wall.

"Not as her doctor," Collin amended. "As a visitor. Would you mind spending some time with her?"

She stepped back. "Me? I'm not really a kid person."

"You see a lot of them in the ER."

That was true. "But that's to treat them." She knew how to do that. "But to visit with them…" She shrugged. "I don't have any nieces or nephews, and I've never really spent that much time around kids."

"Me neither," he said. "But Bailey Ann is different. You'll see. And I heard you were good with Ian and the other little boys when they were in the ER."

"Colton told you that?" she asked. The thought of the paramedic talking about her to his twin had her pulse quickening. Did she cross his mind as often as he crossed hers? Crossed…?

He was usually always on her mind, and she

had no idea why. Maybe just because she saw him so often, in the ER, and around town? Like at Baker's apartment, at the realtor's office and even her own house. Old house. She had no house. She really needed to find a place to call her own. Becca had called her indecision about buying a house or a condo a good thing, that her openness would make it possible for them to tour more properties. They had an appointment to do that soon.

Collin shook his head. "No. I heard it around the hospital that you and Colton gave the kids a tour."

"So you listen to hospital gossip?"

He chuckled. "Guilty." The humor left him as he frowned and continued, "I've been worrying about Colton as much as I have Bailey Ann."

"Why?" she asked.

He shrugged. "I don't know. He's just been *different* ever since the fire at the ranch."

"That's understandable," she said in Colton's defense. "Your childhood home burned down, and you learned about being part of the Haven family. That would be a lot for anyone to process."

"Not Colton," Collin insisted. "He's always been the most resilient of all of us. He stayed positive and upbeat through every one of Dad's health scares and through Mom's death."

"That's a lot," she pointed out. "And everyone must have a breaking point." She hated to think of Colton breaking, not that he seemed broken but he did seem burdened. She didn't know him like his twin did, though. What she did know of Colton reminded her of her grandfather, always helping everyone else while handling his own troubles alone.

What was her grandfather's breaking point? How much could he handle before it became too much for him? Sadie? Could he handle his relationship with her?

Probably better than Livvy could handle a relationship with anyone right now, especially someone as troubled as his twin thought Colton was. The swish of the automatic doors had her turning toward the lobby. Two men walked in; one was her grandfather, the other man towered over him. Colton.

He was laughing at whatever Grandpa Lem was telling him, and he didn't look the least bit troubled until he noticed her standing beside his brother. Then the smile left his face… almost as if he was jealous.

But if he was, it had to be just because of that sibling rivalry thing…which was probably even more intense between twins. It couldn't have been about her…because Colton barely knew her. Although he had caught her in some vulnerable moments, so maybe he knew more about her than she'd realized. More about her than she wanted him to know…

ONE MINUTE COLTON HAVEN had been laughing and joking with Lem, the next he'd gone silent and still, his long body tense. And then Lem saw where the young man was staring… At Lem's granddaughter and Collin Haven.

A smile tugged up Lem's lips with the amusement coursing through him, especially when Collin leaned a little closer to Livvy and gave his brother a challenging stare, purposely goading him. Colton audibly sucked in a breath, almost as if his twin had sucker punched him.

Lem didn't want them to actually come to blows over Livvy, though, so he stepped around Colton and hurried toward his granddaughter. "Livvy, honey, I hope I'm not interrupting anything."

"No, of course not, Grandpa," she assured him. "Is everything okay?"

He nodded. "I just need to speak to you for a minute." Privately so that he didn't embarrass her in front of the Haven twins. He'd promised to pass on a message from another suitor; her ex-fiancé had called him with a plea to help him get Livvy back. That was the last thing Lem intended to do because he knew that if Steven got her back, they would lose her... just as their family had lost her during their engagement.

He suspected Livvy had lost a bit of herself then, too. But he knew better than to keep secrets; he'd seen firsthand what it had done to the Haven family. So he waited until Livvy stepped out from behind the intake desk and led her into the lobby. "I don't want to tell you this."

Her face got pale, and her green eyes widened with fear. "What, Grandpa? Are you okay?"

He nodded. "I'm fine, honey. This is about you."

"What about me?"

The twins hadn't started talking yet; they appeared to be listening, blatantly eavesdropping on their conversation. That smile tugged at his lips again. "You remind me so much of your grandma Mary..."

Her brow furrowed now and she stared at him with confusion and concern. "Are you really okay?"

He nodded.

"But I don't look anything like Grandma Mary."

"You do," he said. "Your features, your petite size…and most especially the way all the boys flock around you."

She blushed now and laughed. "Oh, Grandpa…"

"I was lucky to win my Mary," he said. "She could have had anyone."

"She had the best," Livvy assured him with a loving smile.

She was such a sweet girl.

"Don't you settle for anything less," he advised her.

"I don't intend to settle at all," she said but she glanced back at the twins.

"Steven called me," Lem admitted.

"You? How did he get your number?"

He shrugged. "I'm easy enough to track down, honey. The point is he's trying to track you down. He says you're not returning his calls or texts. He's worried about you."

She snorted. "He's worried that he screwed up and he won't get me back."

"He did screw up," Lem said. "And I hope he's right that he won't get you back."

Livvy hugged him and whispered. "Don't worry about me, Grandpa. I'm fine."

But he was worried. Because Steven had sounded a little too desperate. He'd manipulated her before, and he was obviously trying to do it again. He was trying to get her to go back to him. To leave Willow Creek because there was no way a man like him would ever settle here. Would Livvy? She'd just said she had no intention of settling down. But she'd been talking about relationships.

Had her engagement with Steven made her unwilling to risk her heart ever again?

CHAPTER ELEVEN

STEVEN...

The name brought on another wave of the nausea that had already been roiling around Colton's stomach when he walked into the hospital and saw Collin and Livvy standing so close together at the intake desk. And now her grandfather had taken her aside to tell her about her ex-fiancé contacting him, trying to contact her. The man was an idiot; surely she had to see that now. She wouldn't give him another chance.

"What did you want to see me about?" Collin asked him, then followed his gaze across the waiting room to Lem and Livvy, and he chuckled. "Ohh, you didn't come to see me."

Heat rushed to his face, and he purposely turned away from her to remove the distraction. "It's not like that." It couldn't be like that; he knew it was better to stay single than to risk people worrying about you, losing you...

"What? You're here to work?" Collin asked.

"You're dressed kind of casually for bringing in patients." He peered around him to the parking lot. "And I don't see your rig. Picking up patients in your truck now?"

Colton glared at his twin. "Dad always says you're too smart for your own good."

"Not smart enough to figure out what's going on with you," Collin said as he intently studied Colton's face. "What's been eating you since the fire?"

Colton had worried more about Marsh picking up on his secret-keeping than Collin. They'd never had twin-tuition. Despite being twins, Collin had always been more of a loner.

"Nothing." He couldn't tell Collin about the lighter; his twin was more by-the-book than he was and would want to report Cash. Colton couldn't do that until he knew for certain that their missing oldest brother was responsible.

He didn't want to think he was, but Cash had hurled such ugly words at Dad, disowning him and swearing he was never coming back. But had he? Colton needed to find Cash and talk to him, find out where his head was and more importantly his heart. Was it still so full of bitterness that he would have burned down the house? Colton needed to know, before the insurance adjuster did, if the fire was arson. He needed to know so he could protect Dad.

Hopefully Becca would at least get a message to his big brother for him.

"Is this about Livvy?" Collin asked.

Colton shook his head. "No."

"Maybe it should be," Collin said. "She's pretty amazing."

She was, and he felt a pang of jealousy that his brother had noticed. "Grandma?" Colton teased his twin. "Is that you?"

Collin snorted.

"No, seriously, don't you start matchmaking, too," Colton said. "I told you I'm never getting married."

"We all vowed that," Collin said.

And maybe all for the same reasons.

"It's not right to put a kid through what we went through," Colton said with a heavy sigh. What the little Haven boys had gone through…

"But you're not sick like Dad or Mom," Collin said.

"No," Colton said. "But I have a dangerous job. I go into burning buildings for a living."

Collin held up his hands. They weren't bandaged any longer, but the skin was still pink from the burns. "You don't have to tell me how dangerous your job is."

"I love it," Colton said. "And I don't want to give it up like Baker did. I don't want to settle down with a wife and kids." But when once he would have stated that with unwavering certainty, he wavered a bit. Because now he could see what he was giving up in giving up a family. In his mind, he could see Livvy with the Haven boys and imagine...

He shook his head. "No, I'm never settling down."

"And you think that's what Livvy wants?" Collin asked.

"I don't think she wants that any more than I do," Colton admitted. It was probably another thing they had in common, like losing their mothers and loving their families. But the things that they had in common were also the things that would keep them apart.

LIVVY HAD BEEN struggling to focus on her grandfather because her attention kept straying to the twins who appeared to be having an intense conversation. Over what? Her?

Her face heated with embarrassment over her thinking that they might be talking about her. They barely knew her, but then she did catch the last part of their conversation. And it was about her...

And she tensed as she realized Colton knew her better than she'd thought. Certainly better than Steven had ever known her. And certainly better than she wanted Colton to know her. But he was as committed to never committing as she was, and while that should have made her happy, she felt a twinge of regret. Not for herself…

But for the wife he could have made happy, the kids who would have loved having him as a dad.

She released a shaky sigh.

"Livvy," her grandfather said, and he patted her shoulder as if in commiseration.

Over Colton? Over his never wanting to settle down? Did Grandpa think she cared? That she was disappointed? Since she didn't want to settle down either, she should have been relieved. Happy. She summoned a smile now, for her grandfather, hugged him and kissed his cheek. "I need to get back to work, Grandpa. And please, just block Steven. Don't take any more of his calls." She'd done the same; she just wanted to forget him and how stupid she'd been.

It was good that she'd decided not to date for a while and work on herself. It was past time that she did that.

Apparently she wasn't the only one who thought so as she noticed Nurse Sue peering over the intake desk at them, her face contorted with its usual disapproving frown, and her icy blue eyes as cold as ever.

"I have to get back to work," she said again, and she started to head into the ER, which had been empty the last time she'd checked. That was why Collin had found her out at the intake desk again, waiting for patients to walk in seeking treatment. She wasn't sure why Colton was here. He wasn't dressed as either a paramedic or a firefighter right now. But she didn't want to assume that he was there to visit her; he had to have been looking for his twin.

But as she passed them, Colton reached out and encircled her wrist with his long fingers. "Aren't you missing something?"

"What?" she asked, trying to ignore how her pulse leaped from his touch.

He pulled his other hand from his pocket and uncurled his fingers to show the bracelet lying across his palm.

"My charm bracelet!" she exclaimed. "Where did you find it?" She hadn't seen it since she'd moved home. And she'd been careful not to wear it when she'd realized that Steven hadn't gotten the clasp fixed like she'd asked him to when he took her engagement ring in to be re-sized.

"I didn't find it," he said. "The little boy staying in your old bedroom did." He released her wrist but then proceeded to wrap the brace-let around it. "Do you want it on?"

She wanted nothing more than to wear her bracelet again. Her mom had gotten it for her for her thirteenth birthday and had added charms to it over the years in celebration of Livvy's accomplishments. She blinked against the sudden sting of tears and shook her head. "No…"

"Oh, you're still working," he said.

"Yes, but the clasp is broken," she said. "I don't wear it because I don't want to lose it." And maybe that was why Steven hadn't fixed it like she'd asked. He'd known that bracelet had meant more to her than the big diamond ring he'd bought her. He'd been jealous of it, just as he'd been jealous of any time she'd wanted to spend with anyone else.

She took the bracelet from his hand, and her skin tingled where it touched his. But she forced herself not to react, not to show her at-traction to him. The last thing she wanted was to jump out of one bad relationship and into another…one that might hurt her even more because Colton had made it clear he had no intention of ever settling down.

Not that she wanted to either. No, she needed to stay single, to be independent and strong.

"Thanks," she said before turning and walking away.

She wasn't just grateful for his returning the bracelet; she was grateful she'd overheard what he'd said. It had just strengthened her resolve to stay uninvolved.

WARMTH FILLED SADIE'S CHEST. Lem was here, sitting where he belonged, in the chair next to hers in her suite. His blue eyes sparkled with happiness as he related how Colton had found Livvy's missing charm bracelet.

"That's a wonderful development," Sadie said, hopeful that her plan was finally working.

Lem released a slight sigh then, and the sparkle dimmed in his eyes.

"What is it?" she asked with concern.

"That ex-fiancé of hers keeps calling, begging me to get her to call him back."

"You didn't, did you?" she asked.

"I told Livvy that he was calling," he said.

"Why?" she asked with alarm. "You said he's manipulated her in the past. Why would you let him do it again?"

"Because I don't want to manipulate her..." he sputtered and blushed. "Any more than I already have. I don't want to keep any secrets from Livvy."

Sadie sighed now. "Yes, they have a way of coming out and causing more pain." She pressed a hand over her heart.

"Are you feeling all right?" Lem asked with concern.

"Yes, I'm fine," she assured him. But then a rap on the door startled a little cry from her lips, and she jumped like Feisty jumped up from her lap and rushed toward the door. "Come on in," she said with irritation at the quickness of her heart rate. That was how it had started that day Baker and Taye had saved her life.

"Grandma!" Colton exclaimed after opening the door and stepping inside. "Are you okay?" he asked as he rushed forward and dropped to his knees in front of her.

She smiled, touched again that he called her Grandma. "Yes, yes," she assured him. "I'm fine."

And she was now, her heart rate slowing back to normal. She was being a silly, old woman...her fear of having another attack bringing on the attacks. Anxiety. That was what it was, but she wasn't about to admit that to anyone else.

She wasn't the only one who was anxious. She could feel the nerves in him, in his fingers, when he touched her wrist, like Baker so often did, taking her pulse.

"A little fast," he murmured.

"Blame him," Sadie said. "He was telling me about how that ex-fiancé of Livvy's is harassing her."

He glanced at Lem then. "He is? Is that what you were telling her today?"

Lem nodded. "Yeah, he's desperate to get her back."

"He should be," Sadie said. "Any man would be a fool to let her go without trying to win her heart."

Colton narrowed his eyes as he stared at her, not quite glaring, but suspicious. "You are manipulative," he said. "I was warned but…"

"You let my age fool you," she guessed, "into thinking I'm some sweet little old lady."

Lem chortled while Colton chuckled and shook his head. "I'm not a big enough fool to think that."

"You're not foolish at all," Sadie insisted.

Colton smiled, but then with obvious curiosity, he asked, "How would you know? You don't really know me."

"I know you're a Haven, and no Haven has ever been accused of being foolish. Now, stubborn…"

"Amen," Lem said. "And this one here is the stubbornest."

She glared at him, or she tried…but just having him here with her again made her so happy that a smile tugged at her lips instead.

He grinned back at her, as if he knew that he was getting to her. Lemar Lemmon had never been accused of being foolish either, at least not by anyone but her, and she hadn't really meant it.

"So that's where we get it," Colton remarked. "Dad is stubborn, too, or he wouldn't still be here."

"Strong and stubborn," Sadie said with pride. He'd made it; despite all the odds, Jessup had fought to live…and she knew why. For his kids. And maybe to spite her a little as well.

"But I've learned you should never be so stubborn that you stick to the wrong idea about something," she added. Or someone. Like she had Lem. "You know…like if you decide as a kid that you don't want to get married, but as an adult you meet someone that makes you want to change your mind…"

Colton's handsome face flushed a little, and he glanced over at Lem. "What did you tell her? And what all did you overhear today?"

Lem chuckled. "Same thing Livvy did, that you never intend to settle down and you don't think she wants to either."

Colton nodded. "That's all true."

"Like I said," Sadie reminded, "don't be so stubborn that you don't change your mind when your heart changes." Like hers was changing where Lem was concerned. She'd deal with that later, though. She focused on her grandson now. "So what brings you out to Ranch Haven?"

"You," he said.

But she hadn't summoned him this time. He'd come on his own, and her heart flooded with love and relief that he had.

He continued, "I wanted to check in on you, see how you're doing."

"I'm well," she said. And she was now that Lem was here. And her family of course. Lem was beginning to feel like family, too, though.

"That's good," Colton said, but he seemed distracted.

"What else is bothering you?" she asked.

He shook his head. "Nothing…" But then he glanced at Lem. "You were talking about that ex-fiancé of Livvy's harassing her?"

Lem sighed. "Yeah. He keeps calling everybody who knows her, trying to get them to get her to give him another chance."

A muscle twitched along Colton's jaw. "Would he ever make trouble for her?" he asked with concern. "Ever try to hurt her?"

Lem snorted and shook his head. "He never wanted to set foot in Willow Creek, had no interest in small towns because he considers everyone who would choose to live in one beneath him."

Sadie bristled. "Why was Livvy with someone like that?"

"He's all slick charm on the surface," Lem said. "But underneath…" He grimaced with disgust.

"She deserves better," Colton said.

Lem smiled. "That's what I told her."

"You should tell her that, too," Sadie suggested.

He chuckled and shook his head. "Give it up, Grandma."

Despite his grin, the smile didn't quite reach his dark eyes. "Is there something else you wanted to talk to me about?" she wondered.

He shrugged, but his shoulders bowed slightly, like he was carrying a heavy burden. "Just wondering how you searched for Dad and Darlene…"

"Are you asking me why I didn't find your dad earlier?" she asked. "I tried. I really tried to find him and Darlene. But once she found out from mutual friends in the rodeo that he was married and to whom, it was easier for her to find him and hide with him." She felt a twinge of guilt as she acknowledged that she hadn't tried hard enough to find Darlene. She'd been upset when her daughter-in-law abandoned her sons; she hadn't realized how deeply Darlene had been hurting, how she'd been blaming herself for Michael's death and thought that everybody else, including her sons, were blaming her, too.

"I just wondered how and where you looked for somebody who doesn't want to be found…"

"Oh…" Sadie said as realization dawned. "You want to find your brother Cash."

That muscle twitched in his cheek again, and he nodded. "He should know…you know… about all the family secrets…"

Sadie nodded in agreement. "Yes, he should. I'll help you look."

"Me, too," Lem offered.

He'd found out more than she had when she'd been looking for Jessup and Darlene. Lem would be a good resource for Colton and maybe a way for Colton to get closer to Livvy.

But she had a feeling that Colton had another reason for wanting to find his oldest brother now. A reason he was keeping secret…

CHAPTER TWELVE

COLTON KNEW HE was falling in with the octogenarians' plans, their blatant attempt at matchmaking, but he wasn't worried about succumbing to it. He knew that he and Livvy were on the same page regarding relationships. Or at least he hoped she was and that she wouldn't give her ex another chance.

Concerned that she might, Colton had taken Lem's suggestion to go by his house, and now he pulled up behind the SUV parked at the curb. After shutting off the truck, he reached across the console and picked up the picnic basket from the passenger's seat.

When he'd declined Sadie's dinner invitation, Taye Cooper and Miller had packed him a basket with enough food for two meals. Or for him and Livvy.

Maybe the cook and his seven-year-old cousin had been enlisted in Sadie and Lem's matchmaking scheme. Ian, the five-year-old, had wanted Colton to stay for dinner and tell him firefighting stories. He'd been tempted; those little kids were something special. So was Livvy.

The picnic basket seemed very heavy as he carried it to the door; it pulled his shoulders down and settled a pressure onto his chest. He couldn't understand this sudden fear over seeing Livvy. The highlight of every day since he'd started working for the Willow Creek Fire Department was seeing her. And maybe that was what was scaring him now, that and all Grandma's talk about not being too stubborn to change his mind about things he'd decided long ago…

But he wasn't being stubborn about this; he loved his career and wasn't going to change it. Knowing the worry it could put people through, he wasn't going to change his mind about marriage and family either. He almost thought about turning around and walking away, but he forced himself to knock on the red front door of the stone Cape Cod house.

Then the door creaked open and she leaned against the jamb, blocking the entrance. She arched a reddish-blond brow over one of her pretty green eyes and gestured at the picnic basket. "I didn't leave that in my old room."

"No, this is dinner I got from Ranch Haven."

"That was a long way to go for dinner," she remarked. "There are closer places in town."

"But not as good as Ranch Haven."

"You and my grandfather have that in common," she said. "He thinks Ranch Haven has the best cook in all of Willow Creek as well."

"Our appreciation for Taye Cooper is not the only thing your grandfather and I have in common," he said. "We both appreciate you and hope you don't give that loser ex-fiancé another chance."

Her face flushed, and her body tensed, as she blocked the entrance. "You and my grandfather were talking about me and Steven?"

"He's worried about you," Colton said then added, "I'm worried about you."

"You don't know me," she said.

"I know you love your dad and your grandpa and Willow Creek," he said. "I know you're happy here, and I would hate for you to give that up for anyone."

"I won't," she said. "I won't give up anything for anyone ever again." She expelled a shaky breath. "I gave too much of myself before, so much that I lost myself. I can't risk that again."

She said it with such intensity that he nearly shivered.

"I understand that," he assured her. "My

brothers and I watched how my mom lost herself when she was married to our dad, how she struggled so hard to keep him healthy that she sacrificed her own health. And us kids… we were always so scared. No. It's better to stay single."

She sucked in a breath as tears sparkled in her eyes, but then she blinked them back. "So this isn't a date."

He shook his head. "Nope, this is two friends sharing dinner. We can be friends, right?"

She studied his face for a long moment, as if she doubted his intentions.

At the moment, he doubted his intentions, too. Was he letting Grandma get to him?

"Seriously," he said. "I'm too big a mess right now to offer anyone anything more than friendship. And dinner."

The scent of fried chicken mixed with cinnamon and apples wafted from the basket. His stomach growled.

And hers echoed it.

She stepped back then and gestured him inside. "Now, that I can relate to…"

"What?" he asked. "Dinner?"

"Being a mess," she said.

He chuckled. "You're not a mess."

She pointed at her hair, which was half up

and half falling out of the clip on her head. If she'd been wearing any makeup, it was gone, and there were dark circles beneath her green eyes. "I am a mess."

"You're still beautiful," he said. "You just look tired. Did it get busy after I left?"

She nodded. "Bunch of people suffering from food poisoning."

"Where did they eat?"

"Local diner," she said. "I guess my grandpa is right about Ranch Haven being the best place to eat."

He wrapped his arms around the picnic basket, acting as if he was carrying treasure. "Then I guess it's lucky I went out there today."

"Why did you?" she asked as she closed the door and led him through the foyer into the kitchen. "Did Sadie summon you?"

"Not this time," he said as he settled the basket onto the oak tabletop. "I sought her out."

"So you're getting used to being a Haven?" she asked.

He shrugged. "Honestly doesn't feel any different than I've always felt." That wasn't the secret that was eating him up inside. He needed to share it with someone, but...

"Your brother says you've been acting differently," she said. "That's what we were talking about when you walked up. You and Bailey Ann."

"Bailey Ann?" He tried to place the name. "Is my twin seeing someone?" He and Collin really were lacking in twin-tuition.

She smiled. "He has been seeing a lot of her."

"Did Sadie set them up?" Colton wondered.

"No, she's his patient," Livvy said.

Colton gasped. Collin breaking a rule? What in the world had happened to his family? But then maybe they'd always been like this, keeping secrets.

"She's seven," Livvy said. "And recently had a heart transplant. She has no family and only an overburdened social worker."

Colton nodded in sudden understanding. "That's why he's spending so much time at the hospital."

"Yes." She stepped through an arched doorway and opened a bright blue cabinet. Then she carried in some plates to a round table that had been positioned inside the curve of a big bay window.

"So what was Collin saying about me?" Colton wondered, although he probably shouldn't have asked.

"Just that you've not been yourself, that something's bothering you."

Colton swallowed a groan, but he couldn't deny it.

"I told him you have a lot of things on your mind," she said. "Losing your family home to a fire, finding out that you're a Haven..." As she made the suggestions, she studied his face as if trying to gauge which thing it was that was affecting him.

She wouldn't come up with the real reason. Hopefully nobody would. He had to protect Cash...even if Cash was the one who'd put them in danger. Weary from all the hours he'd been working and the weight of carrying the burden of his secret, he staggered a bit.

Livvy rushed to him, clasping his forearms, steadying him. "Are you okay?" she asked with alarm.

He nodded. "Yeah, yeah...just probably didn't eat today..."

"Sit down," she said, and she pulled out a chair and pushed him onto it. Then she opened the insulated picnic basket and pulled out the bounty, loading up a plate that she placed in front of him. "Eat. I'll get some drinks."

But when she started away from him, he caught her wrist in his hand...like he had at the hospital. She was wearing the bracelet, but instead of the clasp, she'd wound a piece of wire through it to hold it together. The end had poked a tiny hole into her skin. He ran his finger over it. "You need to get this fixed."

"I thought I had…" she murmured.

"A jeweler didn't do the job?"

She shook her head. "My ex-fiancé didn't bring it to the jeweler's when I asked, when he was resizing my engagement ring."

He ran his fingertip over the slight indentation on her ring finger. "You must have just taken it off."

She nodded and released a shaky breath. "I never should have put it on." She stepped back until his hand dropped away from hers. "That's why I would say no…if you asked me for more than friendship."

He nodded. "It's too soon for you to get involved with anyone else."

"I'm not sure that I want to ever get involved with anyone else," she said. "I just want to focus on me." Her face flushed. "That sounds incredibly selfish."

"No," he said. "It sounds sensible."

"You're not focused on you," she said. "Something is bothering you… What?"

He thought about continuing to deny that there was anything on his mind. But he found himself admitting, "Cash…"

"What? You need money?" she asked. "Is it because of the ranch, your dad's medical bills?"

He chuckled. "Not money. Cash…he's my oldest brother."

She nodded. "That's right. I remember… Becca, the realtor, knows him…"

"I wish I did…" Colton said. He wished he knew him well enough to know if he could have started that fire, if he would have burned down the family home and risked their lives as well. And Dad's freedom…if the insurance adjuster thought Dad had committed arson. Then Colton would have to produce the lighter.

THERE WAS MORE.

More food left in the picnic basket despite the fact that they'd both had seconds. And there was more that Colton Cassidy had left unsaid. About his brother… Why was he so worried about him?

The man had been missing for years; why was he so determined to find him now? Was it just because of the secret that had come out? Because they were Havens?

Livvy suspected that just like the food, there was more…more to Colton's concerns about

Cash. "Since we agreed we can be friends, you can talk to me," she said.

His mouth curved into a slight grin. "I think we talked all through dinner."

They had. About the disapproving ER nurse, about her grandfather and Sadie, about Collin falling for a tiny patient. But they hadn't talked much about themselves.

"You know what I mean," she said. "If something's bothering you, you can share it with me."

He paused for a moment, his jaw clenched so tightly that a muscle twitched in his cheek. Then he smiled wider. "Ditto."

She smiled and shook her head. "If you're talking about my ex…I don't want to talk about him anymore." All she'd ever talked about was him, his current cases, his articles, his research, his goals and plans for the future. He'd never considered hers. Had never considered her at all.

"Good," Colton said. "I don't want to talk about him either."

"What about Cash?" she prodded.

He shook his head. "Nothing to talk about. I haven't seen him in nearly twenty years."

"Then why are you thinking about him so much now?"

He shrugged. "Maybe it was Grandma finally finding her runaway son that made me think about the other runaway in my family."

She didn't know why but she didn't believe him, which was presumptuous of her because she didn't really know him. But she couldn't help thinking about what his twin had said, that something was bothering him. She could see it, too, and even more than that, she could feel it…as if she was somehow so attuned to his emotions that his worry niggled at her as well. That unsettled her because she'd never felt so close to anyone, not even her family.

"I should go," he said, and he jumped up from his chair "You've had a long day."

She had, but she wasn't anxious for it to end now that he was here. She really didn't want him to leave, which was dangerous thinking. He was already getting closer to her than she'd intended to allow anyone ever again.

It was good for him to leave. So she quickly stowed the last of the leftovers in the basket and handed it to him. "Thank you for bringing dinner."

"It was your grandfather and my grandmother's idea," he reminded her.

Irritation nagged at Livvy. "I really wish

they would leave me out of their matchmaking schemes."

"You're still not over your ex?" he asked, his deep voice gruff.

"No," she admitted. "I'm not over how I let him control my life for so long. I'm not over his jealousy and manipulations. And I just want to be alone."

"I'm sorry you went through that," Colton said. "And I hope you know that I'm not part of their scheme."

She pointed toward the picnic basket.

And he grinned. "Okay, I did bring over the dinner like they suggested. But like I told you, I decided long ago to never get married."

"Because of your parents," she said. "That must have been hard growing up like that. Maybe I should be grateful my parents didn't tell us when my mom was sick the first time."

"I prefer knowing the truth to being kept in the dark," he said, and there was a hardness to his voice now that she'd never heard before.

"Are you mad at your dad for not telling you about the Havens? About who he really is?"

His breath hitched a bit, and he just nodded. "But I feel guilty for being mad," he admitted. "When I should just be grateful that he's alive. And I'm beginning to understand that some-

times you think it's better to keep a secret…
even if you're wrong."

There was definitely something going on
with him, which was another solid reason to
keep him in the friend zone. They both had too
much in their lives right now. She held out her
hand. "Friends…"

He took it in his and slid his thumb across
her knuckles.

A shiver of awareness raced over her. Why
did he affect her so much…even when she'd
just resolved that he wouldn't?

"Friends," he agreed. But then his gaze
dropped to her mouth, and there was no mis-
taking the longing in his dark eyes. He wanted
to kiss her…maybe as badly as she wanted him
to kiss her.

LEM HAD A picnic basket, too. One he'd brought
to his son, Bob, Livvy's dad. He'd called ahead
to make sure Bob waited for him at the accounting office. It was all part of Sadie's ploy
to give Livvy and Colton time alone.

Colton was at his house; he'd seen the truck
on his way through town to Main Street where
the accounting practice Bob was running for
Katie Morris-Haven was located on the first

floor of one of the buildings. When he pushed open the office door, it smelled faintly of cigars.

"Smoking?" he asked his son.

Bob glanced up from his desk, and his brow furrowed slightly with annoyance. "No. But even if I was, I'm old enough now."

Lem sighed. "I wasn't judging," he assured his son. "And I wasn't complaining. I don't mind the smell of a cigar now and then."

Bob's lips curved into a slight grin. "Just the smell?"

Lem grinned, too. "Yes, and the memories…" Of his friend Big Jake. Jake had loved his cigars almost as much as he'd loved his wife. Lem could understand Sadie…now…but back then…

"You okay?" Bob asked.

Lem nodded. "Yes, I'm just a bit worried about our Livvy."

Bob sighed. "Steven been calling you, too?"

A pang of concern struck Lem. "He's been calling you?"

Bob nodded. "Not messages that I care to pass on to her, though."

"I did," Lem admitted.

"Why?"

"I've recently learned that very little good comes of keeping secrets."

Bob groaned. "Did you find out what I'm up to?"

Lem stared at his son in shock. "You're having Steven murdered?"

Bob chuckled. "No. I'm looking at buying into Katie's practice as well as buying this building."

"Really?"

Bob nodded. "I'm going to remodel the apartment upstairs and move up there."

"You're selling your house?"

Bob nodded again. "Too many memories."

Lem's heart ached. "There are never too many memories," he said. "Sometimes there are not enough."

Like when his sweet Mary had lost hers.

"Oh, Dad," Bob said. "I don't know how you do it. I haven't lived in that house since the kids were small, and I struggle to be there where Elizabeth and I first started out our lives together, started our family... It's too much." He drew in a shaky breath. "And JJ and Darlene... they need the place more than I do."

"What do you need, Bob?" Lem asked. He and his son had never been as close as he'd wanted. Probably because Lem had been too much like Sadie. Trying to hold Bob too close had pushed him away. Lem had wanted him to go into politics like he had, had wanted him to help him run the town like Ben Haven was running it now.

"I need for my kids to be happy," Bob said.

"Me, too," Lem said. But he wasn't sure how to make that happen, how to make his son and all of his grandkids happy...unless he could find them their perfect match like Sadie had found for Michael's sons.

Lem figured that Colton might be Livvy's perfect match, but he was worried that that mess with Steven had made her unwilling to risk her heart on another relationship.

CHAPTER THIRTEEN

COLTON STARED DOWN at the bracelet lying across his palm, the one he'd found in the bottom of the picnic basket when he'd pulled out the leftovers last night. The thin piece of wire must have caught on something and snapped and the bracelet, with its charms, dropped into the basket with the leftovers Livvy had packed up for him.

Colton studied the little mementos of Livvy's life. She'd said her mom had bought her the bracelet and the charms. But had anyone else added to them?

Her ex?

Steven had done some number on her, had made her doubt herself, lose herself. And she wasn't going to risk a loss like that again. Colton understood that and had decided long ago that he wouldn't risk a relationship either, but still he'd dreamed about her, had dreamed that the two of them were together and were watching his young cousins.

And Bailey Ann…

He didn't even know who the little girl was, hadn't met her, this little person who'd come to mean so much to his twin that Collin had mentioned her to Livvy. But not to him.

When the family home had burned down, it was as if Colton's family as he'd known it had been destroyed as well. Now everything was different, and he felt so isolated…alone in that little apartment he'd just sublet from Baker. Baker had given him the keys the night before, leaving it up to Colton if he wanted it or if he wanted to offer it to Livvy instead. Then Taye had given him the picnic basket for dinner for him and Livvy.

Dinner had been fun. He'd asked then if she'd wanted the apartment, but she'd insisted he sublet it from his cousin instead. They'd also talked about the hospital, about the people they both knew. He could imagine many more dinners like that…which was probably why he'd dreamed of her last night. But those dinners would be just as friends because she'd made it very clear that was all she was looking for…a friend.

Colton needed one now. His brothers had always been his best friends because they were the people who'd understood him best. And even now they would understand why he was upset about finding Cash's lighter, but it was how they would react that kept him from sharing with them.

Marsh was now the sheriff of Willow Creek; he couldn't cover up a crime. And Collin was nearly as hung up on doing the right thing as Marsh was.

Usually Colton was, too, but he was also loyal to his family, so loyal that he couldn't get one in trouble without talking to him first, without giving him a chance to explain. But how in the world was he going to find him…

He could try Becca again. He shoved the bracelet into his pocket and pulled out his cell. But before he could find Becca's contact, the doorbell rang. He wasn't sure who'd seen Baker hand him the keys the night before, so he wasn't expecting any visitors yet. But when he opened the door, he found Baker standing outside, the little boys gathered around him.

"Why are you ringing the bell?" Colton asked. "It's still your place."

Baker shook his head. "You're the one living here."

"You live here now?" Miller asked.

"I thought you lived at the firehouse," Ian

said, his mouth sliding down into a disappointed frown.

"I spend a lot of time at the firehouse," Colton assured him. There was a bruise on the little boy's cheek and on his arm from where he'd taken the tumble in the barn. "How are you feeling, little man?"

Ian's brow furrowed as if he was confused. "Good. Why wouldn't I be?"

"Because you got knocked down in the barn," Miller said with exasperation.

"I remember that," Ian said. "But it didn't hurt that bad."

It had really just knocked the wind out of him. But his injuries could have been worse. Fortunately Livvy had confirmed that they weren't, that the little boy hadn't been suffering from another concussion or any broken bones.

"I'm glad you're fine," Colton said, but his shoulders sagged a little with the weight of guilt that the kid had gotten hurt because he'd been distracted.

"It wasn't your fault," Baker said as if he'd read his mind.

"I should have—"

"No," Baker interrupted. "You can't beat yourself up for something that just happened."

"Bad things happen all the time," Miller said. The seven-year-old was so wise beyond his years, but then he'd experienced too many of those bad things already. "It's not our fault."

"No, it's not," Baker agreed, and he looped his arm around his nephew's shoulders for a quick hug.

The love between them all awed Colton. He loved his dad and his brothers and Darlene, but the bond Baker shared with these little boys was something special. Made Colton almost yearn for something like this for himself.

For kids. These kids were amazing, so resilient. They'd survived losing both parents. And their parents hadn't been sick or in dangerous professions. They'd just gotten into an accident that could happen to anyone.

So was Colton's reason for not risking a relationship valid? He'd never questioned it before, but now Sadie's words about not being too stubborn to change your mind played through his mind.

Caleb shoved between Miller and Baker and walked up to Colton. He wasn't one of the orphans. While he had his mom yet, he had lost his dad. But he had Jake Haven now and the entire Haven family. And he was a happy kid, like his cousins. Well, usually he was happy.

Now his mouth was pulled into a little frown as he said, "Taye made some cookies for you."

Baker added, "She wanted to make you something special for how you helped with Ian last week. That's why she asked your favorite cookies yesterday."

"Snickerdoodles," Colton said.

"Those are Grandma's favorite," Caleb told him.

"While his are chocolate chip," Baker said. "So he's a little disappointed that Taye made your favorite and not his."

"Your grandma Darlene makes these," Colton said.

"My mom bakes?" Baker asked. "I don't remember that."

Colton felt a pang of regret for all this family had suffered. While he didn't know if there was anything he could say to make it up to Darlene's kids for her staying away, he had to defend the woman he knew and admired. "She worked really hard around the ranch, keeping it going while Dad was sick. I don't know what we would have done without her. I don't know that any of us would have survived." But they had. Well, at least he and Marsh and Collin had. He didn't know anything for sure about

Cash, but he'd taken off already before Darlene had showed up.

Baker nodded as if he accepted the explanation. And maybe he did. As he and Miller had said, bad things just happened sometimes. And there was no way to prevent them or to protect anyone no matter how much you loved them. So why not give love a chance?

"Are you going to try a cookie?" Caleb asked.

Colton nodded and reached inside the bag the little blond-haired boy handed him. He pulled out a cookie and took a bite then moaned as cinnamon and nutmeg exploded inside his mouth. The outside of the cookie was crisp while the inside was gooey. "Oh, don't tell Darlene, but this is the best cookie I've ever had. And dinner last night…" He moaned again as he swallowed the snickerdoodle. "You're a lucky man, Baker."

Baker's eyes widened with surprise for a moment then he nodded. "I am. Now. I am very lucky…that Taye fell for me and for these guys and that we're all going to be a family."

Colton felt a twinge of envy that he could not deny. Maybe he was beginning to change his mind about not having a relationship and a family. Or maybe he just wanted the one he already had to be closer, to have no more secrets. But right now he was the one keeping the biggest secret.

Cash.

If the runaway had returned to the ranch, maybe he was hanging around somewhere. While the house was gone, the barn and outbuildings were still weatherproof if not exactly well-maintained. Someone could be staying in one of them.

Colton needed to check it out...when he had a chance to head back to the ranch. He dreaded making that trip, though, dreaded seeing the ruins of the home where he'd grown up...much too fast.

"Do you ever want to be a dad?" Ian asked the question. "Can firefighters be dads?"

Baker chuckled and saved Colton from having to answer. "Of course they can."

"Then why did you quit?" Ian asked.

Baker crouched closer to his nephew's level. "I quit because I want to work the ranch with Uncle Jake."

"But you want to be a dad, too," Miller stated with absolute certainty. He wasn't asking a question; he knew.

These kids had no doubt that Baker wanted them, that he wanted to be their father now.

Colton was impressed; the Havens were all

very impressive. At first he'd been shocked that he was one of them; now he was honored. And he wanted to uphold the family honor. So maybe he needed to be honest about everything…especially with himself.

"What about you?" Ian persisted. "Do you want to be a daddy?"

Colton sighed. "I didn't think so…" Because he hadn't thought it would be fair to put anyone through that same uncertainty with which he'd grown up. But there was no certainty in the world; kids like these could lose their parents with no forewarning, just from a freak spring storm.

Baker studied him for a long moment. "Hey, guys, remember I'm paying you to work. You have to pack up my clothes in these bags." He handed them a few garbage bags.

"Nice luggage," Colton teased.

"Where's your stuff?"

"In a duffel bag on the bed."

"Don't touch that," Baker told the little guys as they rushed off to the bedroom, the toddler following behind them.

"You're great with them," Colton praised.

"They're great kids," Baker said.

The sounds of squabbles drifted out the bedroom door and Colton grinned.

"Well…" Baker began.

Colton laughed. "They are great and also incredibly strong."

"Resilient," Baker said. "That's what Taye says. Kids are resilient. So you wouldn't have to be afraid to have some…"

"You think they could handle however much I might screw them up?" Colton joked.

Baker grinned now. "Yeah. Is that why you didn't think you wanted any of your own?"

He was older than Baker and he'd never even had a real serious relationship. "I didn't think it would be fair to get involved, not with the job I have and with so much always going on with my dad and the ranch and my brothers."

"Do you ever take any time for yourself?"

He thought of last night, of eating that picnic dinner with Livvy on her grandfather's kitchen table. "I do sometimes."

"And then you feel guilty when you do," Baker said. He was astute. Or maybe he just understood Colton really well because he'd had so much loss in his family, too.

"Sounds like you know a thing or two about guilt."

Baker groaned. "I know too much about it. But I'm putting that all behind me now. I'm going to focus on the present and the future, not on the past that I can't change."

"Your present and future are going to be really busy," Colton said. "It's brave of you to take on all the boys, to become their primary guardian."

"It's not a burden," Baker said. "It's a privilege. I am so lucky to be able to do this, and I'm so lucky that it's what Taye wants, too. She and I are on the same page about everything. I never believed in that soulmate BS until now, until I met mine."

An image of Livvy Lemmon, her strawberry blond hair falling down from the clip she wore, popped into Colton's mind. They had so much in common, too, but the biggest thing was their desire to stay single and only be friends. At least that was what Colton had thought he wanted. Now he wasn't so sure...about anything anymore.

FRUSTRATION GNAWED AT Livvy as she and the realtor returned to her office on Main Street. "I'm sorry there isn't more to show you," Becca said. "Willow Creek currently has a bit of a housing shortage. New construction isn't keeping up with everyone moving into the area."

"I'm sorry I couldn't get excited about any of those places," she said. "I think it's just because I saw this cute little apartment that I could have sublet."

"The one Colton took?" Becca asked.

She nodded.

"I'm sure he would have given it up to you," Becca said. "He's always been a sweetheart. He would sacrifice anything for family."

"Just because his grandmother is dating my grandpa doesn't make us family," Livvy said. Would Grandpa marry Sadie someday? She'd worried about him getting too involved in the Haven family drama but instead he'd gotten involved in hers with Steven. "Colton did offer to let me take the apartment instead." Which had been sweet of him. He truly was a sweetheart and so self-sacrificing.

Not at all like Steven. And no, she hadn't involved Grandpa in her drama. Steven had. He was also why she needed a place of her own, because of the way her father and grandfather had been watching her, with so much concern. That had to be because of Steven, because he kept contacting them.

She hadn't contacted him in return because she'd figured that was exactly what he wanted. But maybe she should have returned a call or text and let him know that she was going to report him for harassment if he didn't stop bothering her and her family. She had to make it clear to him that she wasn't ever changing her mind. She wasn't ever wearing his ring again or leaving Willow Creek.

"I turned down Colton's offer because I really want to buy," Livvy said. She wanted to put down roots here, permanent roots. She wanted to make Willow Creek the home she'd always remembered it being, when life had been simpler. When she'd been close to her family, to her brothers, and her grandpa and grandma and dad and mom.

"We'll find you something," Becca said as she held open the office door for Livvy. "You're smarter to be patient than to buy something that doesn't really fit."

"Advice you should have taken yourself…" her mother murmured beneath her breath.

Becca gave her a side-eye of exasperation. "Mother…"

"Why do I feel like we're not talking about houses?" Livvy asked with a smile.

"Because *we're* not," Mrs. Calder replied with a smile for Livvy. "And speaking of perfect fits…that Cassidy left another message for you."

A pang struck Livvy's heart. Was Mrs. Calder

a matchmaker like Sadie and Grandpa Lem? Was she trying to match up her daughter with Colton Cassidy?

Or was Mrs. Calder talking about another Cassidy? There were more of them than Colton.

"Which Cassidy?" Becca asked the question burning in Livvy's mind.

Mrs. Calder looked at Livvy now. "The good-looking one."

Livvy laughed. "That doesn't narrow it down." Not with Colton and Collin being identical twins, and Marsh could have been their triplet.

"You haven't met all of them," Becca said.

"Colton," Mrs. Calder replied. "Colton called."

Becca sighed.

"He took Baker's apartment, so he isn't looking for a place," Livvy said.

"I know what he's looking for or for whom, I should say."

"Your English teacher would be proud," Mrs. Calder said with a smile.

Becca responded with a faint smile of her own before leading Livvy into her private office. "I'll put out some feelers," she said. "See if anyone's considering putting their place up for sale. I know Ben Haven recently got engaged. He has a condo in town, and I believe his fiancée has a place of her own, too. One of them might consider selling...especially with Emily staying out at the ranch."

"You know the Havens well," Livvy remarked.

Becca shrugged. "Everyone does, especially with Ben being the mayor now. I just never realized..."

"That your friend was one of them?"

Her brow furrowed for a moment. "Cash?"

"Yes."

"Uh..."

"I'm sorry," Livvy said. "You obviously don't want to talk about him."

"It's not that..." Becca said. "It's just... I don't want to be in the middle of something that's not really my business."

Livvy nodded. "I know. It's not my business either."

"It might be more your business than it is mine," Becca said.

"What do you mean?"

"Just that...Cash and I have only ever been friends. Nothing more."

"That's all Colton and I are, too," Livvy insisted. That was all she could handle right now, maybe ever, without losing herself again.

Becca smiled. "I saw the way he looks at you. Cash never looked at me like that."

Livvy found that hard to believe with as beautiful as the realtor was. But then Collin was identical to Colton, and she didn't look at the cardiologist like she did his twin. "Did you want him to?" she asked with curiosity.

Becca shook her head. "No. We really were just friends."

"Were? You're not any longer?"

"We keep in touch," Becca admitted. Then she released a ragged sigh. "I really need to…" She shook her head. "Keep my mouth shut about the Cassidys and focus on you. We'll find you your perfect place. Don't worry."

Livvy couldn't help but worry although her concerns had nothing to do with finding a property to buy. She was worried that her perfect place wasn't a house or a condo but someone's arms.

SADIE HAD FINALLY stopped worrying about Dale's little boys. She'd thought they were doing better physically and emotionally and that Baker and Taye claiming primary custody of them would be the best for everyone. Her lawyer's voice, emanating from the cell phone she clutched, was telling her something else.

"Who contacted you about them?" she asked. It didn't make sense. Anybody who might have wanted them would have just talked to her directly unless...

Darlene?

Did she want her grandsons?

Surely she would realize that if she fought Baker for custody, she would lose her family all over again and this time forever. Baker wouldn't forgive her for this...even though he'd forgiven her for leaving him and his brothers all those years ago. They'd understood that she'd thought they blamed her for their dad dying...even though she'd been wrong.

Sadie could hear the deep rumble of Baker's voice now, blending perfectly with the excited chatter of the little boys. Their conversation drifted in from the kitchen, sprinkled with Taye's laughter. They were such a sweet family already. Nothing and nobody could prevent them from becoming an official one.

"I don't know," the lawyer replied. "The person who contacted me was a lawyer who wouldn't divulge the name of her client. So I have no idea who's checking out the estate and the guardianship."

"Find out," she said. And she would make some inquiries, too. She would talk to Darlene again. The Haven family had been through too much already; it was time for them to heal and be happy…not to deal with yet more drama.

CHAPTER FOURTEEN

COLTON HAD BEEN waiting for Becca to return his call. So when his cell vibrated in his pocket, he quickly pulled it out and accepted the call despite where he was.

"Hello."

"Colton?"

His pulse quickened as he recognized that voice. Becca wasn't the one calling him. Livvy was. "Yes."

"Collin gave me your phone number."

He swallowed a groan, knowing that his twin was bound to tease him about that. "Is everything okay?" he asked her. Because he couldn't imagine she would be calling him if it was... despite their resolution to become friends.

"Yes," she said. "Well...I can't find my bracelet. The last time I had it on was when you brought that picnic basket the other night, and I don't know what happened to it."

He knew. He held it in his palm as he waited to speak to the busy jeweler on Main Street in

Willow Creek. But the older man was standing further down the case, helping a giddy young couple look at engagement rings.

And he felt a pang of envy.

Which was weird. He'd never had any burning desire to get married. Just as he'd never had any desire to become the daddy that Ian had asked if he ever wanted to be. He hadn't wanted anyone worrying about him like he'd worried about his dad all these years. But now…he had the example of the Haven boys. They hadn't worried about their parents until that day, that horrible day when they'd lost both of them, and they'd survived. They were happy again.

"I'm sorry…did I catch you in the middle of something?" Livvy asked, which prodded Colton into realizing he hadn't answered her.

But he didn't want to lie. He closed his hand around the bracelet. "I don't see it…"

Livvy's sigh rattled through the cell speaker. "I didn't have much hope that you had, but I looked all around the house and couldn't find it anywhere."

"I'm sure it'll turn up," Colton assured her. And when it did, the clasp would be fixed, so that she would be safe to wear it without the risk of losing it again.

"Mr. Cassidy?" the jeweler called out to him.

Colton jumped a bit. "I—I have to go now, Livvy." He clicked off his cell before she could overhear any more of the conversation.

"I'm sorry to keep you waiting," the jeweler told him.

"I just need to get the clasp fixed on this bracelet," Colton said as he dropped it onto the counter.

"That shouldn't take me long," the jeweler replied. But he glanced down the counter at the couple who began to bicker over the rings.

"Take your time," Colton said. "I can pick it up later."

"Thank you—"

"Sir," the young woman interrupted. But she was staring at Colton, not the jeweler. "Can we ask your opinion on these rings? Which one your wife would like?"

"I'm not married," he said, his voice a little gruff. That had never bothered him before, until now.

"Good," the young man said. "Then you can tell her that it's crazy to spend so much money on a ring, right? That it makes more sense to spend it for a down payment on a house."

Colton thought of his house, his childhood home, reduced now just to ashes. But the sterling silver lighter had survived. And his mother's rings had survived, too. Dad had shared that with him as if he thought that Colton might need them sometime soon.

Or ever…

No. It would be smarter for him to stay single. But when once he'd been certain about that, now doubts niggled at him. Hope…

"The house I grew up in just recently burned down," Colton shared. The couple gasped, and their eyes widened. "But one of the few things that survived the fire were my mother's rings. It's all my dad has left of her now besides memories since she died nearly twenty years ago."

Tears filled the girl's eyes. "Oh, I'm so sorry. I'm so sorry I bothered you."

"You didn't," Colton assured her. "I just wanted to point out the things that will last. The things that can be passed on."

The young man nodded. Then he swallowed hard and turned back to his bride. "You're right. You should pick out what you want because I want you to have it forever."

The girl threw her arms around her fiancé's neck and kissed him.

Colton chuckled and turned for the door.

"I should hire you, Mr. Cassidy," the jeweler said.

Colton pointed at his uniform shirt with the Willow Creek FD insignia on it. "I already have a job."

"I'll call you at the firehouse when the bracelet is repaired."

"Thanks." Colton opened the door and stepped out onto the street. But he only made it a few feet when someone else called out to him.

"Colton?" the gray-haired man stared at him as if waiting for confirmation.

"Yes, I'm Colton," he said. "And you're Mr. Lemmon?" Livvy's dad. The man who'd been so kind to give up his home for Colton's family. "Thank you again for what you've done for my dad and Darlene."

The guy's face flushed as if the gratitude embarrassed him. He was very much like his father, Old Man Lemmon, but taller. "I'm happy to do it," he said. "That house is too much for me."

Colton wasn't sure if he was just talking about the size and upkeep or the memories. "What about Livvy?" he found himself asking. She was looking for her own place; Mrs. Calder had told him she was the client Becca had been taking around for showings when he'd called the other day. Becca had yet to return his call. He had to accept that she wasn't going to help him find Cash. Maybe Grandma would be more successful in her search.

"It would be too much for her as well," Mr. Lemmon replied.

Again Colton wondered if he was talking about the size and upkeep or the memories.

"I don't think it's a great idea for Livvy to live alone right now," Mr. Lemmon admitted.

Colton tensed. "Really? Why not?"

"That ex-fiancé of hers isn't giving up on getting her back. He keeps calling me and my father."

Colton's tension increased. "He's harassing you both. That's terrible. Do you think he's dangerous?"

Mr. Lemmon shrugged. "He's a man who's used to getting his way. And he's not reacting rationally right now that his plan, his manipulation of Livvy, didn't work out."

Colton's stomach lurched with dread. "Do you think he would come here? That he would hurt her?" The man was basically stalking her through her family. Would he show up to do it in person? Colton had gone out, too many times, as a paramedic to domestic abuse calls.

The significant other usually got the most dangerous after the breakup.

Mr. Lemmon sighed. "I didn't see Livvy much when she was with Steven, so I don't know him that well at all. But what I do know, I don't like. I should have said something to her, should have warned her, but I didn't want to be one of those overbearing parents…"

Like his father? Like Sadie had been to his dad.

"I should have said or done something." His face flushed a deeper shade of red. "I'm sorry. This is all more information than you wanted to know."

"Not at all," Colton assured him. Everything about Livvy and her life concerned him…even though it shouldn't.

"I just saw you walking past in your uniform and figured you're Colton, and with you going in and out of the hospital as a paramedic, I just wanted to ask for you to keep an eye on my girl."

That concern overwhelmed Colton now. "You are worried about this ex of hers."

Mr. Lemmon released a ragged sigh. "I'm worried about my daughter. And I know if I bring it up to her, she'll assure me everything's fine whether it is or not."

Colton understood that all too well because he kept assuring everyone he was fine. But since they kept asking, obviously he wasn't fooling anyone. And apparently neither was Livvy.

LIVVY HAD SPENT the morning looking for her bracelet, but she hadn't found it. Maybe she'd accidentally tossed it out with the trash. Tears stung her eyes at the thought of having lost it forever. She shouldn't have tried to wear it with the flimsy wire. The weight of the charms must have snapped it.

She'd been foolish to hope that Colton would have found it. And maybe she'd just used the bracelet as an excuse to call him. From the way Collin had smiled when he'd given her Colton's contact information, he'd clearly thought so.

Of course, Nurse Sue had overheard her asking him, and more disapproval had pursed her lips into that perpetual scowl. Livvy had just about had it with her looks and her muttered comments and her constantly questioning her orders. She'd learned as a med student how hard it was for some people to respect females in the medical field, especially ones who looked as young as she did. But she'd studied hard; she knew her medicine and her judgement in it was sound. Much sounder than her judgement in men.

Maybe that was what Nurse Sue disapproved of. Steven kept calling the hospital. He was probably still calling her grandpa and dad, too. She needed to talk to him, to put a stop to it once and for all. Her phone vibrated inside the pocket of her scrubs and she pulled it out to find another text coming in from him.

She had blocked him…until he'd started bothering her grandfather and dad. Then she'd unblocked him because she knew she'd have to talk to him again. She just knew how futile it was going to be because he didn't listen to anyone but himself.

How had she been so stupid to think she was in love with him? He was good-looking and brilliant and she'd been flattered with his attention. It had seemed like they'd had so much in common on the surface. But then she'd realized there wasn't much under Steven's surface. Whereas…

Colton Cassidy walked through the automatic doors from the ambulance bay into the back of the ER. Maybe that was why her eyes were burning. Smoke emanated from his firefighter pants and jacket, and black soot covered the chiseled features of his handsome face.

"Are you bringing in a patient?" she asked as she shoved the phone back into her pocket.

Beneath the soot, a muscle twitched in his cheek and he shook his head. "No, I *am* the patient."

Concern shot through her, tightly gripping her heart. She sucked in a breath, and her throat burned from the smoke. "What's wrong?" she asked, her voice cracking with fear for him. "Where are you hurt?"

He moved his shoulders and grimaced. "A rafter fell on me. I think I'm just bruised, but Captain wants me x-rayed for broken bones before he'll let me clock back in."

"A rafter?" she repeated, her voice squeaking now. "What happened? Where did it hit you?"

"The first one hit my shoulder and knocked me down and the second one fell on my chest…" He coughed. "My helmet came off, too."

"Colton!" she exclaimed with alarm. "You must be hurt!" She pointed him toward an open bay in the exam area and followed him. As he settled onto the edge of a gurney, she reached for his heavy jacket, pushing it from his broad shoulders. He wore a T-shirt under it and his suspenders.

"I'm fine, really," he assured her.

"I should call your fam—"

He caught her wrist in his hand. "No," he said, his voice hoarse. "I don't want to worry them."

"I'm worried," she said.

"I definitely don't want to worry you either."

She furrowed her brow in confusion. "Why not?"

He shrugged then grimaced.

"You are hurt. I need to examine you. You need to take off your shirt, or I can cut it off…"

He was already reaching for the bottom of it, pulling it up over his head.

After a mental reminder that she was a professional, she focused on treating him. A quick exam and an MRI later, she said, "You're a lot like your nephew. Looks like you were lucky enough to get out of this with just some contusions. You're going to be sore, but nothing's broken."

He expelled a breath of relief. "See, no reason to worry my family."

"Why didn't you want to worry me?" she asked.

He shrugged. "I just don't want anyone to worry about me."

"If you figure out how to accomplish that,

let me know," she said. "My grandpa and dad are worried about me."

He nodded. "I know. I ran into your dad just before my shift started. He told me how desperate Steven is acting." His dark eyes were intense as he studied her face.

Livvy realized her dad wasn't the only one who was worried about her. She needed to shut Steven down so he stopped bothering her family. But she'd been avoiding conflict, as she'd often done with him. As her phone vibrated again, probably because she hadn't opened his latest text, it reminded her that she needed to talk to Steven so he knew there was no chance that she would ever change her mind.

"My dad and grandpa don't need to worry about Steven," she said. "I will handle him."

"But if he's dangerous, you need to be careful," Colton advised with concern.

Warmth flooded her heart that he cared. But she smiled and assured him, "Steven would never make the time to fly out to Willow Creek. He's not a threat."

He was just a nuisance and a reminder that she needed to stay strong and independent. Colton was the threat to her independence; she'd been so scared over his getting hurt. She already cared more about him than she had

Steven, and because of that, he could hurt her more. She wasn't sure if she was strong enough yet to risk her heart.

LEM HADN'T SEEN Sadie this scared since she'd been afraid to search out Jessup for fear that she would find out he was dead. That he hadn't survived his illness.

And her fear stoked his. He reached across the space between their easy chairs and squeezed her hand. She had her fingers all knotted together, literally wringing her hands. "You don't know that this is anything to worry about."

"But why would a lawyer be calling around about the boys, asking about custody unless someone was thinking about challenging it?"

"What if they do?" Lem asked. "There's no way they can wrest those kids away from this family, away from Baker and Taye. Even if it went to court, a judge would see that it's in the best interest of those boys to stay here with…"

Us.

He'd almost said it. But he didn't stay here. He traveled back and forth. He wasn't part of the Haven family. He was just a visitor.

A guest.

A friend.

And he wasn't sure that was enough anymore. He wanted more. But now was not the time to pressure Sadie. He wanted to reassure her.

"On a brighter note, Bob ran into Colton this morning," he said.

"It's not tax time," Sadie said. "How did your accountant son run into the firefighter?"

"Outside Katie's office," Lem said. "Colton was coming out of the jeweler's."

Sadie's dark eyes widened and brightened. "The jeweler's? But he's been so adamant…"

"They all were," Lem reminded her. "Jake, Ben, Dusty and Baker."

They'd all claimed they were never getting married, but now they either already were or were soon to walk down the aisle to their betrothed. Lem felt a little jab of envy then…of young love.

But who said old love couldn't be as special? As romantic?

The doorbell rang, and Feisty sprang up from his lap and started yapping as she headed out the door of the suite. "I'm not sure who else is home," Sadie murmured as she started after her little dog, probably to answer the door.

Curious about who rang the bell, Lem followed, and he was glad that he had when Sadie staggered back a step in the foyer as if she was about to collapse.

He grabbed her arms and steadied her. "Hey, are you all right?" He glanced at the open door, to the woman standing on the front porch. He didn't recognize her. She was young and serious looking, with her brown hair bound back in a tight ponytail and glasses sliding down the end of her nose. "Who are you?"

"I'm Elise Shaw," she said. "I'm with child protective services. I need to make contact with Ian Haven over a report of abuse."

Lem gasped now. Sadie had been right to worry about that call someone had made to her lawyer. Someone was up to something regarding the boys and was apparently even willing to file a false report in order to challenge custody.

CHAPTER FIFTEEN

COLTON WAS RESTLESS. While it was always good that there were no fires or accidents, it made for long boring shifts with too much time for him to think.

About Cash and that stupid lighter.

And Livvy and her stupid ex.

So to shut off his mind, he was cleaning the kitchen, which really showed how desperate he was for a distraction because the oven was gross. He had it open, scrubbing at the baked-on grime when his boss called out to him. "Cassidy?"

"In here, Chief," he called back to Chet Maynard. He liked his new boss, liked how focused on the job the man was.

"Man, I'm glad I came up here by myself," Maynard said. "If this CPS worker found you with your head in the oven, you wouldn't be getting a very good report."

"CPS?" He knew what it was from his years

as a paramedic. But fortunately he hadn't had to have many dealings with them in the past.

"Child protective services," Maynard said as if Colton needed the explanation. "I didn't even know you had a family."

"I don't," Colton said. "At least not of my own. I don't have any kids."

"Must be about a call you went on then," Chet said. "She's waiting in my office to talk to you."

Colton hurriedly washed up and headed down the hall to the small, windowless office. He opened the door and startled a young woman sitting in one of the chairs in front of Maynard's banged-up metal desk.

Instead of sitting in either of the open chairs, Colton leaned against the wall. "Hi, I'm Colton Cassidy."

"I'm Elise Shaw with CPS," the dark-haired woman introduced herself.

Colton nodded. "That's what the chief said, but I don't understand why you're here. I didn't make a report."

"No, you didn't," she agreed. "And I wonder why you didn't report Ian Haven's suspicious injuries."

He narrowed his eyes. "What suspicious injuries? He got knocked down by a horse."

She pursed her lips like that nurse at the hospital so often did, with disapproval and skepticism. "And you really believe that's what happened?"

"I know it's what happened," Colton said. "I was there when it happened and saw the whole thing." And sometimes he relived that moment, of the bronco bursting out of the stall, of the little boy knocked to the ground.

"Is there anyone else to corroborate your story?"

Irritation prickled at Colton. "It's not a story. It's the truth. It's what happened, and if you need any corroboration, ask Ian," he said. "He and I were the only ones in the barn when it happened." While a couple of grooms had been present, they hadn't been paying any more attention than he had. Guilt weighed on him that the boy had been hurt, but he couldn't believe that social services had gotten involved.

"Why would the Havens trust you alone with one of their kids?" she asked.

His irritation turned to righteous indignation. Sure, he might not have been as careful as he should have been with Ian, but he hadn't purposely hurt the little boy. "Those kids are *my* cousins. My dad is Jessup Haven. I'm a Haven." He puffed out his chest with the statement as pride suffused him. "I don't know who called you, but they're clearly wasting your time."

"We have to investigate calls like this," she said. "The boy's injuries were serious enough that he was taken to the emergency room."

"I know because I took him," Colton said. "Nobody hurt Ian. Not even the horse, really. The kid just tumbled off a bucket and hit the ground hard."

"Hard enough to lose consciousness and sustain some serious injuries." She sounded skeptical.

"If you have those ER records, you know his injuries weren't serious," he said. "Did someone from the ER call your agency?"

Livvy hadn't. He knew that. She'd heard the whole story from him and from Ian. Even though she wasn't exactly thrilled about her grandfather's relationship with Sadie, she wouldn't have called CPS on them. Was there someone out there with a grudge against the Havens? Maybe against the Cassidys, too?

He was suddenly very conscious again of that lighter he carried in his pocket. Very conscious and very concerned.

LIVVY FELT AS if her shift was never going to end, and that wasn't just because Dr. Brower had called in sick so she'd had to stay to cover the ER until another attending could come in. The slow pace was what had made the day seem never-ending. She'd had only a couple cases of sniffles and a rash to treat the entire shift.

So she'd been hanging out at the intake desk with the receptionist and some of the staff. She was there now when the lobby doors swished open and a young woman walked into the hospital.

"How may we help you?" the receptionist asked her eagerly. They were all bored.

"I need to speak with Dr. Lemmon," the woman replied, staring down her nose through the glasses that were slipping off it.

"You need to see an ER doctor?" the receptionist asked. "I'll need your insurance information—"

"I'm here from child protective services," the woman interjected. "I need to take a report from Dr. Lemmon."

"A report about what?" Livvy asked. She hadn't seen any kids for anything more serious than sniffles or the flu since Ian Haven.

"I need to speak to Dr. Lemmon about that," the young woman replied.

"I am Dr. Lemmon," Livvy said.

The woman glanced from her to the other staff members as if needing confirmation of that; Livvy tried not to get annoyed that her credentials as an MD were so often questioned.

The receptionist nodded. "She is."

"I'm Elise Shaw. Can we speak somewhere privately?" the woman asked.

Livvy stepped around the desk, but she didn't see the need to move any farther away from the rest of the staff. "I didn't call in a report to CPS," she told her. "I don't know why you're here."

"Why didn't you call it in?" the woman asked. "You're supposed to be a mandatory reporter."

"I am," Livvy said. "But I haven't had any cases where I've suspected abuse since I've started at Willow Creek Memorial." That made her so happy and confirmed her decision to come home. Being here had healed her soul. And maybe she'd found someone who might heal her heart as well.

"Despite Ian Haven's injuries, you didn't suspect abuse?" the woman asked as if appalled.

"Ian? This is about Ian?" Livvy asked, and her pulse quickened. Who could have reported that and why? "He got knocked over in the barn at his family's ranch. He had some bumps and bruises from the fall. He's not abused."

"No signs of abuse? Of prior injuries? No other visits to the hospital?"

"For a car crash four months ago. I wasn't living in Willow Creek then, but I and everyone else in this town know what happened. Those poor boys lost their parents in that tragic accident."

"And maybe they aren't in the safest environment right now," the CPS investigator replied. "Ian was in such a dangerous situation that he got seriously hurt."

Livvy blew out an exasperated breath as her patience frayed. "He got bumps and bruises," she said. "He wasn't seriously injured. I don't know who told you that he was or why they would…" She glanced around now, looking for Sue, wondering if she was behind this.

The nurse was probably the only one in the hospital who wasn't gathered around the intake desk right now. Maybe she'd left for the day or maybe she was hiding out in the back because she had reported the Havens. Or Livvy? Was this an attempt to try to get her in trouble for not calling CPS?

"Someone was concerned for the safety of these children," the investigator replied.

"Really?" Livvy asked. "Or are they just trying to stir up trouble?"

"I am not here to cause trouble," Miss Shaw insisted. "I'm just doing my job."

"Whoever called you is the one trying to cause trouble." But for whom? Her or the Havens? "For what purpose?" she wondered aloud. "Trying to get Ian and his brothers taken away from their family to be put into foster care?" Or to take over custody?

"We have to consider that every call is legitimate," the CPS worker replied. "Especially when a child is physically injured."

"I appreciate that you're just doing your job," Livvy said. "And it's a difficult one. I know that. I did my residency in a big city, and I called CPS many, many times." Tears stung her eyes as she remembered some of those times, some of those poor victims.

She'd tried to help them, tried to make sure they wouldn't be hurt again. But once they were released, it was out of her hands. She truly respected and appreciated child protective services. But all too many times those poor kids had returned with more injuries. And Livvy had felt nearly as helpless as they had.

That was partially why she'd wanted to work in a smaller town, so she could keep better track of her patients, to make sure no harm came to them. Ian Haven was one of her patients now.

"But you didn't call this time," Miss Shaw pointed out.

"That's because I know the difference between abuse and accidents. What happened to Ian Haven for both his visits were accidents." Sadness and sympathy overwhelmed her, making tears well up, but she willed them away and added, "What happened to his parents was a tragedy. The little boys are finally happy and anyone who would jeopardize that happiness for them is cruel and does not deserve to be any part of their lives."

Applause broke out, startling and confusing Livvy until she realized she'd raised her voice loud enough that everyone had overheard her... even the man who'd just walked through the lobby doors.

Colton smiled at her as he applauded maybe the loudest of them all. Warmth rushed over her. She wasn't embarrassed, though; this was something else, something far more intense and scary. Something she was not ready for yet, something she might never be strong enough for...

SADIE COULDN'T STOP SHAKING; she felt like Feisty must have when Sadie had smashed the window to free the little Chihuahua from the hot car her previous owner had locked her inside some years ago. She felt like she had that day when she'd heard about the fire at the ranch. That day she'd collapsed alone on her bedroom floor. She would have died if Baker hadn't found her, if he hadn't rescued her. She wasn't the one who needed rescuing now.

Ian did. Maybe all the boys did.

The little boy had answered the CPS worker's questions, though, so the case should be closed. If Miss Shaw believed him. She'd looked so skeptical, though. Like she figured they'd coached the kid. But Ian had matter-of-factly told her the truth.

Who had lied to her?

Who had called and reported the innocent accident as abuse or neglect? Or whatever claim they'd made that had warranted an investigation? Surely the person intended to use the CPS investigation to challenge custody; that must have been why Sadie's lawyer had gotten that call from another lawyer.

Sadie wasn't alone now like she'd been that day of her attack. She was back in her chair in the sitting area of her suite. She didn't quite trust her legs to hold her, as shaky as she felt. Lem was pacing around the room as he shot wary glances at her and anxious ones at the door. When Baker walked through the doorway, Lem let out a breath.

"Do you have your bag? You need to check her blood pressure."

"He's not a paramedic anymore," she reminded Lem. Baker was the ranch foreman instead. But he must have kept his bag because he had it with him, and he pulled a blood pressure cuff from it to wrap around her arm.

"Grandma, are you okay?"

She nodded. "I am. What about the boys?"

"They're fine," Baker said. "They're used to talking to Mrs. Lancaster now, so Miss Shaw's questions didn't surprise or scare them." But from the tightness of his clenched jaw and the deep creases in his forehead, Baker was surprised and scared.

"Someone called my lawyer the other day," she told him. "They were making inquiries about the boys. About custody."

Baker sucked in a breath.

"Maybe you should take your blood pressure now," she suggested when he unwrapped the cuff from her arm.

"It would be high," he admitted. "Thankfully yours is just a little elevated but nothing to be concerned about."

"This isn't either," she assured him. "Those

boys belong with you and Taye and everybody else will have to accept that."

"Who, Grandma? Who could have reported this?"

"I don't know..." she murmured.

He snorted. "You have suspicions."

"The only one I can think is Darlene. Maybe she wants her grandsons."

Baker shook his head. "No. She wouldn't do that, not when she knows that I want them."

"You're certain it's not her?"

"I want to be," he said, but clearly he had some doubts. "I called Colton..."

"I told you that I'm fine," Sadie insisted. She did not want another paramedic grandson taking her to the hospital like Baker had had to not that long ago.

"I didn't call him about you," Baker said. "I called him about Ian. The social worker had just left the firehouse. She talked to Colton, too."

Sadie narrowed her eyes and studied her grandson's tense face. "Did you think Colton reported it? He was the one who was with Ian when the accident happened."

"I know he didn't report it," Baker said. "He feels about it the same as we do, that someone is wasting child protective services' time and resources."

"Does Colton have some idea who might have done this? He brought Ian to the hospital... Did he notice..." she trailed off as she followed Baker's nervous glance at Lem. "Livvy..." she whispered.

Sometimes Lem's hearing was selective in that he missed a lot of what was said, especially on television, but of course he heard her now. And his short body tensed and bristled with defensiveness. "You think my granddaughter reported this?"

"She got her training in a big city hospital," Baker said. "With that kind of background, she's probably seen a lot of abuse cases. She might have gotten into the habit of reporting all injured kids."

Sadie smiled at Baker. He was such a sweet and forgiving man...of everyone but himself. But finally, he was cutting himself some slack, too. Sadie was not about to cut any for anyone who'd threatened her family. She looked up at Lem with a glare.

He was shaking his head, and his mouth was pulled into a grimace. "No. Livvy's a smart girl. She would know that Ian's little fall was just an accident."

"Colton insisted she wouldn't have called either," Baker said. "But I asked him to double-check, just in case…"

Lem shook his head again. "There goes your plan, Sadie. Livvy is going to be insulted and furious, just like I am."

"Lem—"

Baker straightened up from where he'd been leaning over and backed out of the room. Obviously he didn't want to be in the middle of their squabble.

Sadie didn't want to argue with Lem either, but she was furious that the boys' future was getting jeopardized yet again.

"You know someone called your lawyer, too," Lem said. "Do you think that was Livvy? That she suddenly wants custody of your grandsons? That makes no sense."

"Maybe that CPS worker called the lawyer or had their lawyer call mine," Sadie suggested. That made more sense than someone trying to stop Baker and Taye from getting custody of the boys.

"You really want to blame my granddaughter for this?" he asked.

"No," she said. "But I don't know who else to blame." And she didn't want it to be Darlene, not when she'd just come back to their family. "They probably taught Livvy in Chicago to report every incident of a kid getting hurt."

Lem snorted again and shook his head. "And I told you she's smart. She would know the difference. But you want to believe it's her…because it's easier to blame her than one of your family members. It's easier to blame her because she's not family and neither am I."

Lem had been defensive and angry at first, but now he was cold. His voice. His usually sparkling blue eyes were like ice as he stared at her.

Sadie shivered with a strange foreboding. She'd thought she and Lem were becoming more than friends. That they might be family one day.

"Goodbye, Sadie," he said as he stalked out the door, Feisty following close behind him.

"Lem!" she called after him. But he didn't stop. He didn't come back and neither did the little dog.

And once again Sadie was alone.

All alone…even in a house full of other people. Full of family…she was alone.

CHAPTER SIXTEEN

COLTON WAS STILL STUNNED. He wasn't shocked
over what he'd overheard Livvy telling Miss
Shaw; he was shocked over what he felt. Over
the warmth that had flooded and expanded his
heart. He'd already started falling for her, but
in that moment he'd tumbled the rest of the way
in love with her.

She was strong, smart, passionate…such an
amazing woman and doctor and advocate for
her patients. Before he'd had a chance to talk
to her, the CPS worker had showed her a court
order for Ian's medical records and the two of
them had gone up to the administration floor
of the hospital.

The court was involved. How serious was
this allegation? How at risk were the boys of
being removed from Ranch Haven? Colton had
assured his cousin that he'd told Miss Shaw the
truth that he'd claimed sole responsibility for
Ian's mishap in the barn. But he doubted his

word was going to be enough to get this investigation closed.

Livvy's might. She'd been magnificent in her defense of the Haven family and especially the boys, and she'd taken down whoever had called in the report.

Who could have done it? Colton studied the people gathered yet around the intake desk. They all looked excited and happy, like they had when they'd applauded Livvy. Nobody looked guilty.

He doubted any of the staff present today had called in the complaint. But...

He didn't see the nurse who usually hovered around, watching him and Livvy. Sue with the sour expression, that was how he thought of her. She looked like she'd just sucked a lemon every time she looked at Livvy. Maybe her shift had ended. Or maybe...

Hopefully when Livvy showed the CPS worker Ian's medical records, she could find out who had called in the complaint. Baker had asked Colton to make sure it wasn't her, and even though he hadn't thought it was, he'd promised to double check.

Had she realized that was why he was here? Was that why she'd looked at him the way she had when she'd glanced up and noticed him standing inside the doors?

"You're still here," a soft voice murmured as she descended the last step of the stairwell that stretched from the lobby to the second floor. She seemed almost disappointed, or maybe scared, to see him.

Or maybe she was just scared for the boys, like he was. But that wasn't his only fear at the moment. He was afraid he'd fallen irrevocably in love with Livvy. "Where did Miss Shaw go?" he asked.

"She's still talking to hospital administration regarding the records."

"She's really taking this seriously?" he asked. "After talking to Ian and me and you?"

Livvy shrugged. "She's just doing her job."

"Did you find out who called in the complaint?" he asked.

She shook her head. "I don't know. *I* didn't suspect child abuse. You told me what happened and I believed *you*. I accepted what you told me."

"And you think I lied to you now? Are you having doubts?" he asked with alarm. Maybe that was why the CPS worker was still with administration. But then he noticed the woman quietly descending the stairs. She slipped through the automatic doors before they fully opened and rushed out to the parking lot. He wasn't sure if she wanted to avoid another confrontation with Livvy, or if she was hurrying off in order to protect whoever had called in the complaint to her. He'd noticed the reappearance of sour-faced Sue.

"I'm not having doubts about that," she said. "I talked to Ian and the other boys. I know it was just an accident. I know those boys are loved, and, more importantly, they know they're loved. I would never do anything to jeopardize their happiness." She looked over at the intake desk, too, and as her gaze met the nurse's, Sue turned away and pushed through the swinging doors into the ER.

"Do you think it was her?" he asked.

She shrugged. "I hope not. But if she did, she was probably trying to get me in trouble for failure to report."

"What could she have against you?" Colton asked.

Livvy shrugged again. "I don't know. My age. My gender. There is a lot of misogyny in medicine, and sometimes it comes from unlikely places."

"But to bring the Havens into it? To bring the boys into it..." He shuddered as he recalled how worried and scared Baker had sounded. But in the background he'd heard the kids chattering happily away, without a concern in the world. Colton's family had done a good job helping those boys recover and feel secure again after their devastating loss. "I need to talk to Miss Shaw's supervisor. To make sure that she closes this complaint."

Guilt weighed heavily on him. If only he'd been paying more attention to Ian that day, to the barn…to the talk about the bronco…he could have prevented the little boy from getting hurt then and him and his brothers being hurt now.

"That's a good idea," she agreed. "You should go…talk to the supervisor. You should go…" And that look was back on her face, like she was afraid. She stepped around him then.

Was she just busy? Or was there something else going on?

He opened his mouth to call her back, but before he could say anything, someone else urgently called out, "Livvy!"

She whirled around. "Dad? What's wrong?"

Bob Lemmon ran through the lobby doors before they fully opened and passed Colton. "Is your grandfather here?"

She tensed. "No. Why would he be?"

"He called me from his car. He was having trouble breathing. Chest pains. I told him to pull over and wait for an ambulance."

"Where was he?" Colton pulled out his cell and checked it for a call. He was still on duty; he would have been called out.

"He was heading back from the ranch, Ranch Haven." Tears welled in the older man's eyes. "I've never heard him like that…"

A little sob slipped out of Livvy's throat. Colton wanted to reach out to her, to comfort her, but she turned to her father instead, hugging him tight.

"I'll grab a rig and head out," Colton said. "I'll go find him."

"Thank you," Bob Lemmon said.

But Livvy didn't even look at him; she just hugged her dad tighter.

Colton had thought she was afraid before, but now she was clearly terrified for her grandfather. He was worried, too, about the old man and about whatever was going on with Livvy.

But there was only one thing he was sure he could help her with, so he rushed off to find Old Man Lemmon…hopefully alive. For Lem's sake, for his granddaughter's and for Colton's grandmother's sake as well.

LIVVY COULDN'T REMEMBER the last time she'd been this scared. It must have been when her mom was sick…or at least when Mom and Dad had finally told them that she was sick, that the cancer Livvy hadn't even known about had returned. Mom had fought it, but she hadn't been able to beat it a second time. Tears stung Livvy's eyes as she thought about that and worried about her grandfather. She'd already been afraid of her feelings for Colton, when her dad had shared his fears about her grandfather.

Where was he?

Colton had gone to find him. He hadn't been gone long yet, but if Grandpa had called 9-1-1, the dispatcher usually kept the ER apprised of incoming medical emergencies. Unless…

No. He had to be fine.

Livvy studied her dad who paced the waiting room area of the ER. "Why was Grandpa so upset?"

"He got into a fight with Sadie," he replied.

"I remember the way he used to talk about her," she said. "I thought they fought all the time until she was brought here, and he thought he was going to lose her." Then she remembered peeking through the crack in the door and seeing the love between them. "What were they fighting about?"

Her dad's face, which had been pinched and pale with his worry, flushed now, and he avoided meeting her gaze.

She expelled a shaky breath. "Me. They were fighting about me?"

He hesitated before finally nodding. "She thought you called in the suspected child abuse complaint."

"And of course Grandpa knew better," she said.

Bob snorted. "If he knew better, he wouldn't have been getting involved with a woman at his age. He's too old to be dating."

Livvy snorted now. "No, he's not. He's still working. Still vibrant." And from what she witnessed, still very capable of falling in love. He loved Sadie Haven.

Livvy didn't love her right now. Not if something had happened to her grandfather because of her...

"Your grandfather was furious with her," her dad said. "I don't remember the last time I ever heard him this upset..." His voice cracked and he blinked rapidly for a moment.

"Can I get you anything, Bob?" Nurse Sue asked.

Livvy hadn't even noticed that she'd been hovering nearby until now.

He glanced up, as if trying to place the woman.

Livvy was having a little trouble herself because the nurse's face wasn't pinched with that tight look of disapproval. She looked softer, more approachable…younger, though she was probably about her dad's age. Late fifties.

"I'm Sue Lancaster, well, Sue Masters now," she said. "We went to school together."

Her dad nodded. "Little Susie…"

The woman's face flushed a bright red, but instead of scowling, as she usually did, she smiled almost flirtatiously at him.

Did Livvy's work nemesis have a thing for her dad? Then why give Livvy such a hard time? And the Havens, if she was the one who'd called in that complaint.

"Were you the one who filed the report?" Livvy asked.

That scowl started pulling down her mouth as it usually did until she darted a glance back at Livvy's dad. He wasn't smiling at her now; he was intently studying her, too, so she looked back at Livvy. "That's your job to do. You're the attending."

"Yes, I am," Livvy said, her voice going

sharp as her patience with the woman's attitude evaporated. "And you need to respect that and respect me. I graduated undergrad and med school with honors. I matched with my top pick for residency. I know what I'm doing, and if you can't trust my judgement, then maybe you shouldn't be working with me anymore."

The woman's eyes widened with shock and her mouth dropped open. "I—I don't know why you think…"

"You question my every order," Livvy said. "And I've heard you call Dr. Brower at home to check with him before you do what I've told you."

The woman's face went from pale to dark red. "I…" She cleared her throat. "I need to advocate for my patients."

"If that's truly what you were doing, I would appreciate and respect that," she said. "But I've done nothing to make you doubt me. While you…"

"I just advocate for my patients," the woman repeated and then she turned and hurried back through the doors into the ER.

"I would applaud you again," the receptionist said from the intake desk, "but I don't want her going after me like she's been going after you."

"That's probably my fault," Livvy's dad quietly admitted.

"Really?"

"Yeah, we—"

The doors swished open and Colton rushed through them, half carrying her grandfather, who leaned heavily against him as he struggled to breathe. "I found him in the parking lot," Colton said.

Livvy was already racing for a gurney and oxygen, already doing what needed to be done even though she knew she couldn't treat a family member. But she wasn't about to wait for another doctor to show up, so she had no choice.

She was not about to lose her grandfather, not now, not after all the years she'd missed spending with him.

LEM WAS STILL FUMING. Over Sadie…

And over everybody thinking he was so weak and old that he needed to go to the hospital. Bob had shouted at him over the phone. And Colton…

He'd all but dragged him from his vehicle and carried him inside. And Livvy…

Poor, sweet Livvy had been so scared but so stoic and determined to treat him even though he hadn't needed it. Collin Cassidy looked at the read-out from the EKG machine and shook his head.

And a pang of fear struck Lem, making his heart beat a little bit faster. As hard as it beat, it had to be strong.

"How old are you?" the cardiologist asked him.

Lem snorted. "With as many times as you lot in the medical field ask me to tell you my birthday, I think you know. I'm eighty years old, son, same age as your ornery grandmother."

"You have the heart of someone half that age," Collin praised him. Then he chuckled. "Probably even younger than that."

"Make sure you say that loudly enough for my son and granddaughter to hear," he said with a pointed glance to where he could see their feet beneath the curtain of the ER cubicle. They had insisted on having the cardiologist come down to check him out. To make sure that he wasn't dying.

He was too ornery to die. Especially now, especially when he was so mad.

Livvy pulled back the curtain, maybe so she and her father could see the cardiologist as well as hear what he'd been saying.

"So much for medical privacy..." he muttered.

She glared at him...a little, but a smile curved her lips and love filled her green eyes. She was such a sweet girl and so smart and strong.

Colton had told him that in the parking lot, told him how she'd set that CPS worker straight...that Ian Haven was not abused. Lem was prouder of her than he'd already been, and he wouldn't have thought that possible.

How dare Sadie March Haven speak a word against her.

"If his heart is fine, why was he so short of breath?" she asked.

Collin glanced from him to Livvy. "I think you can figure that out..."

"An anxiety attack."

Lem shook his head. "That's ridiculous. I'm not anxious. I'm angry."

And maybe a little scared...

That he'd made a mistake. That he shouldn't have trusted Sadie. That he shouldn't have started falling for her...

Because he would never be family. He would never mean as much to her as the legacy she'd built with Big Jake, as the family they'd started.

And maybe she would never mean as much

to him as the family he and Mary had started...
that lived on with grandchildren like Livvy.

"You need to calm down, Grandpa," Livvy
said.

Despite his foul mood, he smiled slightly.
"Are those doctor's orders?"

"Yes," she said. "But also on granddaughter's orders, too. Please don't be upset on my
account."

He drew a deep, albeit unsteady breath. "I'm
upset on account of Sadie, not you. But don't
anyone tell her that. I don't want to give her
the satisfaction. Nobody better tell her that I'm
here either!" He glared at Collin, who held up
his hands as if he needed to fend him off.

"I'm not saying a word to her," Collin assured him.

"Neither am I," he said. "Ever again."

It would be better that way. Safer for all of
them.

But then Lem narrowed his eyes and gazed
around the small space. "Where did Colton
go?"

"He was working," Collin said. "He probably had to leave for another call."

Lem hoped that call didn't involve Sadie,
either professionally or personally. As angry
as he was with her, he didn't want anything to

happen to her. He also didn't want her to know how upset he'd gotten, how much he cared... not when it was still so one-sided. And even if it wasn't...

He wasn't sure what to do, how they could make it work when their families meant more to them than anything or anyone else.

CHAPTER SEVENTEEN

COLTON HAD BEEN admonished so many times about ringing the doorbell that he couldn't bring himself to push it now. He couldn't just reach out and open the front door either, though, so he followed the wrap-around porch past the formal front of the house to the patio in the back and the French doors that looked into the kitchen. He didn't have to open those because once Ian spied him through the glass, the little boy rushed out to greet him.

"Did you come from a fire? You got on a uniform, but it doesn't look like fireman clothes. Where's your coat and your boots? Are you going to get a dog?"

"Take a breath," Baker advised the little boy with a chuckle. "And give Colton a chance to answer." He reached out and clasped Colton's shoulders, pulling him in for a hug. "Thanks for coming out here."

Moisture welled in Colton's eyes for just a second, but he blinked it back. "I came out here to check on everyone," he said. "Are all of you all right?"

Baker released a shaky breath. "A little worried…"

Ian looked from one to the other of them. "What are you worried about, Uncle Baker? The ranch?" He frowned. "Or us? We're good now. I remember everything, and Miller isn't mad at us anymore. We're good now. I told the new lady that today." He turned back to Colton. "She asked a lot of questions about me getting hurt in the barn when Midnight got out."

"That was my fault," Colton said. "I should have been watching you better." Guilt, over his negligence, churned in his stomach.

"Don't go there," Baker said. "I know that road leads to nothing but pain. You don't need to go there."

Ian shook his head; maybe he didn't understand what they were saying. Then he stated calmly and vehemently, "It was my fault. I know I'm not supposed to go near Midnight's stall alone. But I was showing off." His face flushed. "I told the lady that."

Moisture flooded Colton's eyes again, and it was harder to blink it away. He picked up the little boy and hugged him close. "You are one amazing kid," he said. "And this is one amazing family."

"You're family, too," Ian said. "You're our cousin."

Colton smiled. "Yes, I am. Now I need to check on Grandma."

"It's almost dinner time," Ian said. "She should be coming out of her room soon."

"You need to go wash up before dinner," Baker said, and he swung Ian down from Colton's arms.

The little boy hesitated. "Will you sit next to me?" he asked Colton.

"You're taking my spot," Baker said, but he grinned.

Colton shook his head. "I don't think I'll be staying for dinner."

"There's a lot of food," Ian said. "Taye and Miller always make a lot."

His stomach roiled with emptiness now, not just the guilt and anxiety he felt. But that overpowered his hunger. He waited until the little boy rushed off before turning back to Baker.

"Was it Livvy?" Baker asked.

He shook his head. "No, like I told you." His lips curved into a slight smile. "She made it very clear to Miss Shaw that there was nothing to the complaint except malice on the part of whoever made it. It might have been a nurse in the ER. She's had an attitude with Livvy since she started."

"You think this was to get her in trouble?" Baker asked.

He shrugged. "I don't know. I'm not here about that. I'm here about Grandma. Is she really all right?" Because he didn't want to tell her about Lem if she wasn't.

Baker nodded. "I checked on her a little bit ago. Her blood pressure is under control now. I think she's more concerned about this fight she had with Lem than about the bogus call to CPS."

Colton could almost feel the color drain from his face. He should have stayed at the hospital, should have made sure the old man was okay. But Livvy and Collin could do more for him than he could.

He could do more here…with his grandmother.

"What is it?" Baker asked.

"It's Lem," a female voice answered before Colton could, and he looked toward the house to find Sadie standing between the patio doors Ian had left open. And her face was as pale as Colton's probably was. "What happened? Did that old fool have a car accident? He went tear-ing out of here with gravel flying behind him. It's going to kill him if he cracked up that old Cadillac of his." And from the look of fear on her face, it might kill her, too, if something had happened to him.

Colton shook his head. "No accident. But he must have driven fast to get to town as quickly as he did. Bob made him come to the ER. He was having trouble breathing."

Sadie staggered back a step, and Colton rushed forward to catch her. But Jake was already there, sliding his arm around her. "I got you, Grandma. I'll take you."

She shook her head. "No, Colton will take me."

He nodded. "Yes."

"We can all go—"

Colton shook his head now. "I don't think that's a good idea. I had a hard time convincing him to get out of his car and go inside the ER. He's really mad."

"At me," Sadie said.

"And at himself," Colton said. "He's mad at himself for getting so worked up. He won't want a lot of people there."

"Proud old fool," Sadie said. "But he's right. The rest of you need to stay here. Colton and I will go."

Baker nodded. "Makes sense for the paramedic to take you." He grinned, but it was obviously forced, his face tense. "In case you and Lem get into it again, Grandma."

Baker might have been joking, or he might have known what Colton did. He grimaced as he admitted, "He probably won't want you there, Grandma."

Sadie flinched, but then she pulled away from Jake and stood tall and proud. "Too bad. I'm going to be there for him, just like he's always been there for me. Even when we hated each other, we always had each other's backs."

He suspected Sadie didn't hate Lem anymore. In fact, it looked like it was quite the opposite. She loved him. And maybe Colton recognized that because he'd fallen himself for a Lemmon, one who was as determined to stay single and uninvolved as he'd once been.

LIVVY JUST WANTED to go home, even more so now…after what had happened. But nobody had come in to take over the last of Dr. Brower's shift. Even Nurse Sue had tried to get someone else to cover her.

Livvy didn't know if the woman had done that because she couldn't stand working with her or because she felt guilty over reporting the Havens to CPS…if she'd done that. She hadn't admitted it, but she'd started acting so much nicer for *some* reason.

Livvy would hate for anything to happen to the Haven family. Those little boys didn't deserve to suffer any more than they already had. Tears stung her eyes as she thought of them being separated from the ranch, from their uncles and grandma and maybe even from each other.

She remembered one case that she had reported at her old hospital and how the poor battered teenage girl had been so angry with her for calling CPS because she'd been separated from her younger siblings. She'd been so worried that there would be nobody there to protect them like she'd tried…which was why she'd been the battered one. A sob burned the back of her throat as she remembered that girl, just one of the many reasons why she'd wanted to come back here to what she remembered as the innocence of Willow Creek.

The sweet nostalgia and caring of a small town. She remembered spending holidays here and how everyone had gathered in the town square to visit Santa. Everyone loved her grandfather. Everyone had seemed to love each other.

Even after her family had moved away, Grandma and Grandpa had told her stories of kindnesses. Of one of the teachers taking in an orphaned child, and that child had become a teacher, too. She was currently engaged to marry the mayor.

Livvy would have thought that town she'd remembered so well would have gathered around and embraced the Haven orphans, doing everything they could to help them. Not hurt them.

Her chest ached with the fear they must have felt. She'd been so afraid for her grandfather, but that was nothing compared to what those children had endured.

"You're still here?" the nurse asked. Sue. She stood in the doorway to the doctor's lounge.

Livvy closed her eyes, not wanting to see the look of judgement that was always on the older woman's face. No doubt she would think negatively of Livvy lying on the couch even though there were no patients now. At least there hadn't been when she'd left the floor.

"Did someone come in?" she asked.

"Dr. Porter is on his way in to take over the last of Dr. Brower's shift."

So Sue had found someone. She really was desperate to get rid of Livvy. "Did a patient come in?" she asked. She couldn't leave the

ER with no coverage even if Dr. Porter was on his way.

"No, but…"

"What?" Livvy prodded her, her voice getting a little sharp with impatience. She was so very tired.

"That Cassidy paramedic is back with his grandmother," Sue reluctantly reported. "I can tell them that you've already left if you want me to…"

Livvy opened her eyes then and stared at the woman with surprise. Was she trying to protect her now? Or trying to make up for what she'd done? Or was it another trap? Another attempt to try and get her in trouble?

"I will talk to them," Livvy said. Not that she wanted to see Colton again. Or Sadie…

A groan replaced the sob that had burned in her throat, but it managed to escape. She was just so very tired…too tired to fight her feelings.

She rolled to her side, ready to swing her legs to the floor, when a deep voice said, "Don't get up. You look exhausted."

"That's because I am," she wearily admitted, too tired to be proud at the moment. The emotions of the day, more than the length of it, had taken their toll on her. She had to close her eyes to shut out his face, to shut him out, so that she didn't jump up and rush to him for a hug. She'd never felt as comforted as she had in those brief embraces he'd given her in the past. His strong arms, his chest beneath her head...she needed the warmth and comfort of him so much right now.

"All you have to do is tell us which room is Lem's," Colton said.

She shook her head. "I can't do that."

"He really doesn't want to see me..." That voice was deep but it wasn't Colton's.

Sadie Haven had a very deep voice for a woman. She was tall, too, with such an intimidating presence. But at the moment Livvy was too tired and too irritated to be intimidated by anyone. She opened her eyes and studied the older woman.

Sadie looked as tired as Livvy felt, with dark circles beneath her eyes, and more lines in her face since the last time they'd met. And her shoulders that were always so straight and strong were stooped now with age or the same exhaustion Livvy felt. Or maybe guilt.

"Your grandfather probably told you why he was so upset with me," Sadie said.

Livvy tensed and nodded. And because she felt small and vulnerable sitting down, she stood up, but the Havens were so tall, she almost felt as if she was still sitting. But from her grandfather she'd learned how to stand tall despite her height. She lifted her chin and stared proudly at them.

"I'm sorry," Sadie said. "I shouldn't have doubted you...even for a moment. You're a smart girl, like your grandfather says, and would have known the difference between abuse and a stupid accident."

"Stupid on my part," Colton said. "I should have been watching him."

"Ian told you not to blame yourself," Sadie said, as if reminding him. "He took full responsibility for going near Midnight's stall when he knew he wasn't supposed to."

In appreciation of the little boy's honesty and integrity, Livvy let a smile curve her lips. "He's a sweet kid. And if for any reason I thought he was in danger, I would have called. But it's clear how much he and his brothers are loved and protected."

Tears welled in Sadie's dark eyes, and she nodded. "So much that the investigator showing up like she did, without warning or cause, scared me, especially since someone has also been calling my lawyer about them and the estate."

Livvy tensed now, with concern. She doubted Sue had done that. Sue hadn't even admitted to reporting the incident to CPS. Maybe it hadn't been her. Livvy felt a flash of guilt for thinking it was her without proof, and her irritation with Sadie slipped away as she acknowledged her own hypocrisy.

"I wouldn't have called CPS about that and certainly wouldn't have called your lawyer," Livvy said.

"I know. I thought for a moment that maybe CPS had called the lawyer…" Sadie released a ragged sigh. "Seriously, I just don't know what to think. But I should have never considered that it might be you, and I'm sorry."

Livvy shrugged off the apology. "I understand why you might have thought it. You don't know me."

"I know Lem," Sadie said, and her voice cracked on his name. "I know him probably better than I know myself. And he was certain you wouldn't have done it. That should have been enough for me. I shouldn't have upset him like I did. I need to see him and apologize to him now. And I know he's here because his Cadillac is still in the parking lot. So please tell me what room he's in."

Livvy shook her head.

Sadie gasped and touched her heart, as if she'd felt a jab in it. "He really doesn't want to see me?"

Livvy stepped forward and took the older woman's wrists in her hands, checking her pulse. "Are you okay?"

"Baker and I have been monitoring her pressure," Colton said. "She's fine."

But she wasn't. She was obviously upset, very upset over Livvy's grandfather. "I can't give you his room number because he's not here."

Sadie's eyes widened for a moment with fear but then she shook her head. "If something had happened to him, you wouldn't be here yet. You'd be with him and your dad."

Livvy would like to think that she would, but too many times in the past she'd let her career and Steven keep her from her family. From what had mattered most.

"He's fine. The difficulty breathing must have been due to an anxiety attack although it would kill him to admit that," she said with a smile. Sadie smiled, too, but faintly, as if she'd had to force it. "His heart is great." Sadie's was not, and Livvy should have been more sensitive to that. "You don't need to worry about him."

But those tears welled in the older woman's eyes again. "I can't lose someone else I…"

"Love," Livvy finished for her. She'd seen it herself just a few weeks ago…in this very hospital. She'd seen how they'd looked at each other, how they'd touched each other. "I know he feels the same way. That's why he got so upset."

Because he was scared and Grandpa was always so brave, so in control. Livvy was pretty sure she hadn't really even loved Steven, and she'd given up control of her life to him. That was why she was scared of falling truly, deeply in love.

Because she was worried that she would do everything to make her partner happy and not do the things that made her happy. She couldn't take the risk of loving someone and losing herself.

"Dad drove Grandpa home a while ago, after Collin did a whole bunch of tests confirming that he was perfectly healthy. He wanted to drive, but Dad insisted on driving him." She smiled as she recalled their argument, their bickering, and how they'd had their arms around each other. Dad had been as scared as she'd been, as scared as Sadie was now. Despite all his complaining about his father, he loved him.

"I need to see him," Sadie said, and there was an almost desperate note in her voice and on her face when she turned toward her grandson. "Give me your keys."

Colton shook his head. "I'll drive you over there."

"I need to talk to him alone," Sadie said, her hand held out between them for his keys.

"How will I get home?" Colton asked.

She pointed to Livvy.

Despite her exhaustion, Livvy's pulse quickened. "I—I'm still working."

"Dr. Porter walked in with us," Colton said. "He's taking over your shift, so you can get some rest. You've had a long day. Why don't you let me drive you home in your vehicle… after we give the grandparents some time alone first?"

That sounded wonderful to let someone take care of her. "I do have to finish up my charts first anyway." That would give them some privacy.

Colton dropped his keys into his grandmother's hand and advised, "Don't get any speeding tickets with my truck. I've heard about your driving."

Sadie smiled as she closed her fingers around the keys. Then she kissed his cheek. "Thank you, sweetheart." Then she turned back to Livvy, hugged her and kissed her cheek, too. "And thank you, honey."

Once his grandmother was gone, Livvy gave Colton a warning. "After I brief Dr. Porter, I just want to drop you off and go home to sleep, so I don't intend to give them very much time alone. I'm also not sure Grandpa will even talk to her."

He sighed. "I hope they can work it out. Will you give me some of your time tomorrow? I checked the schedule. You're not working and neither am I. We can go out to the ranch...just as friends."

He'd been sweet to drive his grandmother to town and sweet to worry about her. Livvy knew she shouldn't take the risk of spending that much time with Colton, but she was too tired to come up with an excuse why she couldn't. Maybe in the morning, after a long night's sleep, she would come up with a reason she could share with him that wasn't her real reason. That she was too afraid that she was going to fall for him to spend any time alone with him.

SADIE HAD BEEN to Lem's house before, many times, to help with Mary. But then she'd always thought of it as Mary's house. While Lem had been running the town, Mary had run her little stone cottage on Main Street. She'd taken care of the house and the garden and Lem…like the perfect homemaker Sadie had never been.

Sadie would have rather been out riding around the ranch, fixing fences, feeding cattle, breeding horses than spend any time in the kitchen or the garden. She still would. But she couldn't sit in the saddle as long as she used to.

She was getting old whether she wanted to admit it or not. Her recent health scare had proven that; she wasn't as strong as she'd once been. Was she strong enough to risk her heart again?

At the moment she wasn't sure she was strong enough to lift her arm from her side and ring the bell, so she just stood there, in front of the arched, oak door which suddenly creaked open.

"You selling magazine subscriptions?" Lem asked as he stared up at her. "Or Girl Scout cookies?"

A laugh sputtered out of her. He was the most frustrating, funny, wonderful man. She threw her arms around him and hugged him tightly as tears streaked down her face. "I'm sorry," she said. "I'm so sorry…"

He patted her back for a moment, almost awkwardly, and he didn't step back. He didn't let her inside.

And Sadie realized she wasn't forgiven. She pulled back and stared at him. "What's wrong?"

"I'm fine," he said. "Got a clean bill of health."

"That's what Livvy said. I apologized to her," Sadie shared. "And she forgave me...so why won't you?"

He sighed. "It just seems like it's your family or my family..."

She sighed, too. "I was just thinking that this was Mary's house."

"Is that why you didn't ring the bell?"

"Feels weird to be here to see you and not her," she admitted. Almost like a betrayal. But Mary had been gone for a few years already, more years if you counted when she'd first started forgetting...everything but Lem. Some part of her had always seemed to recognize the husband she'd loved so much.

"I've been going out to the ranch, and Big Jake is everywhere there and he's been gone even longer than Mary has."

Sadie shook her head. "I changed so much of the house after he died. I built on the whole wing that has my main floor suite and the other wing with the kitchen. It's not the same house that Jake lived in with me, where we raised our sons…while your place is like a shrine to Mary."

Lem glanced around her, at the front yard where Mary had planted so many flowers. They glowed in the setting sun. He sighed. "I know… It's time to move on…"

"Move on with me," Sadie said. "Marry me…"

CHAPTER EIGHTEEN

DESPITE BAKER'S ADVICE to not give in to guilt, Colton couldn't quite shake it. Last night he'd taken a little bit of advantage of Livvy's exhaustion. Once they'd arrived at Grandpa's house to find Sadie already gone with his truck, he'd asked if he could drive her SUV back to his place and pick her up the next morning for the ride out to the ranch to retrieve his truck.

Since Grandma had already been gone when they'd showed up at Lem's house, he probably hadn't even let her inside to apologize. The Lemmons might be nearly as stubborn as the Havens.

That was why he hadn't been willing to take the chance that Livvy wouldn't come up with an excuse not to see him on her day off. And since he had the whole day off as well, he wanted to spend it with her.

Which was selfish and inconsiderate of him…which probably reminded her of her former fiancé. And that was the last thing he wanted. So he showed up at her door the next morning with a box of donuts and an insulated cup of coffee. From working with her at the hospital, he knew how she took it with cream and a sprinkle of cinnamon and nutmeg. The delicious scent wafted up from the cup.

Her dad and grandpa must have already left for the day because she was the one who opened the door. Her hair was wet, her face damp, as if she'd just gotten out of the shower. She was dressed in worn jeans and a green T-shirt with her feet bare.

Colton's breath stuck in his lungs, burning, as he was overwhelmed with how naturally beautiful she was. "Wow..." he murmured.

She touched her face. "Give me a few seconds and I'll put on some makeup so I don't scare the horses."

"You don't need any," he assured her.

She traced the shadows beneath her eyes with a fingertip. "I look like a raccoon."

"You should have slept in," Colton said, that twinge of guilt striking him again.

"I did," she said. "I can't remember the last time I slept so many hours in a row. That's a luxury I didn't have at my last job."

"It seems like you're always at the hospital here, too," he remarked.

"I thought yesterday was never going to end," she admitted. "But it was still better than any day in the city. And I'm actually looking forward to seeing the ranch."

His guilt increased because he intended to take her to another ranch first before Ranch Haven. He had plenty of time to tell her during the ride out that way, but they talked of other things instead, of the little Haven boys, of Sadie and Lem and what might have happened between them since she hadn't seen her grandfather yet to ask why Sadie had left so quickly.

Any time during the conversation he could have told her where he was taking her...since she'd asked him to drive since he knew the way and she didn't. Clearly she didn't or she would have noticed that he'd headed in the opposite direction from Ranch Haven.

It wasn't until he started down the bumpy gravel road toward the house that she tensed as she peered out the passenger window. "Uh oh, why do I feel like this scene has been played out on every true crime show I've watched? The male acquaintance driving the hapless woman out to the middle of nowhere? This doesn't look like Ranch Haven."

"It's not," he said. "It's the Cassidy Ranch."

"Where you grew up?" she asked.

He snorted. "Sometimes I don't feel very grown up."

She turned toward him then, her green eyes wide. "What do you mean?"

"It just feels like part of me is stuck here, at the age I was when my mom died and I was so afraid that my dad was going to go next. And then Cash was gone and…" His voice cracked, and he had to clear his throat. "I don't know."

She reached across the console and touched his hand. "I do. It's like I've been so focused on starting my career all these years that I wasn't living my life. I spent all that time in school and in hospitals and even when I wasn't, I was talking about medicine."

"Even with your ex?" he asked.

"Especially with my ex," she said. "That was really all we had in common."

It was more than she had in common with Colton, but he didn't want to point that out to her. And maybe they had more than they realized. They'd both lost their moms and maybe a little bit of themselves along the way, too. "I might have gotten lost out here, years ago," he admitted. "But that's not why I brought you out here. I'm not looking for me."

"Then why did you bring me here?" she asked.

"I'm looking for Cash."

"You said he ran away years ago. He's been gone a long time."

"I think he's come back," he said. "At least once." The day the house had burned down. But maybe he was wrong about Cash. Like maybe he was wrong about that decision he'd made so long ago to stay single...

He'd been assuming that whoever he loved wouldn't be tough enough to handle his career, the risk, the danger...and that it wasn't fair to put someone through that. But what if he found someone smart? Someone strong?

"I know I can trust you," he said. "That's why I brought you out here." He pulled her small SUV up to the crumbling foundation of the ranch house.

"Wow..." she murmured with shock as she stared through the windshield at the blackened shell of his childhood home. "That must have been some fire."

"It was," he said.

"Did you ever find out how it started?"

"The Moss Valley fire chief determined it

324 THE FIREFIGHTER'S FAMILY SECRET

was mechanical. We were always so busy taking care of dad…medically and financially… that the house fell into really poor repair," he admitted, sickness churning in his stomach with guilt and the despair he'd felt then.

Her hand tightened on his. "I'm sorry, Colton, that must have been a difficult time for you."

He tried to shrug off her sympathy, but the weight was too heavy, bowing his shoulders. With another attempt at humor, he asked, "What? My childhood or the fire?"

"Both," she said. "Collin thinks it didn't affect you. That you've always had a positive attitude despite what you were all going through."

"You and Collin talk about me?" he asked.

She nodded. "You and Bailey Ann."

"I can't wait to meet Bailey Ann," he said with a smile of his own. "She sounds very special."

"She is," Livvy said. "I've gone up to see her a few times."

"My twin is a good guy."

"So are you," she said.

But he shook his head. "I've been doing the same thing everyone else has been doing," he said. "As much as I've hated all these secrets I've found out about, I have a secret of my own."

Two secrets actually.

The first was that he'd fallen for her. Despite her warning that she didn't want to get involved with anyone, despite his resolve not to get involved with anyone…he'd fallen hopelessly in love with her.

And it was hopeless. He knew that. But he had to know something else…

He had to know if his brother had burned down their family home. The insurance adjuster hadn't made a final determination, and Colton hoped to figure it out before they did. Or at least be prepared if arson was the determination.

He took the lighter out of his pocket and put it in her hand. Then he pushed open the door to the SUV and stepped out, needing the air and the sun on his face.

But the scent of smoke hung yet in the air… and Colton felt like even though the house had burned down, he would never be free of it.

Never be free of the past and all his conflicted feelings over it.

LIVVY STARED AT the lighter Colton had put in her hand. The silver was slightly tarnished and maybe even a little charred with something like soot deep in the etching of the horseshoes that spelled out: CC.

She was thoroughly confused. She opened the passenger door and stepped out on the gravel drive. "What is this?" she asked, her heart pounding hard. "Are you confessing that you burned down the house? Is that your secret?"

He shook his head and looked at her, his dark eyes holding so much pain along with those secrets. "No, how could you think that of me?"

She felt a twinge of regret that she'd even asked him such a question. But then she held up the lighter. "You're the one who handed me your lighter."

"It's not mine," he said, his handsome face tense.

"The CC?"

"Cornelius Cassidy. My grandfather," he said. "He died when I was so young that I don't remember him."

"I don't understand then… Did you just find this in the house?"

"Yes, during the fire," he said. "I can't think what else it would have been doing in the cellar. It must have fallen through a hole in the kitchen where I'm pretty sure the fire originated."

"But the poor maintenance…"

He shrugged. "I don't know…"

"Who do you think started the fire, Colton?"

"My brother Cash took that lighter when he left," he said, and his eyes glistened with a hint of tears. "That was the last time I saw it."

This was it, what was bothering him…why he wasn't as happy-go-lucky as his twin said he was. "Oh, Colton," she murmured, and she approached him, sliding her arms around his waist to offer him one of the comforting hugs he'd given her in the past.

His arms closed around her, holding her tight as his breath shuddered out in a shaky sigh. "I haven't dared to say anything to anyone. I haven't seen him. I don't know that he's back, and I can't imagine he would do this…" He gestured at the blackened remains of his childhood home. "But he loved the ranch. He probably would have been furious to find out that Dad was selling it. As the oldest son, it would have been his birthright."

"He left it," Livvy reminded him. "He left all of you. You were all struggling after your mom died, but he ran away instead of staying to help. Why are you protecting him?"

"Because he's still my brother, and because I don't want to think the worst of him."

Always looking for the positive. That was what his twin had said about him. That was the exact opposite of Steven, who'd found the negative in every situation, in every person. And maybe his attitude had started rubbing off on her.

She'd been so wrong about him. About herself...

She stepped back, pulling away from him. "What about me?" she asked. "What do you think of me?"

Her heart beat faster, and her skin flushed. The way he was looking at her...

She shouldn't have asked. It would be better if she didn't know. But she had to know so she repeated her question, her voice all soft and breathless sounding. "What do you think of me?"

"That you're perfect," he said, and he closed that distance between them to skim his fingertips along her jaw. "You're so smart and beautiful and strong and caring..."

Wishing she was really all those things, she shook her head in denial—knocking his hand away from her face. "I guess you don't know me..."

But he shook his head now. "You're the one who doesn't know you."

And she froze, stunned with what he'd said and with the knowledge that he was right.

"That was true for a long time," she said. "But being back here, being *home*…" And despite only living here for the first six or seven years of her childhood, Willow Creek was home. "… I think I'm getting myself back."

He grinned. "The way you handled the CPS investigator…" He whistled in appreciation.

"And Nurse Sue," she said. While he'd witnessed her standing up for the Havens, he'd missed her standing up for herself.

"I wondered why she was being so nice to you last night," he said with a smile. "You scared her."

She shook her head.

"You scared yourself?"

"No," she said. "Surprisingly. It felt good to speak my mind. To shut down the disrespect. I should have done that a long time ago." With Steven she'd learned to just agree since he'd always been able to argue or manipulate her into doing what he'd wanted. She needed to talk to him the way she had Nurse Sue; she needed to make it clear to him to leave her and her family alone. And to respect that she knew what she wanted…and whom…

"You're thinking about your ex," Colton said, and his shoulders bowed slightly again.

She sighed and shook off those thoughts. "I'm thinking about you." She held up the lighter. "What are you going to do about this?"

He sighed now. "I don't know. I don't know how my dad and my grandma kept secrets for so long. The heaviness of them…" He smiled at her. "I'm sorry I shared that weight with you."

"I'm not," she said. "You needed to talk to someone." And that he'd chosen her, that he respected her opinion, filled her heart with warmth.

He released another shaky-sounding breath. "I think I need you…and that scares me."

She could relate. But even though she knew she should turn and run away, she leaned closer to him, and he lowered his head and covered her mouth with his…in a gentle, almost reverent kiss.

She was falling for him…despite all the reasons that she shouldn't. Despite her fear of losing what she'd just found: herself.

WHEN THE UNFAMILIAR vehicle appeared on the long driveway leading to the house, Baker was glad that he'd headed back early to the barn, leaving Jake alone in the pastures. He'd had this niggling feeling, this fear…

That even though everyone had told the CPS worker the truth, that the boys were not being abused or neglected, that she hadn't believed them. That she was still going to take them away from them, from him.

He'd already lost so much…he couldn't lose them, too. He nudged his knees against the horse's sides, urging the mare to hurry as he tried to catch that vehicle. The small SUV continued toward the house, pulling up behind some other vehicles.

A lot of people were at the ranch…which was odd for a weekday. The doors of the SUV opened, and Colton and the ER doctor stepped out. "Is everything okay?" Baker asked with concern. "Is your grandpa doing okay?"

Because his red Cadillac was conspicuously missing from the driveway.

She nodded. "He's fine." She glanced around the driveway, too, as if looking for his vehicle. "I thought he'd be here. He was already gone when I woke up this morning."

"It's a weekday," Colton said. "He's probably at his office."

"The mayor isn't," Baker remarked as he noticed his brother Ben's Lincoln SUV parked in the drive. And his dread knotted in his stomach. Ben had a law degree, but as busy as he was with his mayoral duties, he hadn't been handling Dale and Jenny's estate. Was he taking it over now?

Baker dismounted from his horse just as a bunch of little boys ran out of the front door of the house, down the porch steps and across the yard toward them.

"Grandma's here!" Ian exclaimed.

Baker's brow furrowed with concern for a moment. "Of course she is." Sadie's truck was parked in its usual spot near those front steps, and the one she'd used to get home last night, Colton's, was parked behind it.

"He's talking about Grandma Darlene," Miller exclaimed.

That dread churned even harder in Baker's stomach. Was she the one who'd started all this? His mother? Was she going after her grandsons?

CHAPTER NINETEEN

COLTON WAS GETTING used to Ranch Haven, to the Haven family, *his* family…but he could tell that Livvy was overwhelmed. He wanted to reach for her hand, to hold it to comfort her, and to comfort himself.

Ever since their kiss at the Cassidy Ranch, she'd been quiet, withdrawn. Maybe she was still just tired, but he suspected he'd shared too much. He shouldn't have burdened her with his secret; he shouldn't have shown her the lighter. Or maybe she was worried that he was going to try to take over her life like her ex-fiancé had.

She seemed more at ease now, in the chaos of the Haven kitchen, than she had with him in her SUV. Little Jake had even somehow managed to make it into her arms, and Colton felt ridiculously jealous of the toddler.

Collin chuckled. "You're looking at that little kid like you looked at me the last time I talked to Livvy."

Colton wasn't the only Cassidy-Haven at

the ranch. He wasn't sure why his twin, his dad and Darlene had made the trip out. But then Collin must have heard about the CPS visit when he'd treated Lem at the hospital. The old man was fine; Colton's grandmother didn't look as well. She sat in her chair at the head of the long table, her back to the hearth of the fireplace. It was July, so no fire burned in it. The smoke Colton smelled was from the Cassidy Ranch. When he'd kissed and hugged Livvy, he'd noticed it in her hair.

He shouldn't have brought her there, shouldn't have told her about the secret he was keeping.

"She's fine," Collin said, his gaze trained on their grandmother, too. She was across the enormous, noise-filled room from them. "I checked her out again when Dad, Darlene and I got here. I think she's just worried about the CPS investigation."

"Is that why you're here?" Colton asked.

Collin nodded. "Yeah, Darlene was worried that someone might think she was behind it."

From the way Baker had been staring at her since he'd joined them in the kitchen, it was clear that someone did think that.

"I still can't get over all the secrets..." Collin muttered. "All the things we didn't know about Dad and Darlene and…us…" He turned toward Colton then, studying him intently.

Colton knew his twin was well aware Colton was keeping something from him.

"I'm surprised you dragged yourself away from the hospital," Colton remarked.

Collin chuckled. "Not jealous of me and Livvy, are you?"

"Nothing to be jealous of there," Colton said with certainty. "Your heart belongs to another. Little Bailey Ann…"

Collin grinned. "She is a sweetheart," he admitted. "What about Livvy's heart?" he asked. "Where's hers?"

"It's not mine," Colton said. No matter how much he wished it was. But clearly she wasn't ready.

"Have you tried for it?" Collin asked. "You two have so much in common. You're both first responders."

"But she's a doctor."

"And if you don't keep the patient alive on their way to her, she'd have nobody to treat," Collin said. "I know you're good at what you do. You're a good man, Colton."

Colton narrowed his eyes. "It's not like you to be this nice to me," he said. "Did you take my EKG without me knowing? Do I have a bad heart?"

"You have a good one," he said. "I heard about you rushing out here to get Sadie after you got Lem inside the hospital. And the way you've always been there for Dad and Darlene while Marsh and I were off to college and Cash was…"

"Gone," Colton said.

"Yeah, he disappointed us all."

He might have done more than that. But maybe that wasn't Colton's problem. Maybe he had to just let the insurance investigation play out and see what they determined had caused the fire. Maybe his former boss was right, and it had been a mechanical failure.

"You've never disappointed anyone, Colton," his twin said. "You've always been there for all of us."

"Don't put me at saint status," Colton said with an uneasy chuckle. "I'm doing what I want to do with my life. I didn't make any sacrifices." Maybe until now…until he'd decided to carry this secret alone without sharing it with his family.

But Collin could barely say their oldest brother's name. No. It was better that he hadn't told him. That he'd only told Livvy…

But would she keep his secret, Cash's secret, for them? She'd moved around the room, still with Little Jake clasped in her arms. Now she stood near the patio doors with his dad and Darlene. And the way they talked and glanced over at him made him uneasy.

Made him wonder what they were talking about...

No. He didn't wonder. He knew. They were talking about him.

LIVVY COULD BARELY believe that Jessup JJ Cassidy Haven had recently had a heart transplant. He looked so strong and healthy, like an older version of his sons. He stared across the room at where they stood in the doorway between the kitchen and the hall that led back to the front of the house.

"The twins look exactly alike, but they couldn't be more different," their dad said. "Collin has always been so serious and driven, and Colton has been the light...the one who kept us all smiling..." His brow furrowed, though.

And Darlene finished for him, "Until the fire..."

Livvy knew why he'd changed since then, because he was carrying a secret that shouldn't have been his to carry. It wasn't hers to share either, though, so she floundered around to find a way to change the subject.

Little Jake snuggling against her shoulder while he played with her hair gave her the perfect switch. "He's such a friendly, happy kid," she said.

Instead of beaming with pride, Darlene's hazel eyes widened, and her face got pale. And Livvy wondered what she'd said wrong. The little boy was shy with his grandma, though. He would only sneak glances at her before hiding his face in Livvy's shoulder again.

"There's the little flirt," Baker said as he approached them. "He goes for the blondes every time."

"I'm not quite blonde," Livvy said. But she wasn't as much a redhead as her granddad had once been. She wondered again where he was. City Hall?

After last night, she'd expected him to take the day off. After Sadie had been so desperate to see him, she'd expected him to be here.

"It wasn't me," Darlene said, her voice cracking with emotion.

Livvy turned to her in confusion. She wasn't talking to her, though; she was focused on her youngest son.

"It wasn't me, Baker," Darlene said. "I wouldn't try to take the boys from you."

"You don't even know them," Baker said. "You don't even know me."

Heat rushed to Livvy's face; she wanted out of this conversation, of this family drama, but Little Jake clung tightly to her, as if she was the safe haven in the storm of family drama.

"I'm sorry," Darlene said, tears pooling in her eyes. "I never meant to hurt you. I stayed away because I thought my presence would cause more pain, that you blamed me for your dad dying. I hated myself for what I did, for distracting him, and that tractor…" Her voice cracked with emotion, but she cleared it and determinedly continued, "I would never want to hurt you or these little kids any more than you've already been hurt." The tears spilled over, sliding down her cheeks.

As if Little Jake felt sorry for her, he stopped being shy and reached for her. She hesitated before taking him, looking over his head at Baker.

He hesitated, too, before nodding. "You can hold him."

Her arms shook as she reached out and took him from Livvy, but then the grandmother drew his small, chubby body against her. She closed her eyes and released a shaky sigh.

Tears stung Livvy's eyes now.

Jessup reached up and touched her hand, lightly squeezing it. "You are as special as my son thinks you are," he murmured.

Now Livvy knew why Colton was so special...because his whole family was. But they were also overwhelming, complicated, dramatic and maybe just all too much for someone who was still struggling to find herself.

She smiled at him. But she couldn't say anything for the lump of emotion that had risen in her throat. She just waited for the first opportunity to slip out the open patio doors, around the porch to the front. To her vehicle...

And before anyone could stop her, she hurried away...from Colton and the temptation of falling for him. But even as fast as she drove back to Willow Creek, she couldn't outrun the feelings she'd already developed for him.

Even before that kiss at the Cassidy Ranch and everything they'd shared, she'd started falling for him. Now she was afraid that she'd fallen so hard that she might not be able to pick herself up again.

THE EERIE SILENCE of his house, of Mary's house, unsettled Lem. He'd already gotten used to Bob and Livvy living with him. That must have been why the quiet unnerved him, because they were both gone.

Bob was at the office. He was always at the office. And Livvy was always at the hospital. So really the empty house was nothing unusual for him.

He heaved a heavy sigh as he had to admit that wasn't the problem. The problem was that he'd gotten used to the chaos of Ranch Haven, to all the kids and adults running in and out of Sadie's suite. To Feisty yipping at him with excitement…

The little dog had seemed to want to leave with him last night when he'd rushed out of Sadie's suite. No. She didn't want to leave the ranch. She just hadn't wanted him to leave either.

Neither had he.

But he'd been so mad. And he was working hard to hang on to that anger. To protect himself.

A door opened and shut, and he jumped.

"Hey, Grandpa," Livvy greeted him. She looked a little unsettled, too, until she forced a smile. Then she crossed the kitchen where he'd been standing by the microwave. And she gave him a big hug.

She trembled a bit in his embrace. And he wondered...

Was she worried about him? Or was she worried about something else?

That idiot ex of hers had called City Hall today. That had been his mistake to catch Lem in the mood he was in. "Leave her alone, Stevie," he'd told the obnoxious surgeon. "She's making a life for herself here in Willow Creek. She's happier without you. If you cared about her at all, you would let her be happy. And you'd be happy for her finding happiness."

Steven had suspected she'd found someone else and moved on. Lem had only meant that she was happy with her job, with her family, but he'd thought of Colton Cassidy, too, of how his granddaughter looked at the paramedic firefighter. But she wasn't ready to move on that way.

She pulled back from Lem's arms and peered at him, and she didn't look happy. She looked like she'd been crying, her face a little pink, her eyes a little red. He didn't think Colton had made her cry; it must have been that persistent pest of an ex of hers.

"Did he bother you, too?" he asked.

"Who bothered you?" Then she gasped and

shook her head. "Steven? I'll take care of it, Grandpa. I'll make sure he stops bugging you."

She reached for her cell phone, but when she pulled it from her pocket, Lem took it from her. "I might have taken care of him today myself. He caught me in a mood," he admitted.

"Didn't Sadie apologize last night?" Livvy asked, as she studied his face as intently as he'd been studying hers.

He shrugged. "I'm not the one she owed an apology to."

"She apologized to me," Livvy assured him. "Before she left the hospital to come and talk to you, she explained everything, and I totally understand. I didn't get a chance to tell you this morning because you were already gone when I woke up. I thought you two had made up. But you don't look happy and neither did she when I saw her earlier at the ranch."

"You saw Sadie today?" he asked with surprise. "You were out at Ranch Haven?"

She nodded. "And the Cassidy Ranch…" Her teeth nipped at her bottom lip as if she was nervous.

Maybe as nervous as he was over what he was feeling. Too much…

From the tears she must have shed today, it was obvious Livvy was feeling too much, too.

She must have been with Colton; nobody else would have taken her to both those ranches, probably not even one of his brothers.

"Are you okay?" he asked her. He liked Colton, thought he was a good man. But if he didn't make Livvy happy, he wasn't the right man for her.

She nodded, but her teeth seemed to sink a little deeper into her bottom lip, as if she was holding something back.

So was he, so he decided to come clean first, hoping it would inspire her to do the same. "Sadie did more than apologize last night..."

Livvy didn't ask; she just waited.

"She proposed to me." Maybe that was what had galled him; he was an old-fashioned guy. He was supposed to do the proposing, with a ring, and the whole down-on-one-knee thing. But if he got down on one knee, he might not make it back up again.

"Does that bother you, Grandpa? Surely you aren't so chauvinistic as to think a woman can't propose?"

"Not at all. I thought it was charming when Emily proposed to Ben. And...it's Sadie March Haven. I should have known she would just go after what she wanted. She wouldn't wait around to be asked." But did she really want him? Or was she just lonely, like he was?

The funny thing was that he hadn't realized he was lonely until he'd started spending so much time with her. After Mary had died, he'd kept himself busy; he'd had things to do. Always. But when he'd started spending time with Sadie, he was lonely when he wasn't with her...lonelier than he'd been even when he was on his own.

"Were you going to ask her, Grandpa?"

"At our age? With my life here in town and hers out at the ranch?" But he'd been thinking about asking, even hinted at making an honest woman of her...which might have been a little insensitive given everything she'd been keeping from her family. Jessup.

She hadn't told her grandsons about their uncle; she hadn't known about their cousins... until Baker had gone out to that fire at the Cassidy Ranch.

But with all that going on, he hadn't thought it would be the right time to ask her. The problem was that he wasn't sure there would ever be a right time.

"So what did you say when she asked?" Livvy wanted to know.

Heat rushed to his face. "Nothing," he admitted. He'd been so surprised, and still a little mad at her, and he hadn't been sure why she'd asked. If she'd just been trying to make it up to him for insulting Livvy...

But that would have been kind of drastic, even for Sadie. But she'd said nothing about feelings. About loving him. But then neither had he.

Instead they'd both gotten embarrassed. She muttered something about it being late and a long drive back to the ranch, and she'd hurried off.

"Don't you want to marry her?" Livvy asked.

"Yes. But..."

"But what?"

"I'm just not sure we can figure it out. That ranch is her life, her family is her life."

"And you're not sure she has any room for you?"

"I'm not sure I can move to the ranch, away from town. Away from my job. Away from you and your father. And now I'm hearing that a couple of your brothers might be coming home."

Her eyes widened with shock. "What? When did you hear that?"

"You didn't know?"

She shook her head. "I kind of lost touch with them over the past few years."

"Because of Steven?"

She nodded. "I lost myself with him. I don't want that to happen to you with Sadie. I don't want you giving up who you are to make someone else happy."

"I won't do that," he assured her. "And I don't want you doing that either." Not even for Colton Cassidy.

CHAPTER TWENTY

A FEW DAYS had passed since Colton had burdened Livvy with his secret about finding the lighter, and he wished he'd kept it to himself. Because she didn't talk to him…except about the patients he brought her.

He was bringing one in right now. The sirens wailed and lights flashed on the rig as they rushed the patient toward the hospital. The guy had collapsed while mowing his yard. His heart was beating, but he was still unconscious. Could have been a heart attack or maybe heat stroke.

Colton had already called ahead to alert her, so probably she and Collin would be waiting. While Colton's pulse had quickened at the sound of her voice, she'd been cool and professional.

Like that day never happened, like they'd never kissed near the ashes of his old childhood home. She hadn't even said goodbye when she'd left Ranch Haven. He'd seen her slip out the patio doors, but before he'd been able to follow her, Ian had stopped him and then his dad.

"Give her time," Dad had suggested, gesturing around the kitchen. "This family is a little overwhelming."

"This isn't…" Me. He'd started to say, but he'd realized that it was. He loved the ranch and most of all, he loved the people. While he'd only just discovered this part of his family, he already loved them. Especially Sadie…

She'd commiserated with him. "That's not easy to do," she'd said. "But your dad's right."

"What?" Jessup had teased his mother.

"This time," she'd clarified. "About this… You can't overwhelm someone or you'll lose them for sure." Like she'd lost her son.

So Colton hadn't pushed, and whenever he'd crossed paths with Livvy at the hospital, he'd acted as professionally as she did… even though it was killing him to not kiss her again, or at least touch her hand, share a smile with her…

He missed her, and he wasn't sure he'd ever really had her.

The rig jerked to a stop, and Colton reached for the doors, pushing them open. One of them nearly knocked down a guy who was walking up to the back of the building. He wasn't familiar to Colton yet somehow he instinctively knew who he was. The sweater in the middle of summer, the thin little mustache, the superior attitude as he glanced into the back of the rig.

She'd claimed he wouldn't make the trip. But what man wouldn't go all the way around the world to get Livvy back if he'd ever been lucky enough to really have her?

Steven probably had that engagement ring with him, burning a hole in his pocket, whereas Colton only had her bracelet that he'd picked up from the jeweler's a couple of days ago. The clasp was fixed now. She wouldn't lose it again.

Colton ignored the stranger as he focused on helping his partner unload the gurney and rush the patient through the open doors into the ER.

"Hey!" the guy called out, and he squeezed through the doors behind them. Willow Creek Memorial didn't have the security they should have, the security necessary to keep out dangerous lowlifes like this guy.

"This is authorized personnel only," Nurse Sue said and stepped in front of the intruder.

Colton had never liked her more.

"You need to go in through the doors from

the parking lot," she told him, "and sign in at the desk."

But the guy ignored her, looking over her like he couldn't even see her. Then Colton realized who he was staring at as Livvy let out a soft gasp of surprise as she came down the hall toward them. Colton knew his instincts were right; the stranger was Steven.

"Olivia—"

Colton interrupted, speaking over him to fire off the patient's blood pressure, pulse and oxygen levels.

Livvy focused on him, nodding that she'd heard. Then she fired off orders to Nurse Sue, ignoring Steven. And when Collin rushed up behind her, Steven was the one who gasped— looking from one to the other of them.

Once Colton pushed the patient into an area and helped Nurse Sue hook up the machines, he stepped back, making room for his brother and for Livvy. She turned to look at Steven.

"Not now," she said.

Colton waited for the *Not Ever* but she didn't add it. She and Collin focused on the patient. So did Sue, pulling the curtain closed around them. Then she mouthed the words, "Get rid of him."

He suspected Sue knew who he was, too.

Colton stepped out and nearly fell over Steven. "You need to leave," he told him.

Steven shook his head. "I'm a neurosurgeon."

"Not here," Colton said. "You don't have staff privileges. So you need to get out of this restricted area."

"Are you an ambulance driver and security? That's how backward this little speck on the map is?"

Ambulance driver? That didn't bother Colton, but he was upset about the guy insulting his new home. Willow Creek was much more than a speck on the map, a lot of that owed to Colton's cousin Ben and to Livvy's grandfather.

"If that's how you feel about this town, you shouldn't have come here," Colton said.

Steven gestured at the curtain. "I am here for my fiancée."

"Ex-fiancée," Colton corrected him, and he balled his hands into fists, tempted to throw one at the guy. But he hadn't been in a fight since he and Collin were young, and that had been to defend his twin. Now he just tended to stop fights, usually with humor.

"You two need to get out of this area!" Livvy called out the order like she'd asked Nurse Sue for labs and meds.

"You heard her," Colton said, and he pointed

toward the doors that opened onto the public area. "Out."

The guy glared at him. "How dare you speak to me with such a tone."

"You're lucky he's talking and not punching your face," Collin said from behind the curtain. Maybe that infamous twin-tuition had finally kicked in and alerted him to how badly Colton wanted to hit this guy, or maybe he felt the same way.

Colton pointed toward the doors again. "Don't make me have to shove you through them."

Steven looked up at him…way up at him. The guy wasn't much taller than Livvy or Lem. And he must have realized that put him at a disadvantage because he finally turned and walked away.

"We have another call," Colton's partner said as he headed toward the doors that opened onto the ambulance bays.

When Colton stepped through them, he found Steven standing next to the rig instead of in the waiting room. "She's out of your league," he taunted him.

Maybe he wanted Colton to hit him. He wouldn't give the surgeon the satisfaction of making Colton lose his temper. Instead he handled Steven the way he'd always handled things that upset him, with humor. He grinned at the guy and said, "She's even farther out of your league, buddy."

Steven looked like he was the one thinking about swinging at him. But Colton jumped into the rig and his partner peeled away from the hospital with lights flashing and siren wailing.

But as they drove away, Colton didn't feel like he was heading to an emergency situation; he felt like he was leaving one. That Livvy was the one who needed his help.

But then he remembered how she'd handled the CPS investigator, and how she'd brought Nurse Sue around to show her the respect she deserved.

And he felt a twinge of pity for Steven. He was the one who was going to need help because he had no idea how strong and fierce Livvy really was.

EVEN THOUGH LIVVY focused on her patient, who fortunately hadn't had a heart attack, she couldn't get the visual out of her head of Steven standing next to Colton. Her ex-fiancé had looked so small and petty and insignificant standing there in the shadow of the bigger, better man.

She knew Colton had left because she'd heard his partner call out to him. She suspected Steven had left as well because he hated to be kept waiting. *His time was too valuable for that...*

She'd thought he'd considered it too valuable to make the trip out here as well. He was probably at the house with her grandfather and dad. He would have been able to figure out where it was. Grandpa had a publicly listed landline, so that he was always available for those who needed to contact him. Steven needed to stop contacting him, though.

So she was actually glad that he was in Willow Creek; maybe it would be easier in person to get through to him that they were over. *Really* over.

She pushed open the doors to the waiting room and walked past the intake desk, only just taking note of Steven leaning over it. When he stepped forward, she ignored him and called out for the family of her patient. The wife rushed up and Livvy assured her that her husband only needed to be treated with an IV; that he'd passed out due to the heat and dehydration.

The woman hugged her. "Thank you, honey.

You are just as sweet and smart as your grandpa always says you are."

Livvy didn't know the woman, but just like everyone else in town, the woman knew her… because of Grandpa. Livvy smiled and hugged the older woman. "You're welcome and very sweet as well. Nurse Sue will show you where your husband is if you just want to step through those doors."

Once the woman disappeared into the back, Livvy drew in a breath and turned toward her ex.

"Well, that was awkward," he said.

"What?" His being here, his standing next to Colton, the man she…

She what?

Loved?

No. She'd been fighting against that feeling, fighting the fall…because she wasn't sure she would recover from it like she'd recovered from her breakup with Steven. She'd also rediscovered herself here in Willow Creek.

"The woman hugging you," he said as if disgusted. "That was totally uncalled for."

Steven wasn't affectionate, and Livvy had always respected that that just wasn't part of his clinical nature. But now she pitied him.

"That was sweet," she corrected him. "Everyone here is."

"That ambulance driver?" he asked. "Do you think he's sweet?"

"I think he's a firefighter and an exceptional paramedic," she said. "One of the best I've ever worked with."

"He works for you, not with you, Olivia," he said, as if correcting her. "He's *beneath* you."

Her fingers curled into her palms, and Livvy was tempted to swing her fist into his face. But she didn't want to hurt her hand. "You don't know anything about Colton Cassidy," she said. "So don't you dare disparage him!"

"You know him?" Steven asked.

She nodded. "I know he's a good man. Honorable, loyal, protective, kind and patient—"

Steven laughed. "Sounds like you're describing a dog, not a man."

She really wanted to hit him, but Collin nearly beat her to it. He charged toward the smaller man. She hadn't even realized he'd stepped through the doors behind her, but as he started past her, she reached out and grabbed his white jacket, pulling him back. "He's not worth it, Collin. Let me handle this."

"But the way he's talking about Colton—"

"He's just jealous," Livvy said.

All the color drained from Steven's face.

Collin laughed then. "You're right. And he has good reason to be. Colton is more than twice the man he is. How he's always taken care of and protected his family—"

"Stop," Steven interjected. The color rushed back into his face, turning it red as he focused on her again. "I didn't come here to talk about some ambulance driver. I came to talk to you, Olivia. To get you to come to your senses and come home with me."

"Willow Creek is my home," she said.

He sniffed disparagingly. "When you were a child," he said. "But you're an adult now, it's time to move on."

"I have," she said and almost pityingly she added, "It's time for you to move on. You need to stop texting and calling me. And please don't harass my dad or my grandpa anymore either. I'm staying here."

"Because of *him*?" he asked.

She smiled. "Which him?"

Steven's face flushed a deeper red. "The ambulance driver or the doctor, Olivia? Which one are you seeing?"

"I moved back here for my dad and my grandfather originally," she said. "Or at least that was what I thought."

"Because you felt guilty for putting yourself and your career over them," Steven said. "They wouldn't have wanted you to do anything else."

"No," she agreed. "They have no problem with my not being there for them like I should have been. But I do. I regret that, and I regret all the time I wasted with you."

His neck snapped back like she had slugged him. It was probably more satisfying than if she physically had because she hadn't had to hurt her hand.

"I mentored you," he said. "I helped you prepare for your career. I've done more for you than anyone else has. You owe me your loyalty."

That was how he'd manipulated her all this while. She saw that so clearly now. And she laughed at how foolish she'd been and how foolish he still was. "I'm not a dog, Steven," she said. "Any more than Colton is. I'm a good person. Not as good as I want to be yet." Not as good as Colton was. "But I'm working on it."

"Olivia—"

"No, my name is Livvy," she said. "That's what everyone who knows me calls me."

"It's a child's nickname. You're an adult now," he said. "It's time you grew up and put your childhood behind you."

"Can I punch him?" It wasn't Collin who asked but Nurse Sue. She'd joined Collin and the receptionist at the intake desk as they all blatantly eavesdropped.

Instead of being embarrassed, Livvy laughed. "We don't need security here," she said. "We have Nurse Sue. You better leave before I let her escort you out."

"Olivia—"

"Nothing you say or do is going to change my mind," she said. "You can't manipulate me anymore. And you don't want to be with someone you can't control, Steven. I'm not who you want anymore."

"You can be," he insisted. "When you come to your senses—"

Sue literally growled.

Livvy laughed again. "I came to my senses when I gave you back your ring. I'm never wearing it again."

"So you're choosing someone else… The ambulance driver or the doctor?" he persisted.

"Me," she said. "I choose me."

Applause erupted behind her again as it had the day she'd defended the Havens to the CPS investigator. But this time she'd defended herself.

"Now get out," she said. "Before I throw you out myself."

And the applause got louder, especially when Steven turned and walked away.

LEM'S CELL VIBRATED with an incoming text. He'd left it sitting on the counter...in the jewelry store. He glanced at the screen to see if it was Ben; he was usually the only one who texted him.

Although sometimes Sadie did...with a quick reminder about something, usually one of her schemes.

But she hadn't texted or called him since that night she'd proposed. Maybe she regretted it; maybe she wished she'd never asked him.

Steven won't bother you anymore.

That was what the text said, and Lem chuckled aloud as he read what Livvy had sent. She'd apparently gotten her message across to that stupid ex-fiancé of hers. His chest swelled with pride for his granddaughter.

She'd come home so tired, so broken, but she'd healed herself. She was whole now.

Lem wanted to be whole again. He hadn't even realized anything was missing until he'd started spending more time with Sadie, until she'd filled a hole he hadn't even known he had. Not just in his life but in himself. She gave him more purpose and passion than he'd ever felt.

And here he was, like a nervous potential bridegroom, poring over rings in a jewelry case. "Did you make a decision yet, Lemar?" the jeweler asked.

The bell dinged as the door opened behind him.

"You can take care of that customer first," Lem said, borrowing more time to choose something that was just right. Something befitting Sadie.

"Was there a problem with the bracelet, Colton?" the jeweler asked. "Didn't the clasp hold?"

"No, it's fine," Colton said. "I was looking for something else…"

Lem turned to grin at the young man. "Are you looking for rings, too?"

Colton shook his head before his eyes widened in surprise. "You are? For Sadie?"

Lem nodded. "Long overdue, but I have no idea what to get her. Sadie gave up her rings to Jake, for Katie. She stopped wearing them a while ago because of her arthritis." He sighed. "Maybe we're both too old for this nonsense… too old to start over."

Colton snorted. "You and Sadie old? You are

the most vital, alive people I've ever met. You have a lifetime yet to live, Lem. Do it right."

Tears of gratitude stung Lem's eyes, and he reached out to clutch Colton's arm. "You're quite a man. I know why your grandmother is so proud of her family."

"Yours, too, once you seal the deal," Colton said.

Lem chuckled.

"And I have an idea for you…"

Lem heard him out and loved it…a lot more than the disgruntled jeweler did. Before he turned to leave, he suggested, "Maybe you should look for a ring, too."

Colton shook his head. "Livvy's not ready."

"Livvy? What about you?"

"I would marry her tomorrow," Colton said. "But I know if I push, I'll lose her…just like Steven did."

Colton hadn't seen the text, but he must have seen the man. And he'd known, instinctively, that Livvy wasn't going back to him, wasn't leaving Willow Creek.

"You know my granddaughter well," he said.

Colton nodded. "Maybe better than she knows herself, but she's getting there. And I can wait…"

CHAPTER TWENTY-ONE

COLTON KNEW LIVVY would be home because he'd seen the ER schedule and her shift ended when his had. He also knew she would be alone because when he'd run into Lem at the jeweler's, her dad had been at his office. Colton had a pretty good idea of where Lem was headed now. To Sadie…

Thinking of the old man and his grandmother had him grinning even before Livvy opened the door. When she did, his grin widened over how beautiful she looked…in her scrubs, with her hair falling down around her shoulders.

"You look happy," she said.

"I just ran into your grandfather."

"He told you I got rid of Steven?"

He shook his head. "He didn't have to tell me. I knew you would."

She arched a reddish-blond brow. "Really?"

He nodded. "I know you, Livvy Lemmon. You make yourself very clear."

She grinned now…with obvious pride. "I

certainly did." She leaned against the jamb of the open door, not letting him inside, so maybe she was making herself clear to him, too.

"I just stopped by to bring you something," he said. And he pulled her bracelet from his pocket. It had tangled around the lighter, so he'd pulled them both out. And his grin slid away.

"You're still carrying that..." She'd handed it back to him that day at Cassidy Ranch...when he'd kissed her and had never wanted to stop.

He sighed as he shoved it back into his pocket. "I don't carry it alone anymore...but I shouldn't have burdened you with my secret."

"I'm glad you did," she said. "But it's really not yours to keep."

He didn't know if she was talking about the lighter or the secret, but he nodded his head in agreement. "I'm going to tell Collin."

"Good."

"But this is what I wanted to give you..." He held out the bracelet again, but this time he held either side of the clasp.

"I thought you didn't find it."

"I lied."

Her eyes widened in surprise that he had. But not anger. Maybe she knew him as well as he knew her; she knew that lying wasn't something he did unless he had a good reason.

Like protecting his brother. Or… "I wanted to get it fixed before I gave it back to you," he explained.

"Oh…" Tears welled in her eyes. "That's so sweet." And she held out her arm toward him.

He linked the silver chain around her wrist and clasped it. Then he stepped back, knowing that if he didn't he would pull her into his arms and never let her go. He loved her so much. So very much…

But as he'd told her grandfather, she wasn't ready. And he wasn't going to disrespect her like Steven had. "I know how much this means to you," he said. "And you mean so much to me, but I know you just want friendship right now. And I'm grateful for that." He wasn't going to push for more.

But she threw her arms around his neck and clasped them behind his head, which she tugged down as she rose up on her toes.

And she kissed him…

GRATITUDE AND SOMETHING else flowed through Livvy, warming her heart…heating her lips where they moved over Colton's. She kissed him deeply, passionately…until he pulled back, panting for breath, his long, strong body shaking slightly.

"Livvy…" he murmured, his voice gruff. Then he cleared his throat and said, "You're very welcome."

"That wasn't even my thank you," she said.

"Then why did you kiss me?" he asked, his dark eyes intense.

"Because I've fallen in love with you."

He sucked in a breath and looked as shocked as Steven had when she'd finally gotten through to him that she wanted nothing more to do with him. But she wanted just the opposite with Colton.

Did he not want the same?

"Not what you wanted to hear?" she asked.

He shook his head. "Not what I expected…"

"Why not?" she asked.

"I didn't think you were ready," he said. "Not after Steven. He told me you were out of my league today, and I said you were farther out of his."

"He said that?" she asked. "Now I really wish I'd hit him. When did he say that to you?"

"He was waiting by the rig when I left," he admitted. "I really wanted to hit him, too, but he wasn't worth it."

"No, he wasn't," she agreed with a wistful sigh for all the time she'd wasted on him. But she had learned from the relationship; she'd learned to recognize real love when she saw it.

Like when she'd watched Sadie and Lem interact at the hospital her first night in town. And what she hoped she saw now in Colton's eyes as he stared at her.

"After meeting him, I can understand why you'd hesitate about entering another relationship," he said. "Did you notice anything about the bracelet?"

"That it's fixed, and you were so sweet to do that," she said.

"I know how much it means to you."

Tears stung her eyes again like they had when he'd first told her he'd had it repaired. He knew her. And he cared about what she cared about.

How could she not fall for such a wonderful man?

"So I hope you don't mind that I added something to it," he said.

She lifted her arm and studied the bracelet. So many charms dangled from it. Charms her mother had painstakingly picked out. She remembered every one of them but a shiny little dagger. She frowned. "I don't understand. It's not a scalpel." Her mother had already given her one of those.

"A dagger symbolizes strength and fierce independence. You, Livvy, it symbolizes you."

She didn't feel particularly strong right now as the tears streaked down her face. "You are so amazing."

Colton closed his arms around her and pulled her against his chest, where his heart pounded hard and fast. "You're the amazing one, Livvy. You're strong, so very strong. So I don't have to worry about your worrying about me getting hurt as a firefighter or getting sick like my dad…"

That was why he was still single. "No, I won't worry," she said. "I'll just fix you up myself."

"I think Steven might have been right that you're out of my league," he said. "But I love you so much that I will aspire every day to deserve you."

She sniffled back her tears. "Oh, Colton, I love you so much. And we deserve each other."

"I'm not going to argue with you," he said. "Not when I know how fierce you are, my love. And I know that Dad and Darlene and Grandma all hurt the people they were actually trying to protect. I love you too much to ever hurt you, and I respect you too much to think that you can't handle whatever comes your way."

She smiled as that strength surged through her. "I am fierce," she agreed. "I'm stronger than I even realized I was." Until she came home to Willow Creek. "I'm strong enough to love, as deeply and completely as I love you, and not lose myself. I think loving you is what made me realize who I really am and where I belong. In your arms…"

"Forever," Colton said as he tightened those arms around her.

Forever.

FOR ONCE IN her life Sadie didn't know what to do. She usually had a plan, some purpose, and some way to get what she wanted or at least handle what she had to…

Over the eighty years of her life, she'd had a lot to handle. She'd been handling Lemar Lemmon since they were little kids. But maybe that was the problem.

She'd known him so long that she'd taken him for granted. She'd just assumed that he would always be around when she needed him or even when she didn't.

She hadn't expected him to drive off mad and then never come back…even after she'd proposed to him. He'd looked so shocked, and she'd shocked herself with the question.

But that was what she wanted. She knew it. He was what she wanted. While he'd once been her schoolyard enemy, he was now her very best friend, and she couldn't imagine her life without him.

She closed her eyes against a sudden rush of tears and leaned back in her chair. She fisted her hands on her empty lap. Feisty sat in Lem's chair as Sadie thought of it now. As Feisty must have thought of it, and she spent most of her time in it now, as if she was keeping it warm until he returned.

Would he?

When Sadie had built onto the house after Big Jake was gone, she'd moved her suite to the main floor and had added this sitting area. And at the time she'd bought two chairs to go in front of the fireplace and TV, she hadn't figured on anyone but one of her grandsons and granddaughters-in-law using the other chair.

She certainly wouldn't have imagined Old Man Lemmon making that chair, making her heart, his.

"Dang old fool…" she admonished herself. And as if Feisty agreed with her, she began to yip.

Then a familiar voice murmured, "Hey, at least give me a chance…"

She opened her eyes to find Lem at her feet, literally. He knelt beside her chair with Feisty jumping all around him now. Sadie pressed a hand over her heart which almost seemed to leap in her chest; she was startled at his sudden appearance. Was she losing it?

She reached out and touched his face, sliding her hand over his soft white beard. And her fingers trembled. "You're really here…"

"You better get used to it," he grumbled, "because I'm probably never going to be able to get up again after getting down here…"

She laughed even as tears began to trickle down her face.

"I figured this was a mistake…" he grumbled some more.

And she sucked in a breath. "Proposing?"

"Getting down on my knees," he said. "Proposing is the smart thing to do. The thing I intended to do before you beat me to it, just like you've beaten me at everything our whole lives, Sadie March Haven."

She smiled. "I intend to keep doing that," she said. Because she wouldn't be able to handle it if he went before her, she wouldn't be able to handle life without him. At the thought, a sob slipped out.

He closed his arms around her. "Sadie, what's the fuss? What's wrong?"

"I love you, you old fool," she said. "I love you so very much."

He softly kissed her cheek, his beard tickling her skin. And then he kissed her lips.

Sadie's pulse quickened, and her breath escaped her and she felt like a girl again.

"I love you," he said.

"Then what's wrong with you?" she asked. "Why didn't you say yes the other night? Why did you keep me waiting? We're old. We don't have that kind of time to waste."

He chuckled now. "I just had to come around to your way of thinking, like usual…"

"What do you mean?" she asked.

"That I'll move out here…with you…give up town."

She pulled back and studied his face. "You love town. You gave most of your life to that town."

"Now I want to give what's left of it to you."

She swiped away the tears that kept falling. She couldn't remember ever crying this many happy tears before. "Are you sure, Lem? We could split our time between town and the ranch. We can figure it out."

He nodded. "I'll be fine with whatever you tell me *we've* decided."

She laughed at his very deliberate choice of words. Nobody, not even Big Jake, had ever known her as well as Lem did. "I love you so much."

"I love you, too, probably always did even when I thought I hated you," he said.

She laughed again because she'd so often thought the same thing of him.

"So will you marry me, Sadie March Haven?"

"I asked you first," she reminded him with a smile.

He grinned and nodded. "Of course, I will marry you."

"Then I will marry you and become Sadie March Haven Lemmon," she said, and she waited a little expectantly. "You got down on one knee."

"Actually both of them," he pointed out. "I thought it would be easier to get up."

"I'll help you up," she said. Just as he'd helped her after she'd lost Dale and Jenny and her family had been reeling. He'd helped her so much. "But before you move from there, you should get out the ring. I assume you got me one." Because Lem was old-fashioned that way. That was why he hadn't been able to accept when she'd proposed to him first. She hadn't worn a ring in a while and wasn't even sure she could fit one over her knuckles anymore. But for Lem, she would try.

He sighed. "I was at the jeweler's but nothing in that case suited you."

"I don't know whether to be flattered or offended," she admitted.

He shrugged. "No dainty little piece of jewelry seemed to fit you. Nothing did…until your grandson made a suggestion…"

"Uh, oh, what did Ben tell you to do?" Ben was the most like her, which was why she and Lem had finally gotten together, because Ben had turned her matchmaking scheme on her.

"Not Ben. Colton…"

"You saw Colton?" she asked. "Does that mean he's been coming around Livvy?"

"I saw him at the jeweler's."

Sadie gasped. "Was he buying a ring?"

He shook his head. "He doesn't think Livvy's ready yet."

"But he is," Sadie said with satisfaction. She hadn't been wrong yet with her matchmaking.

"She is, too," Lem said. "And she'll tell him so."

Sadie nodded in agreement. "Yes, she will.

She's a smart girl." Just like Lem had always bragged. "So what did Colton tell *you* to do?"

"Make an appointment for us at the tattoo parlor."

"What?" she asked, taken aback at her grandson's suggestion. "You want to get tattoos? At our age?"

"Let's get our rings tattooed on," Lem said. "This is it for me, Sadie. You're it for me. I want to go into my grave with the symbol of my love for you and your love for me tattooed on my hand and in my heart."

"You…" A sob choked her before she could call him an old fool again. She could only nod and wrap her arms around him and pull him close. She intended to never let him leave her again. And since he was unlikely to get up from the floor on his own, it wouldn't be hard to keep him here with her.

Forever.

* * * * *

THE NORA ROBERTS COLLECTION

40% OFF!

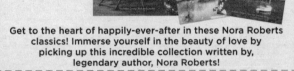

Get to the heart of happily-ever-after in these Nora Roberts classics! Immerse yourself in the beauty of love by picking up this incredible collection written by, legendary author, Nora Roberts!